ALSO BY LAURIE GELMAN

Class Mom: A Novel

You've Been Volunteered: A Class Mom Novel

Yoga Pant Nation: A Novel

Smells Like Tween Spirit

Smells Like Tween Spirit

a novel

Laurie Gelman

HENRY HOLT AND COMPANY
NEW YORK

Henry Holt and Company
Publishers since 1866
120 Broadway
New York, NY 10271
www.henryholt.com

Henry Holt® and Ⓗ® are registered trademarks of Macmillan Publishing Group, LLC.

Library of Congress Cataloging-in-Publication Data is available.

ISBN: 9781250777591

Our books may be purchased in bulk for promotional, educational, or business use. Please contact your local bookseller or the Macmillan Corporate and Premium Sales Department at (800) 221-7945, extension 5442, or by e-mail at MacmillanSpecialMarkets@macmillan.com.

First Edition 2022

Designed by Meryl Sussman Levavi

Printed in the United States of America

10 9 8 7 6 5 4 3 2 1

This is a work of fiction. All of the characters, organizations, and events portrayed in this novel either are products of the author's imagination or are used fictitiously.

For all the class moms, volunteers, and yoga pant enthusiasts, this one's for you

Smells Like Tween Spirit

To: Mat Moms
From: Franny Watson
Re: Mat Mom Get-together
Date: September 13

Hello,

My name is Franny Watson and I'm back as head of the Pioneer Middle School Wrestling Team's Mat Moms.

Our first meeting is this coming Tuesday, 8:30, at the Donut Hole near school.

See you there.

Franny

P.S. I've attached some wrestling reminders and an order form for the new Mat Mom team T-shirt.

So *disappointing!* I think to myself as I push back from my laptop and roll my neck from side to side. After so many years of putting my heart and soul into my class mom emails, I can't help being a little judgy when it comes to other people's offerings.

"I mean, come on!" I say out loud. "Would it kill you to put a little razzle-dazzle in your emails? A little song, a little dance, a little seltzer down your pants?"

I take a deep breath and click reply. For my eyes only, I promise myself.

> To: Franny Watson
>
> From: Jen Dixon
>
> Re: Mat Mom Get-together
>
> Date: September 13
>
> Dear Franny,
>
>   Way to whip us all into a frenzy! I for one can't wait to hit the Donut Hole! In anticipation of next week's klatch, here are some thoughts . . .

> 1. *Let's start with the name. Do we really have to be called Mat Moms? Why not call us what we are? Doormats. Or maybe we could call ourselves the Matt LeBlondes and all wear wigs to the games. I mean, if we're going to do this, let's have some fun with it!*
> 2. *As the mothers of tween boys, please consider how much money we could all make by starting our own towel and tube sock company.*
> 3. *Do we all wish our boys chose another sport or is that just me?*
>
> *Let's think about how we can put the "rest" back into wrestling, shall we?*
>
> *I'm only here to help.*
>
> *Jen Dixon*

I smile. It's kind of fun to take the snark out of storage and give it a spin. I should write fake responses that no one sees more often. I'd get in a lot less trouble.

I take a sip of my one and only cup of coffee for the day. Thanks to a recent diagnosis of acid reflux, I've had to reduce my favorite vice to a single shot in the morning. At the ripe old age of fifty-five the hits just keep on coming.

Just the other night I had shared with my husband, Ron, that I was feeling a little isolated and out of touch because I wasn't involved in anything at the new school my son Max started last year. Don't get me wrong, I thoroughly enjoyed his sixth-grade year— what I like to call my year of liberation from the grind of OPOs (Other Parents' Opinions)—and filled my time teaching more spin classes, doing an online sushi-making course, and generally enjoying the freedom of no obligations beyond my family and friends.

I only started feeling out of touch when Max kept referring to kids I didn't know and wouldn't be able to describe to police if it ever came to that.

"Can I go to Spike's house?" he asked last week.

"Who's Spike?"

"Mom, I've told you. That's what we call Sam Spiner."

I actually have heard Sam Spiner's name a few times, but as I mentioned before, I couldn't tell you what he looks like.

"Where does he live?" What I'm really asking is how far am I going to have to drive.

"I don't know." Max shrugged. And really, why would he? When I was a kid, I rode my bike everywhere, so I always knew where people lived. I don't think Max would even know how to get to his own school because he just sits in the back of the car and looks at his phone. Teaching him to drive should be interesting.

After a short back and forth about my comfort level with Max's visiting the house of a kid whose parents I don't know, I convinced him it would be easier if Spike came to our place. Apparently, he's lucky enough to have a mother who doesn't care what her son does. At least that was Max's takeaway from the whole thing. He was not happy because Spike has the newest Xbox, and they were going to play Fortnite. All we have is the original Wii, but I made it up to them by ordering pizza.

So, when I shared my feelings of being a bit out of the loop, Ron, being a man, decided then and there to "fix my problem" by making all kinds of suggestions about how I might be able to fill my time. These included going back into the PTA cesspool (I'd rather listen to "Baby Shark" on repeat for the rest of my life), volunteering in the cafeteria (raise your hand if you can see me as the lunch lady), or hosting a moms' coffee klatch once a week (I'm still laughing at that one).

I told Ron I just wanted empathy, not a grocery list of suggestions, and the conversation ended with a hostile good night to each other.

So this morning's email is the fruit of my attempt at *getting involved*. As a mat mom. For the school's wrestling team. I couldn't be more shocked if I were posing nude in *Playboy*.

Our son has never displayed any interest in joining a sports team no matter how many times Ron waved a ball or a stick in front of him. So you can imagine our surprise when he announced at dinner after his first day of seventh grade that he'd decided to wrestle.

I'll admit, at first I laughed because when anyone mentions wrestling, I immediately think of Hulk Hogan and Randy "Macho Man" Savage, the two heroes of WWE wrestling from my youth. I was confident Max would outgrow this little whim and continue on his path to greatness as a computer genius, or mid-level accountant.

Of course, Ron was thrilled.

"That's great, buddy!" he said, and I swear to God he had tears in his eyes.

"Why wrestling?" I couldn't stop myself from making a *Someone just farted* face as I asked it.

"Coach D said the team could use a guy like me," Max said with a big smile, then shoved an overflowing forkful of mashed potatoes into his mouth.

I frowned at his bad manners.

"I need to make weight," he informed me with his mouth full.

"What does that even mean?" I asked him. I looked to Ron for support, but he had his mouth full of chicken cacciatore. What a pair.

"I was flattered," Max said earnestly after he wiped his face with a paper napkin. "No coach has ever asked me to join a team before."

"So you've been waiting for an *invitation* to join a team?" Ron asked.

"No, but he said they need me."

I was about to point out that no one at this table gave a royal rip what Coach D needed, but Ron cut me off.

"Do you know anything about wrestling?"

"We did it in PE last year."

"And you liked it?" Ron encouraged.

"I didn't *not* like it," Max replied with a shrug.

"Buddy, I think it's great. It's a tough sport but a good one. Just be prepared to work hard."

"I will."

"Are any of your friends on the team?" I asked him.

"Nope. They all play soccer in the fall." He stood up. "I have homework."

"Take your plate to the sink, please."

Judging from his groan, you'd think I had just asked him to scrub all the toilets in the house. He grabbed his plate with exaggerated ennui and dropped it in the sink with a bang.

"Max!" Ron rebuked him.

"Sorry," he mumbled and walked out of the kitchen.

"What's your problem with wrestling?" Ron asked me when he was gone.

"I don't have a problem with wrestling. I just don't get the appeal." I picked up our plates and took them to the counter. "I mean, does he even have the build for it?" Max is in the awkward growth spurt phase of life, and right now the best way to describe him is gangly.

"He's probably hoping it will help him build some muscle." Ron pulled out his phone and started typing.

"Who are you texting?"

"I'm not. I'm making notes about what he'll need."

I looked over his shoulder and read the list: shoes, headgear, singlets, and a grappling dummy, whatever that is. I had already lost interest and Ron could tell.

"You know, wrestling takes incredible discipline. If Max gets into it, we could see some better behavior around here."

"Really?" I asked hopefully. As evidenced by his dinner conduct, Max had recently been exhibiting all the delightful attributes of a pubescent boy.

Ron shrugged. "We can only hope."

Now, as I try to warm to the idea of being a mat mom, I turn back to Franny's email, click on the attachment, and look at the helpful hints. It's literally shouting at me thanks to Franny's use of ALL CAPS.

1. NEVER COME TO PRACTICE SICK!
2. IMMEDIATELY NOTIFY THE COACH OF ANY SKIN RASHES OR INFECTIONS.

3. WRESTLERS MUST SHOWER AFTER EVERY PRACTICE, MATCH, AND TOURNAMENT. USE OF ANTIBACTERIAL SOAP IS PREFERRED.
4. WASH ALL WRESTLING CLOTHING (SHIRTS, SHORTS, SINGLETS) AFTER EVERY PRACTICE, MATCH, AND TOURNAMENT—SPORT LAUNDRY SOAP IS PREFERRED.
5. WASH OR DISINFECT HEADGEAR, SHOES, KNEEPADS, ETC., FREQUENTLY AND DON'T SHARE EQUIPMENT OR WATER BOTTLES WITH OTHERS.

As I'm absorbing the sheer amount of laundry I'm going to be doing, I scroll down further and am treated to a photo of the mat moms' team shirt they want me to buy—a red T-shirt with *Pioneer Middle School Mat Moms* emblazoned across the front. However, they've chosen to *really* accentuate the first letter of each word of the school's name so what you really see is

Pioneer Middle School
Mat Moms

If this is on purpose, I may have finally found my people. If it isn't, then I have my work cut out for me. There is also a picture of the back of the T-shirt on which is printed in bold letters **GET OFF YOUR BACK!** I'm given the choice to personalize it with my son's name.

"Well, I won't be wearing that," I assure my computer screen. I decide to add a P.S. to my fake reply to Franny.

P.S. "Get Off Your Back" has a whole other meaning in our house.

I look at the clock and swear. I'm expected at Fusion Fitness to teach my Wednesday spin class in fifteen minutes. I slam my laptop shut, down the last of my coffee, and run to get my things.

✦ ✦ ✦

As I pull into the gym's parking lot, I see one of my regulars hurrying from his car. Jeff has been with me since I first started teaching two years ago. I nicknamed him Tour de France because he used to come to class in really colorful and logoed cycling clothes. But he toned it down after a few months and now just looks like any other rider. We've become quite friendly mainly because my friend Peetsa Tucci is dating his brother, Greg. We set them up on a blind date, and they have been going strong for over a year.

I jump out of my SUV and sprint to catch up to him.

"Hey, Tour de France, don't worry, you aren't late!"

"Well, I guess not if you're behind me! Here, let me get that." He holds the door for me.

"Thanks. Can I ask you a question?"

"Sure."

"Did you ever wrestle?"

He frowns. "You mean like in high school?"

"Or whenever." I shrug.

We stop outside the double doors to the spin room. "I didn't, but Greg did. He loved it. I think he was all-county his senior year."

"What did he like about it?" I reflexively wrinkle my nose.

"Uh, well, at first he didn't, but it was the closest thing he could do to martial arts in school. But later he loved it for what it was. He says it taught him a lot about self-discipline."

"Ya, I keep hearing that," I mumble.

"Thinking of taking it up?" he asks with a laugh, as he opens the door to the spin room and gestures for me to go in. I'm not surprised to see most people saddled up and ready to roll in the mostly full class. The early classes are like that. People want to get in and get out.

"Good morning, eight o'clock!" I pause so that Bob, one of my loyal riders, can tell me it's actually 8:03 or whatever, but I don't hear him and conclude he must be out today. I make a mental note to check in on him later. He rarely misses a class.

I switch on the first song—"Hold On Loosely" by 38 Special—and crank up the volume as I put my shoes on.

"Nice comfortable jog to start—everybody up."

As I get on the bike, I scan the room and smile at the realization that I know everyone in here. I'm so happy I started teaching. Sometimes it's the only fun I have in a day, unless of course I'm spending that day with my granddaughter, Maude. But that doesn't happen as much as it used to because she just started pre-K five mornings a week.

If there really is such a thing as karma, it's coming back to bite my daughter Vivs hard for the years she tortured me with her titanium-strength stubbornness. It turns out Maude is just like her mother. Willful, headstrong, and sooo bossy. What drove me nuts about Vivs when she was young I find delightful in my little four-year-old ray of sunshine. She really didn't talk until she was almost three, but now she makes her feelings known in no uncertain terms.

I think it's safe to say we all wish Maude had inherited more of her father's gentle sensibilities, but Raj's is sadly not the dominant gene in her DNA. Thank goodness both Raj and I have had years of dealing with Vivs's bitchiness, so we are prepared for whatever Maude throws our way. I'll be curious to see how she navigates in a classroom situation. I've always said school is the great equalizer of big personalities. Our little type A might be the big boss at home, but throw her into circle time with other type A's and we'll see who is all bubble and no gum.

✦ ✦ ✦

After the final stretch in class, I thank everyone and hightail it home to shower and get on with my day. My hip flexors are unforgivably tight, so I do a few extra lunges while I'm drying my hair. Thank God we don't have cameras in the bathroom, because that's a sight you wouldn't be able to unsee.

My cell rings as I'm donning the mom uniform of yoga pants,

T-shirt, and long cardigan. "Jen's Boogie Basement!" I answer because I know it will annoy my mother.

"Jennifer, I know you think it's amusing to answer the phone that way, but I find it a bit off-putting. Sometimes I think I've dialed the wrong number."

"Oh come on, Mom. You get some of my best material."

"Lucky me," she says dryly. "When are you coming over?"

"In a few minutes. Do you need anything?"

"Just for you to be on time. I'm playing bridge at Riverview at twelve-thirty."

"You got it. See you soon."

Kay spends a surprising amount of time at the Riverview Assisted Living facility considering she doesn't live there. My younger daughter, Laura, is currently working there as a chef, and my parents actually stayed there for a few nights when we found out they had a carbon monoxide leak in their old house a while back. During that brief stay, my mother made friends with a bunch of the residents and even bumped into an old boyfriend who lives there. Since then, she goes at *least* twice a week to play cards or take people to appointments if they don't have a family member available. Leave it to Kay to turn her visits into an opportunity to help.

When she goes, we take turns either sitting with my dad or taking him out. He's really slowed down over the past year and is very forgetful. After he randomly turned on all the taps in the house this summer and left them on, we realized Ray couldn't be left alone anymore. So, between me and my daughters and Amelia, their cleaning lady, we try to spell Kay as much as possible.

My parents' apartment is about ten minutes from us in Overland Park, Kansas. It was a relief when they sold their house and downsized to a condo, but my mother had a little trouble purging their things. As a result, there is a two-story, three-bedroom house crammed into eighteen hundred square feet of living space at the Hickory Leaf condo complex. I find the main room suffocating, what with two sofas and coffee tables anchoring the entrance, not to mention the table that seats ten touching three walls of the dining area off the kitchen, but I don't have the heart to push them to give up any of the things they are attached to . . . yet. I'm waiting for someone to call my mother a hoarder to her face and shame her out of this nonsense.

"Jennifer, finally!" is how she greets me. I hug her and go to the kitchen to kiss Ray on the head.

"Hello, you," he says, smiling.

"Dad's already had lunch, so you don't have to worry," Kay informs me as she grabs her purse and car keys. "I'll be home by two-thirty." And she's out the door before I can even tell her to have fun.

Taking my father out is slow going. He can still walk on his own, but pretty much at a snail's pace. And you can't rush him! He gets really upset if he's asked to hurry. It can make things like going to the grocery store excruciating, but I like to give him a change of scenery, so when I have the time, I take him with me.

"How does grocery shopping sound?" I take his hands and lift him out of his chair.

"Okay, I guess." He pats his pants pockets like he's looking for something. "Where are my shoes?"

In the ten minutes it takes to put his shoes on and get him into my Hyundai Palisade SUV, I have had to answer the question "Where are we going?" twenty times, and I'm not exaggerating. His short-term memory is all but gone. It breaks my heart because I can no longer have a real conversation with him. It ends up being the same conversation over and over again.

"Want to listen to some music?" I ask him once we are on the road.

"Okay."

I switch my SiriusXM radio from PopRocks to 40s Junction and Ray is immediately tapping his foot to Tex Beneke's version of "Chattanooga Choo Choo."

"Where are we going?" my dad asks.

"To the grocery store," I tell him as though it's the first time. I don't want to make him feel bad.

"Laser tag," he announces as we drive by a strip mall sign, and I know he's started his reading routine. It's something he does in the car. The doctor said he does it unconsciously to calm himself down.

"McDonald's."

"Post No Bills."

"Shell."

My phone rings and I see its Laura, so I put it on speaker.

"Hi Sweetie!"

"Walgreens."

"Hi Mom, hi Poppy!" Laura chirps. "Are you in the car?"

"Verizon Wireless."

"What was your first clue?" I joke. "What's up?"

"Can Vivs and I come over later? We want to talk to you and Ron about something."

"Red Lobster."

"Is everything okay?" I ask, a little alarmed.

"Oh ya. It's nothing. Well, it's something but it isn't anything bad."

"Aldi," Ray announces as I pull into the parking lot of our destination.

"Come for dinner," I suggest as I park the car.

"No parking."

"Okay. See you around six." She hangs up.

I look at my dad. "Ready to get out?"

"Okay. Where are we going?"

✦ ✦ ✦

Back at my mom's, Ray is taking a nap, so I make a cup of tea and check my emails. The first one I see is from Franny, the mat mom czar with the subject line reading *Thoughts on Your Thoughts*. Oh crap.

To: Jen Dixon
From: Franny Watson
Re: Thoughts on Your Thoughts
Date: September 13

Dear Jen,

First, I don't want you to ever think of yourself as a doormat. I'm sure all the work you do for your family is very much appreciated. And what you do for us most definitely will be.

Your suggestion to change our name is interesting, but I think we're going to stick with good old Mat Moms. But if you'd like to wear a wig to the games, that could be fun!

Tube socks and towel company? Definitely something to talk about!

And I can't speak for everyone, but I wouldn't want my son to be doing any other sport. We are all wrestling die-hards in my family.

I look forward to seeing you at the Donut Hole. I feel like you need a good long hug.

Franny

How the hell? I quickly check my sent file and yup, there it is. For my eyes only found its way to Franny. Thank God I didn't hit reply-all. The only damage done seems to be to her opinion of my self-esteem, considering she thinks I need a hug. Or maybe that's her sense of humor. Franny just might be a comedy genius. Or the most sincere person alive. I'm looking forward to finding out.

My mother gets home just as my dad is waking up, so I leave them to their reunion and head home.

I'm excited both girls will be joining us for dinner—and hopefully Maude too, although I think Raj may have her.

I look at the clock on my car dashboard and see it's 2:45. There was a time when this hour of the day would have had me racing to school to pick up Max like Pavlov's dog salivating at the sound of a bell. But now that Max is in middle school, he takes the bus and gets home around four. And next week when wrestling starts, he'll take the later bus and probably won't get home until six. This has added an extra little nugget of me time to my day, which I usually spend writing my memoir and going to the spa . . . or vacuuming the house and emptying the dishwasher. It's really a toss-up.

✦ ✦ ✦

"I'm starving," Vivs announces as we all take our traditional places at the kitchen table. We usually try to have dinner together on Sundays, but it's a nice treat to have the girls here on a random weekday.

"Don't you have lots of food at work?" I ask her. Vivs is the manager of the Jenny Craig in Overland Park, and she usually fills herself with their protein bars and snacks.

She scrunches her face. "It's all processed. I way prefer fresh and organic food."

Oh for the love of God, I want to say, but I don't because that's the type of comment that can set Vivs off, and I don't want to have a fight. Instead, I say, "Well I'm glad I didn't defrost the Swanson Chicken Pot Pie."

"Mom! That stuff is poison." Laura frowns.

"Oh, girls, please. It was good enough for you when you were growing up."

"When we didn't have a choice," Vivs points out.

I ignore the comment and ask how Maude's trip to the dentist went.

"Much better, thank God." She shakes her head in disbelief. "I would never have pegged her as a biter!"

Poor Maude has a bit of a reputation in Dr. Siebert's office ever since she drew blood the first time she went. The second time he was ready for her with a dam to put in her mouth so she couldn't bite down. On seeing it she declared in her little three-year-old voice, "You're not putting that thing in my mouth." And she refused to open wide.

"So third time's a charm, I guess? You were the same way, you know," I remind her.

"So you keep mentioning," she grouses.

We all dig into the daughter-approved dinner of grilled lamb chops, spinach salad, roasted broccoli, and sweet potato fries done in my brand-new air fryer.

"Tell me about your day," I say to Max, who is eating his lamb chop like it's a corn dog on a stick.

"It was good."

"Don't you guys have to do a musical instrument this year?" Laura asks him.

"They don't do that anymore," Max answers with a mouthful of broccoli.

"Why not?" Vivs asks. "That was like the craziest part of seventh grade."

Max shrugs. He doesn't know it, but we parents received a note from the school board about it in the summer. Apparently the funding for the music department had to be funneled to the science department after a very unfortunate Bunsen burner incident last spring.

When the girls went through middle school, they both chose brass instruments—Vivs the saxophone and Laura the French horn—and it was the truest test of my love for them thus far. The racket they made night after night while practicing sounded like we were torturing cats. I'm amazed no one ever called the police. Neither ever managed to squeak out more than a few notes of anything that sounded remotely like music, and I know for a fact that when I went to the school's concert, they both faked playing so as not to be heard. You'd think their teacher would have been angry, but I'm pretty sure he was grateful.

"I'm sorry to hear that, buddy," Laura says. "What do you think you would have liked to play?"

"Percussion," Max says with a grin.

Thank God for budget cuts. I pick up my plate, which signals the girls to do the same, and in no time at all, the kitchen is clean, and we are all eating ice cream. Max has gone up to his room, so it's a good time to ask them why they wanted to see us. Vivs starts.

"I think you know that I haven't been happy at work for a while now." She looks at me, so I nod. Vivs has been managing our local Jenny Craig for a couple of years but in the last six months has been complaining loudly about how she doesn't buy into their philosophy anymore.

"So I've been trying to think of something else I could do. Something that's more of a career than a job, you know?"

"And I've kind of hit a wall at Riverview," Laura jumps in.

This is news to me.

"You have? Why do you say that?"

"It's just so limiting not being able to cook with salt," she explains with a world-weary sigh, and I bite the inside of my cheek to keep from laughing.

As I'm trying to figure out where this is leading—Are they moving back home? Do they need money? Are they leaving KC?—Ron asks the question I can't seem to.

"So what's this got to do with us?" He asks it kindly. It would have come out as frantic and a bit hostile if I had tried to say it. Ron's velvety voice can make anything sound better.

"We've been talking about going into business together—doing something with healthy food."

I'm waiting for more, but Ron jumps right in with questions.

"What are you thinking about? Launching a line of products?"

"Not at the beginning. We're thinking maybe open a small café that serves vegan and vegetarian salads and sandwiches," Vivs explains.

"Plus fresh juices and snacks," Laura adds in. "All made fresh every day."

"That's a lot of work. And the food industry in general is very tough with all the hoops you have to jump through for the FDA," Ron informs them. "Plus the overhead is a killer."

"We know," Laura assures him. "We've been doing a lot of research."

"Where would you open the café?" I ask.

The girls look at each other, then Vivs nods to Laura.

"Well, this is kind of where you guys come in."

"Do you want us to invest?" Ron asks them.

"Not directly," Laura says slowly with a glance at her sister.

"For the love of God, girls, just spit it out!" This game of twenty questions is getting to me.

"Okay, okay!" Vivs looks squarely at Ron and me. "We'd like to open our first café at the Overland Park Om."

Om Sweet Om is the name we gave our yoga studios. We opened four years ago, and they have really taken off in the past year. But I can't see how a café would fit the low-key vibe.

I look at my husband, and I can tell he's thinking the same thing. He's making the same face he makes when we talk about the Visa bill. This should be good.

"Where in the studio?" he asks them.

"We thought we could take over a corner of the lobby where the kettle and little fridge are now."

"We would do most of the prep work at home, so we'd just need a small space for a refrigerated display case and a sign," Laura adds in.

"So not so much a café as a counter where you'd sell your food," he confirms.

"Exactly," Vivs says.

There is silence from Ron, so I decide to ask a few questions of my own.

"Are you sure you girls want to live together *and* work together? Do I really need to remind you that you argue more than the hosts of *The View*?"

"Mom, we're adults now. I think we can get past any minor disagreements," Vivs says with a huff.

I confess that I do still see them as teenagers, but the reality is they are women—Vivs is going on thirty-one, and Laura just turned twenty-nine. How did my babies get so big?

"How do you see this working?" Ron surprises us by speaking

again. "Will you be your own independent contractor within the studio, or would you become an arm of the business?"

"Our hope is to make it a permanent part of all the studios. I don't know if you've ever talked to your clients, but many of them have told me they'd love to have a healthy food option available," Laura explains. A glance at Ron tells me this was the wrong thing to say.

"Did you just ask me if I've ever talked to my clients?" he asks with a frown.

"Sorry," Vivs jumps in. "Of course, you have. We just weren't sure if you'd ever explored the thought of food with them." She gives Laura an exasperated look.

"Where would you get your seed money for groceries? And do you realize you will have to have your home kitchen inspected and certified?" Ron seems to have moved past his annoyance.

"We've done a lot of research," Vivs reiterates. "And Nana and Poppy said they would front us the money."

"You asked them for money without asking me first?" I blurted out.

"Yes, Mom, we did. We are grown women, and we negotiated a loan with our grandparents. Well, with Nana. And we fully intend to pay them back within two years." She reaches into her purse and pulls out what looks like some kind of contract. Ron starts to read it.

I'm a bit flustered by this turn of events, but before I can tear into Vivs for taking advantage of old people who love her too much, Ron jumps in.

"Well, you've really given us something to think about. I can see you girls have put some thought into this. I want to do a little research of my own and then I'll get back to you."

As Vivs gives us a sincere thank-you, Laura unwisely says, "Could you make it soon? We have other places we'd like to pitch it to."

Vivs punches her arm as I shake my head and Ron lets out a guffaw. These two in business together? With us? What could go wrong?

2

To: Mat Moms
From: Franny Watson
Re: Today's Meeting
Date: September 18

Hello,

Good turnout today. Thank you to those who showed up.

Moving ahead, we have a Pancake Breakfast Fundraiser in the cafeteria every Saturday morning thru December. See below for the schedule of which day your family cooks.

Attached please find the laundry/snack schedule as well. We have twenty-seven games this season, so everyone is going to have to pull their weight.

And remember to order your Mat Mom T-shirts. I think we will all look very sharp in them.

Thanks, and Go BlueHawks!

Franny

Ya, nothing says sharp-dressed woman like a blue T-shirt with "PMS" written on it. I mutter this to myself as I put my phone down and continue to cook dinner.

The meeting this morning wasn't bad at all. We met at the Donut Hole and pretty much took over the back of the restaurant. There were about twenty women there, none of whom I had ever met before. That's usually a recipe for disaster for me—I've been told I'm an acquired taste. Ron says I really need to work on my filter, but I figure why start now? They'll either get used to me or they won't. My level of caring whether I'm liked or not seems to steadily decline every year along with my resistance to chocolate.

That's why this morning was a pleasant surprise. Unlike the PTA where there are rules and decorum and many sticks up asses, the mat moms are a pretty groovy bunch.

Franny Watson is the group's uncharismatic leader. But she is one of the most sincere, lovely people I have ever met who doesn't have any sense of irony. When I introduced myself, she gave me the promised hug and assured me she was still mulling over my idea of a towel and tube sock company. When I explained that the email was a joke and my computer had accidentally sent it, she slapped my arm and told me what a funster I am. I have been called many things in my life, but I think I like funster the most.

Franny confessed that this is her seventh and final year in the mix thanks to her four sons, three of whom now wrestle in high school.

"I should probably be more involved in that program," she admitted. "But it's just too serious. Middle school is way more fun."

Franny introduced me to a couple of seventh-grade moms, inferring that their sons will probably be Max's best friends.

"These kids become thick as thieves."

Maria and Georgina nodded their heads.

"Get used to seeing a lot of us." They laughed. After chatting for a few minutes, I decided that I wouldn't mind that at all.

It felt good to be out among the moms, hearing school gossip, none of which meant anything to me because I don't know the players (although I do feel bad for whoever Deanna is because it sounds like her choosing to bring gum to last Friday's bake sale did *not* go over well). They didn't conduct any business, so I thought I was home free. That's why this email is a bit of a gut punch. Apparently, I'm scheduled to wash the team's uniforms after matches nine and twenty-two. I can't believe that's even a thing.

To: Franny Watson
From: Jen Dixon
Re: Today's Meeting
Date: September 18

Dear Franny,

Thanks for the fun get-together this morning. We really raised the roof off that dusty old Donut Hole, didn't we?

I think I can speak for all of us when I say washing the dirty uniforms of a dozen pubescent boys is a heaven on earth I never thought I'd be worthy of. Match number 9 can't come soon enough!

Suggestion: Instead of a pancake breakfast, what do you think about one week trying a toaster strudel breakfast? And it could be BYOT (bring your own toaster)! Everyone comes, plugs in and makes a morning of it. You can let me know.

Thanks,

Jen Dixon

I hit send. "I hope she knows I'm kidding about that."

"Talking to yourself again?" Ron asks as he saunters in from the living room, all tall and jock-like.

"I find I'm my best audience." I blow him a kiss.

"What was that? I wasn't listening," he says and then bursts out laughing. Ron is of the opinion that some jokes never get old.

"I just got an email from the mat moms."

"Oh yes? Anything interesting?"

"They have a pancake breakfast every Saturday!" I say incredulously.

"You make it sound like they're going to strap you to a chair and force-feed you." Ron laughs. "I'll totally go to that."

"Every Saturday 'til Christmas?"

"Why not?"

My computer pings. It's an email from Franny that says *You're a card!* Along with six laughing emojis.

"Shouldn't Max be home by now?" Ron asks.

"He should," I agree and reach for my phone to track him. Today is his first day of real wrestling practice, and I know how excited he was about it. As if on cue, the back door opens, and Max comes shuffling in carrying his backpack and his wrestling bag. He unloads both on the floor with a *whoof* and goes straight to the sink to wash his hands. Ron and I look at each other across the table and I raise an eyebrow. Max never washes his hands without being asked at least twice.

"How was practice?" Ron asks him.

"Great." He's enthusiastic, but I can tell he's exhausted.

"Dinner's ready. We want to hear all about it." I motion him to sit down, and I serve him some chicken stew. "How many dumplings?"

"Two," he mumbles.

"Two what?" I ask.

He frowns. "Dumplings!"

"What else?"

He looks confused for a moment, then says, "Oh God, Mom, please. *Please* can I have two dumplings, PLEASE! Please and thank you! Jeez!"

"Watch your tone," Ron warns. "So tell us how it went. What did you do?"

Max is slumping over his plate and shoveling food into his mouth at a rate that just might be world record breaking if there were such a record to break.

"We did a lot of drills and exercises, and in the last hour we scrimmaged." He takes a big gulp of milk, and I am treated to the sight of white liquid dribbling out the sides of his mouth and down to his chin. I hand him a napkin.

"They worked you hard, huh?"

"Ya, but it was fun. Can I have more stew, please?" He's coming back to life after a little sustenance.

"Wow. You must have been starving." I bring the pot from the stove and fill his plate again.

"Coach says I need to put on weight."

"What weight class are you shooting for?" Ron asks.

"A hundred forty-five."

"A hundred and forty-five *pounds?*" I exclaim. Max can't be more than 110 soaking wet right now.

"That's a good goal!" Ron seems pleased. "But don't make yourself crazy. Sometimes it's better to be in a lower weight group."

"It isn't if you have to wrestle a girl," Max informs us.

I let out a barking laugh. "Oh sweetie, they'd never let you wrestle a girl."

They both just stare at me.

"What?"

"Jen, it's the twenty-first century. Girls wrestle boys."

I'm horrified.

"How is that even allowed? I mean, their hands are all over each other."

"Mom! Eww!" Max yells. "Can I be excused? I have homework." He takes his plate to the sink, grabs his backpack, and sprints upstairs.

✦ ✦ ✦

"Gee Gee, I have a joke for you," Maude says to me as we are FaceTiming before she goes to bed. We try to do this if I haven't had a chance to see her that day.

"Let me hear it!"

"What do you call a fairy that doesn't like to take a shower?"

"I don't know, what?"

"Stinkerbell!" she yells and then doubles over with laughter. "Do you get it?"

"I do get it. That was a good one. Who told it to you?"

"Miss Dawson." This is Maude's pre-K teacher.

"What did you learn at school?" I know if I just ask her how school was, she will just say "good," so this is my way of trying to get specifics.

"We learned a song and we wrote our names. Then we did art."

"Wow. Busy day. Did you have your bath yet?"

"Yup. Did you?"

"Not yet. Your dad is going to bring you here tomorrow afternoon, okay?"

"Okay. Bye. I love you." Maude kisses the screen quickly and runs away, leaving the iPad askew on the couch and giving me a nice view of the ceiling in Raj's apartment.

"Does noon still work, Jen?" I hear Raj but don't see him.

"Sure."

"Thanks again for taking her a day early. I didn't know about the half day at school tomorrow."

"Are you kidding? It's a treat!"

Raj and Vivs do an excellent job co-parenting Maude, even though they aren't together. Somehow they managed to replicate her room at each of their apartments, so she feels at home wherever she is. They rarely have a hiccup in their schedules, but when they do, I'm usually free to pick up the slack. Raj didn't tell me why he needed the change, but I guess Vivs had plans so she couldn't accommodate him.

"We have Maude tomorrow," I tell Ron as I climb into bed. He nods and then gives me the look that every wife knows. It's the *Are you up for sex?* look. Whatever happened to foreplay or romance or even getting me a bit drunk? I mean, I need more than a look. In fact, these days I don't think even a combo of Spanish Fly and oysters would get my libido to kick in. I've always heard of women eventually drying up *down there*, but I never thought it would happen to me because I love sex and Ron still turns me on. But for the past few months I'm as dry as Utah on a Sunday. I've just lost all interest, and I don't know what to do about it. Even my go-to mommy porn doesn't seem to help. I really don't like to say no to Ron, so I made a deal with myself that I would say yes every fifth time he approached me. Sadly, for him, this is only the third time he's asked.

So I ignore his look and eventually he gets the hint and starts doing that thing with his pillows where he builds a mini fort around his head.

"O-kay," he says with a sigh. "What time will Vivs be by to get her?"

"Probably after work. Does it matter?"

"I want to talk to her and Laura about their proposal."

"Oh great! We're still doing it, right?" Ron and I had decided pretty much the night they pitched it that we would let them give their café idea a whirl.

"We are, but the more research I do, the more I realize they probably don't know what they're getting themselves into."

"Well then maybe they shouldn't do it," I counter.

"I think no matter what happens it will be a valuable learning experience for them."

"No matter what happens?" I climb on top of him so he can see my face despite the pillow barriers. "If you think it's going to fail, you should tell them before they lose all my parents' money."

"Well hopefully that won't happen." He yawns and says groggily, "Now if you're getting frisky all of a sudden, it's too late. I've missed my window." And with that he closes his eyes and is asleep within thirty seconds.

3

I'm up and at it Wednesday morning to get Max on the bus and myself to spin class. I sit in the parking lot of Fusion Fitness and frantically finish putting my playlist together for class. Back when I was a newbie, I would do all my playlists for the week on Sunday night, but these last few months I've been slacking off. However, putting it together in the car five minutes before class is a new low, and I vow I won't do it again.

"Good morning, eight o'clock!" I say into my microphone. I pause for Bob's time check and once again he is not in class. I never did reach out to him to see if he's okay, and immediately I feel guilty.

"Does anyone know what's going on with Bob?" I ask my group. Dead silence. I frown. Surely someone sees him outside of class. I see this group hanging out at the juice bar together once in a while.

"Jeff?" He shakes his head.

"Mary Willy?" I ask one of my longtime riders.

"Maybe he went on vacation." She shrugs.

I promise myself to reach out after class. Bob is in his early forties and in great shape, so I doubt it's a medical thing, but I want to check just the same.

✦ ✦ ✦

I'm dripping with sweat as I poke my head into Jodi's office. She is the manager of Fusion Fitness and the woman who single-handedly changed my life by giving me a job teaching when I was fresh out of spinning school. I cringe when I think back on those first few classes. I so appreciate the people who stuck with me through some truly inexcusable faux pas.

"Hey," I say, and Jodi looks up. "Do you have any contact info for Bob? He hasn't been in my class for a couple of weeks."

"Bob Nolan?" she asks as her eyes widen.

"Uh, sure. Probably." I'm not sure I've ever heard his last name.

She stares at me. "Oh my God, Jen, I can't believe I didn't tell you."

"Tell me what?" I immediately presume I did something in class to turn him against me. These days all it seems to take is an off-color joke or a best of Milli Vanilli ride for people to stop taking a class.

"He died. Dropped dead of a heart attack two weeks ago when he was running."

I gasp and put my hand over my mouth. "Oh my God!" I fall into Jodi's office and sit down on the small sofa in front of her desk. I'm stunned.

"But he was in great shape. He was one of my best riders." I look at her. "How did you find out?"

"His daughter called to cancel his gym membership."

"Where was he? Was he with anyone? Did they have a funeral?"

"I . . . I didn't ask. I was so busy when she called." It comes out as an apology of sorts.

We sit in silence for a moment as I take in this news. Bob didn't have any belly fat or a ruddy complexion that would have suggested he drank a lot.

"Are you okay?" Jodi asks me.

"Uh, ya, just really shocked. I thought he was so healthy."

She shakes her head. "It's the Jim Fixx enigma." She's alluding to the author of *The Complete Book of Running*, who died at fifty-two when he was out for a jog.

I don't want to get up, but I know I have to. "If you hear anything else, could you let me know?"

"I can give you his information if you want to send something," she offers.

"Okay," I say listlessly, still in disbelief. She hands me a scrap of paper with an address and phone number.

+ + +

I pull my sweatshirt on and dash to my SUV. There's a nip in the air that tells me fall is most definitely here. As the car warms up, I look at the phone number and contemplate calling. I've known Bob for two years, but how well did I really *know* him? I had no idea he had a daughter. I don't even think I ever heard him mention a wife. When he started in my class, he told me he was trying to pump up his cardio. He ended up as the guy who always gave me a time check in class.

My phone rings as I'm pulling out of the parking lot.

"Hi Mom, I can't really talk . . ."

"Amelia's sick and can't come sit with your father today, so I was wondering if you could," she blurts out.

"I actually have Maude starting at noon."

"Oh dear." Kay sounds distressed. "I promised Sammy I would take him to his doctor's appointment."

I wasn't surprised to hear that name. Sammy was an old boyfriend from high school my mom had reconnected with during her short stay at Riverview Assisted Living. But I didn't know she was driving him to appointments.

"Doesn't he have like three daughters to help him with stuff like that?" I ask with a bit of attitude in my voice.

"Oh, they're useless," my mom informs me. "They only come around on holidays. I feel terrible for him."

"Well, you might have to disappoint him, Mom, because I'm booked today." I debate telling her about Bob.

"What if I bring your father over to your place? Then he and Maude can have a nice long visit."

I roll my eyes because, sadly, my father isn't very interactive with Maude. She's a boisterous kid, and I think she scares him a little.

"What time?" I ask.

"I can drop him now and be back by two-thirty."

"Two-thirty? That's a long appointment." I pull into my drive-way.

"Well, he's offered to take me to lunch afterward."

"Okay," I say, sighing, and disconnect. I'm going to have to put my thoughts for Bob aside for now.

I have just enough time for a shower before Jen's daycare/eldercare opens. As I run up the stairs, I amuse myself with possible names for my fake business. Cradle to Cane? Diapers to Diapers? Naps "R" Us?

I get myself all cleaned up in record time and am scarfing down a strawberry Activia when my mom comes in the back door holding my dad's hand.

"Here we are!" She singsongs and hands me a reusable shopping bag with my dad's slippers, the newspaper, his glasses, and a few Depends pull-ups.

"Will I be needing these?" I point to the adult diapers and have a small panic attack. I mean, I'm a good and loving daughter, but I have never envisioned myself as having the fortitude to wipe my father's behind. There is truly a special place in heaven for people who can do that without sustaining permanent damage to their psyche.

"Probably not, but just in case." My mother is anything but assuring. She kisses my dad on the head.

"Okay Ray, I'm going. Have a nice visit with Jennifer." To me she says, "He had a late breakfast so he won't be hungry for a few hours."

I nod to my mother and look at my dad.

"Hello, you," he says with a smile.

I smile back. "Don't worry about us, Mom, we are going to have a great time doing puzzles with Maude."

A startled look crosses my father's face, but I can't tell if it's for what I just said or the fact that my mother slammed the back door a little too enthusiastically.

"Dad, I was going to make some banana bread. Do you want to sit here with me while I do it?"

"Okay," he answers then reaches for his newspaper and glasses in the bag beside him.

"Want to peel the bananas?"

He doesn't say anything, so I leave him to his reading and start gathering the ingredients for my super special gluten-free, sugar-free, and dairy-free banana bread. The secret is letting the bananas ripen until they are black and squishy. And don't cheat and put them in the oven to ripen quicker because they won't be as sweet. I measure out all the ingredients and line them up on the counter so Maude can help me when she comes. If I let her do the measuring, there is just too much of a mess to clean up.

"Want something to drink, Dad?" I have almost forgotten my father is here because he is so quiet.

"Dad?" I repeat and notice that he has been reading the front page of the newspaper for half an hour. I wonder if he's fallen asleep. It's hard to tell when he has his glasses on.

The backdoor opens and thirty-six pounds of dynamite comes running into my kitchen.

"Hi Gee Gee!" Maude gives my legs a big squeeze, then turns to my father. "Hi Poppy!" She runs and hugs him from behind, which startles my father out of his stupor.

"Okay, okay," he says and tries to pull away. Maude doesn't notice but I do.

Raj is standing in the doorway holding Maude's purple backpack with unicorns on it. "Maude, don't be so rough with Poppy!"

He walks over to shake my father's hand. "How are you doing, Ray?"

My dad seems a bit rattled by all the attention, but he manages to say, "I'm alright, I guess."

"Thanks again, Jen." He smiles at me.

"Of course. Do you have a big work project or something?"

"Or something," he says and winks. "Maudey Moo, give me a kiss. I'll see you in a few days." He hugs her.

"Okay! Bye Daddy." In the same breath, she turns to me and squeals excitedly, "Are we *baking*, Gee Gee?" She has obviously seen the ingredients on the counter.

"You bet we are. Come over here and start mashing the bananas!" My father has turned back to his newspaper, so I don't bother trying to include him.

✦ ✦ ✦

Later, when my father is watching TV and Maude is in a time-out for not listening when I told her not to touch the stove, I sit down at the kitchen counter office and call my friend Peetsa. Her son, Zach, is still Max's best friend, and they are in school together at Pioneer, but I rarely see her anymore because of her job and my lack of involvement in the school.

"Hey stranger!" She picks up on the first ring.

"Hi, are you busy?"

"No, it's slow today, so I'm catching up on paperwork."

Peetsa sells cars for Hyundai, and business has been really good for her over the past couple of years.

"One of my riders died," I blurt out.

"Oh my God, no! What happened?"

"Heart attack. He was in his forties." I can feel myself getting upset, so I change the subject.

"What's been going on? How's Greg?"

"Really good." I can hear her smile through the phone. I pat myself on the back once again for introducing them.

"Any talk of moving in together?"

"Not yet. I mean, we have five kids between us and not everyone gets along."

"Not quite the Brady Bunch, huh?"

"Not unless the Bradys were a therapy-drenched dysfunctional mess."

"OUCH!" I hear from the other room.

"Oh shit. Hang on, P."

I run into the living room as my father lets out another yelp. Maude is standing in front of him trying to jump rope, but all she's managing to do is whip the skipping rope around and slap my father on the knees.

"Maude, stop that!" I run and grab the rope from her. "You're supposed to be in time-out!"

"The timer went off!" she yells. "Poppy said he wanted to see me jump rope." Her eyes well up with tears. "I didn't do anything wrong."

"It's okay, sweetie. You just need to be careful." I kneel in front of my father. "Sorry, Dad, are you okay?" I rub the part of his leg hit by the jump rope.

"I need to go to the bathroom," he says and starts to get up out of the chair.

"Let me help you." I start to take his arm, but he won't let me.

"I can do it," he grouses, so I let him shuffle to the powder room in the foyer. I figure he'll call if he needs me.

I had left my phone in the kitchen, so I dash back and grab it.

"P? Are you still there?"

"Yes, is everything okay?"

"Ya, it's just I have my father and Maude with me so it's a little hectic."

"I'll let you get back to it, then. Let's try to have lunch this weekend."

"I'd love that. Talk to you later."

"Bye."

When I hang up the phone, I can see Maude standing in the doorway to the kitchen.

"Come here, sweetie." She crawls onto my lap and puts her head on my shoulder.

"You know I'm going to need your help to take care of Poppy."

"I was helping," she says quietly.

"I know. But Poppy is getting older, and he needs things to be calm around him." I can't help but wish she had known him when he was even ten years younger. Ray was always so much fun. He would roughhouse with Max for hours. It's hard to see him like this.

"Maybe I can read him a book?" Maude can read only one book and it's because she has memorized it.

"Hello?" I hear my dad calling from the bathroom.

"Shit," I say under my breath and jump up. Maude's eyes widen to the size of dinner plates.

"You said 'shit,'" she whispered.

"I know," I whisper back. "Don't tell your mother. Stay here, please." I head into the front hallway.

"Are you okay, Dad?"

"Where am I?"

"You're in the bathroom at my house. Do you need help?" I silently pray that he doesn't.

"The door is locked."

"Okay, well, do you see the little pin to the right side of the knob? Just pull that out. Sometimes it sticks."

I hear some movement and then the door opens, and my dad is standing there holding his pants in front of himself with one hand and his Depends in the other.

"I need my bag," he tells me with no indication of whether he is embarrassed or annoyed by his situation.

"I'll get it," I tell him and almost trip over Maude as I run to the kitchen.

"Sweetie, I told you to stay put."

"I was bored." She looks at my dad. "Poppy, why don't you have your pants on?" she asks.

I don't hear the answer as I grab his bag and dash back to the foyer bathroom. I have barely handed it to him when Maude informs me while jumping up and down that she needs to go potty. I look at the closed powder room door and wonder if she can wait.

"How bad?" I ask.

"Really bad."

Of course. I take her hand and we run up to my bathroom, which, for some reason, is Maude's favorite for number two. I know I can't leave her, but I don't want to leave my father alone downstairs.

Maude jumps up on the toilet and starts humming her potty song and swinging her legs around. I tell her to please hurry up.

"I'm not supposed to push hard!" she says with a grunt.

I'm trying not to lose it, but my heart rate is nearing cardio max level. When Maude is finally done, I help wipe her and then swing her into my arms despite protests that she needs to wash her hands.

"I was kidding about the daycare/eldercare," I mutter to the universe.

We find my father in the kitchen, fully clothed and reading the cover of the newspaper. I sigh in relief and take Maude to the sink to wash her hands.

"Poppy, did you wash your hands?" she asks.

"I think so," he says.

Good enough for me. I glance at the clock and see it's 2:40. Where the *hell* is my mother?

"Dad, are you hungry?"

"I think so," he says again.

"I am," Maude adds.

I get them some hummus and pita chips and take a seat at the kitchen table. And that's where my mother finds us when she comes waltzing in at 3:10.

"I'm here!" She singsongs like she did this morning. Back then I found it charming. Right now, I'm ready to rip her throat out.

"Mom, you said you'd be here forty minutes ago!" I blurt out.

"Hi Nana." Maude runs to give her a hug.

"Hello sweetheart!"

I'm not sure which one of us she's talking to, but she is clearly not going to address her tardiness.

"How was everything? Ray, did you have fun with Maude?" She starts to put his newspaper in his bag. My dad just nods and smiles.

"How was your lunch?" I ask her.

"It was nice," she says dismissively. "Okay Ray, let's get going."

"Bye Dad. Thanks for spending the day with me." I hug him.

"Yup. Right. Good." He replies and follows my mother out the back door.

✦ ✦ ✦

Vivs and Laura arrive around six, and Ron comes home soon after with take-out Minsky's pizza, because I couldn't face cooking dinner after my day with Dad and Maude, and with the news of Bob's death still lingering in my heart. As we dig in, Max gives us all the lowdown on his wrestling practice.

"I learned a half nelson hold. Coach says it should be easy for me because I have such long arms."

"Well, that sounds fun," I say because I don't know what else to say.

"Buddy, your grappling dummy showed up today," Ron says.

"Seriously?" Max says way too loudly. "Where is it? Can I see it?"

"It's still in the car."

"What's a grappling dummy?" Laura asks.

"It's a dummy you practice your wrestling holds with," Vivs answers promptly. We all stare at her, surprised.

"What? The guy I went to junior prom with was a wrestler."

I'm trying to remember who that was . . . At sixteen Vivs had kind of a revolving door of suitors.

"Todd Munch?" I guess.

Vivs shakes her head.

"Gary Miller." She turns to her daughter. "Maudey, you're going to love playing with it."

Maude perks up at the sound of her name. "Yayayay!" she squeals.

"It's not a toy! She can't play with it," Max rebukes his sister. "Dad, tell them."

"I'm sure she won't hurt it."

"Max, you can see it when your homework is done," I inform my son.

"Come *on*, Mom!"

"No, Mom's right. Why don't you go finish up and then we can go through a few basic moves?" Ron says, and I give him a grateful smile. "Besides, I need to talk to your sisters for a minute."

Max hotfoots it upstairs to his room and the rest of us clear the table. I love take-out night because the cleanup is so quick and easy.

"So, girls, if you still want to launch your business with us, I'll be happy to have you," Ron begins. "But I have a few questions." Vivs and Laura look at each other and grin.

"Shoot," Laura prompts him.

"First, how do you plan to get all the permits required to make your kitchen eligible for food production?"

"Oh, we're not going to use our kitchen anymore," Laura assures him. "After going on the government website, we realized that there is just too much paperwork involved."

"What a nightmare!" Vivs adds. "So Laura is going to stay on at Riverview and we can use the kitchen there."

"Do *they* know this?" I ask.

"They said we could try it out, and as long as it doesn't get in the way of my other duties, it should be fine."

Ron looks skeptically at them.

"The plan is to stay after my shift so I can make the food for the next day, then bring it home in a cooler."

"Okay. That kind of answers the second question of how you're going to store the food. I don't want to invest in a refrigerated display case until we see how it's going."

"That's fair," Vivs says with a knitted brow. "We can use the cooler."

"Well, if you guys think you have all your ducks in a row, we can start this next week."

"What are you going to charge us for the space?" Vivs asks.

"Nothing at first. Let's just play it by ear."

"Wow, thanks for the vote of confidence." Vivs sounds a bit defensive.

"Not at all. I just want to take it slow. But I'm all in, ladies."
Ron sticks out his hand to shake on the deal.

✦ ✦ ✦

Later that evening, Ron comes into the bedroom all sweaty from his
session with Max and the grappling dummy.

"How was it?" I ask.

"Fun." He flops down on the bed beside me. "He's going to be
in great shape if he sticks—"

"What the hell is that smell?" I interrupt him as a waft of something horribly fishy comes my way.

Ron sniffs himself. "Oh yeah. Gross, right? It's the dummy.
They say the smell goes away."

"God, I hope so." I pause and look at him. "I have something
to tell you. One of my riders died."

"You're kidding!" He sits up. "Who?"

"Bob." I'm starting to well up.

"The time-check guy? How?"

"Dropped dead of a heart attack when he was running." I move
closer and put my head on his shoulder.

"Jesus, how old was he?"

"Forty-five, I think. So young."

"I'm sorry, babe. Is there anything I can do?"

I sigh. "Can you get out of those clothes, please? That smell is
so bad."

Ron jumps up and runs to the bathroom. It occurs to me that
he may be thinking I'm asking him to clean up so we can have the
kind of life-affirming sex people have when someone dies. But all I
really want is a hug, so he's going to be pretty disappointed when
he gets out of the shower.

To: Jen Dixon

From: Franny Watson

Re: Batter Up!

Date: October 2

Hi Jen,

Just a reminder that you are in charge of pancakes this Saturday. You should show up at the school cafeteria at six a.m. with three people ready to set up and cook. We have a standard batter that everyone uses, but if you want to add a little fun (and as our resident funster I know you will), you can bring some toppings. Whipped cream and berries and chocolate chips are popular. Syrup and butter are provided.

Thanks for jumping into the Mat Mom experience with such gusto!

Regards,

Franny

P.S. I was at practice the other day and saw Max do a single leg takedown. He looked good.

Well, I wouldn't call it gusto, but I am happy to step in for Kitty Schmitt, whose turn it was supposed to be this Saturday.

To: Franny Watson

From: Jen Dixon

Re: Batter Up!

Date: October 2

Franny,

So that's a no to my toaster strudel idea?

xo Jen

The mat moms have had two pancake breakfasts so far, and they seem like a big hit. Dozens of people come out to support the team and stuff their faces. Plus, each mat mom tries to put her own spin on things by jazzing up the menu. Last weekend one of the moms put crispy bacon bits in her pancake batter and word has it the result was pure heaven.

Normally I would be sweating it wondering how I was going to make mine stand out, but luckily, Laura happened to be with me when I first got the call to step in. She volunteered herself and Vivs to do it for me.

"We can totally do pancakes! Can we sell sandwiches, too?"

"Uh, probably not, but you can wear your T-shirts."

"Good idea. And I have a great pancake batter recipe."

"They actually provide the batter, so all you have to do is work the griddle and bring toppings," I tell her.

"Don't worry about a thing. We've got this." I'm wondering if she even heard what I said, and decide it doesn't matter. I'm leaving it to the professionals to make it special. The most I will have to do is clean up.

And they *are* professionals if the sales of their food are any indication. For the past few weeks they have been bringing salads and sandwiches to Om Sweet Om, and have sold out every day. I mean, they bring only about eight of each, but people seem to really like their plant-based food. Personally, I'd rather have turkey on whole wheat with mayo, but I'm not going to knock the people who get the same pop from root vegetables and sprouts with hummus aioli on a hemp wrap.

Thank God Laura didn't quit her job. There is no way they would have been able to make money selling a dozen or so sandwiches and salads a day for ten dollars each. The cost of the organic ingredients alone eats up their profits, not to mention they invested in a logo and got it printed on stickers that they put on their products. It's a nice touch, but it was $500 they really didn't have. They call their company Good Clean Grub, and the logo is bright yellow with white letters and three daisies surrounding the words. It's very cheerful looking. They also had T-shirts made, which they wear when they are at Om Sweet Om and sell for twenty dollars . . . or they will if someone ever wants to buy one.

But the biggest thing to come out of their partnership is they have never gotten along better. My concern about them getting into daily fisticuffs has been allayed after watching them coordinate their work/home lives. For the first time probably ever, they are working together. It's hard for me to get used to since I've been playing referee their whole lives, but I will happily hang up my whistle if it means they are finally in sync.

This morning I have promised myself I'm going to call Bob's family and send my condolences. I have been putting it off because one of my true failings as a human being is my inability to know the right thing to say in times of sadness. I'm very uncomfortable around other people's grief, so I try to avoid it. My mind-set is usually *Oh they don't want to hear from me*, but in truth, people *do* like to know they are being thought of during the tough times. Or at least they do until they hear from me.

Bob's death continues to hit me hard, and I've been doing some serious soul-searching trying to pinpoint exactly why. The last person I lost was my grandfather on my mother's side, and that was a good thirty-five years ago. I remember being sad for my mother, but I wasn't especially close with him. He was old-school strict, and a firm believer in the adage that children should be seen and not heard. Truthfully, he scared the crap out of young Jen. I wonder how I'd react if I met him today.

I'm hoping a conversation with one of Bob's family members will help me figure out why his death has been such a trigger for me, so I take a deep breath and dial the number Jodi gave me. After three rings, a woman answers.

"Hello?" Her voice sounds like her throat needs to be cleared.

"Um, yes, hi. My name is Jen Dixon and I'm a spin instructor at Fusion Fitness and Bob was in my . . ."

"I know who you are. Bob loved your class," she says kindly.

"He did?" I feel a flush come over my whole body.

"He really did." She coughs to clear her throat.

"Are you his wife?" I feel like an idiot asking, but I want to know who I'm talking to.

"No, but I've been with him for a long time. I'm Barb. I guess you could say I'm his common-law wife . . . or I was." She sighs deeply with grief and my internal organs start to gather into a knot.

"I'm really sorry for your loss," I say lamely.

"Thank you," she answers, and there is silence between us that I am desperate yet terrified to break.

"I was so surprised when I got the news," I tell her, because let's face it, it's all about me.

Barb chuckles a bit. "Yes, we all were. Bob was so focused on his health. We never thought his heart would give out the way it did."

I'm nodding but not sure what to say. "Well, he was a great rider, that's for sure. One of my best."

"Well, no surprise there, considering . . ." Barb leaves the thought dangling.

"Considering what?" I ask.

"Considering he was in the Olympics for cycling."

"He was?" I'm shocked.

"Yes!" Barb is suddenly animated. "In the 2000 games he was

part of the track cycling team. I'm amazed he never mentioned it to you. He was so proud of it."

"You know, we didn't talk that much outside of class." I'm trying to think of even one conversation I had with him. "I called him my time-check guy because he always let me know how late we were starting class."

Barb gives a genuine laugh. "That's what military training will do to you."

"He was a soldier, too?" I'm starting to feel like a fool for calling. I didn't know this guy at all.

"That's how he paid for college."

Barb launches into a mini bio of Bob's life and accomplishments, which include a tour of duty in Iraq, his first marriage to his high school sweetheart, who died of ovarian cancer just after their daughter was born, and his ultimate career in veterans affairs.

"It sounds like he was an amazing man." I say it as though I've never met him, and in a way I feel like I never have.

"He sure was," Barb confirms. I can hear her voice breaking and take that as a cue.

"Well, I should let you go. I just wanted to give you my condolences. I'm really going to miss Bob in my class."

"It was nice of you to call, Jen." She sniffs. "Take care."

"You, too."

As I hang up, a flood of relief washes over me. I hadn't realized just how much I had been dreading that call. But the relief is quickly followed by an emptiness that directly relates to how little I knew about this man.

✦ ✦ ✦

"And he was a veteran and had a daughter that he raised alone after his wife died, until he met Barb."

I'm sitting with Peetsa at Starbucks later that day and vomiting out my story about Bob. She is listening patiently while sipping her grande Flat White.

"How could I not know anything about him?" I say for probably the seventh time. When she glances down at her phone, I realize I have been bogarting the conversation.

"I'm sorry, P." I acknowledge my rant, but she waves off my apology.

"Don't be. I can tell you're upset. It's just . . ."

"What?"

"Well, I think you're being hard on yourself. I mean, how many instructors know the intimate details of their riders?"

"I know who Tour de France guy's brother is sleeping with!" I grin.

"Yes, and that's way too much. Maybe find a happy medium?"

"Well, I'm going to at least try to get to know something about each of my regulars besides their names," I vow. Peetsa merely arches one perfect black eyebrow at me.

"Hey, will you come to the pancake breakfast for the wrestling team on Saturday? Vivs and Laura are cooking."

"How did you get them to do that?"

"They volunteered, believe it or not."

"I can swing by early with Zach, but I have to work at ten. I still can't believe you're a mat mom."

"Too glamorous for me."

P laughs. "Yes, that's exactly what I was thinking."

✦ ✦ ✦

I take my time getting ready to go on Saturday. Ron and Max agreed to be the advance team along with Vivs and Laura, so I figure I'll just get there for cleanup and avoid the siren song of white flour and maple syrup.

My phone rings as I'm driving to Pioneer Middle School (heretofore referred to as PMS).

"Jen's Bait and Tackle," I answer.

"Where are you?" It's Ron, and it sounds like he's calling from a crowded room.

"I'm just about there," I tell him.

"Okay, good. You might need to do some damage control."

"What? Why?"

"Just get here." As he hangs up, I think I hear a child crying.

I arrive six minutes later to find an unusual number of people milling around instead of sitting and eating. I bypass some of the other mat moms I recognize and head straight to the griddle in the back where Vivs and Laura, both wearing their Good Clean Grub T-shirts, are having a heated conversation with a few parents.

"What's going on?" I ask, and before anyone can answer, I see exactly what the issue is. Beside the griddle are stacks of green pancakes. And not a cheerful green like you might want to make on St. Patrick's Day. No, no. These are a dull and very unappetizing mud green.

"We just want regular pancakes!" a woman holding a toddler is saying to Vivs. "How hard is that? We come here every Saturday!"

"Why are the pancakes green?" I walk right up to Vivs and Laura at the grill.

"I put spirulina in them," Laura says proudly.

"And flax meal," Vivs adds, then shrugs. "They taste the same as any other pancakes."

"No, they don't!" a little girl whines. "They taste like dirt."

"They smell like fish," Max's friend Spike points out with a scrunching of his nose.

"That's the fish oil," Vivs says, and there is an audible gasp of horror from the crowd.

"Mom, you told us we could put our own spin on them." Laura shakes her spatula at me.

"I thought you'd just think of some fun toppings, not reinvent the wheel." I pop a piece of green pancake in my mouth. It has a gritty texture and very little sweetness, but it isn't terrible until the fishy aftertaste makes an unwelcome entrance.

"Why would you change the batter?" asks a mother holding a young boy's hand.

"Uh, because that other batter is poison?" Vivs isn't one to just sit there and take it.

"It is?" The little boy starts to tear up.

"Well, I'd rather eat that poison than this shit," a father lobs in from the sidelines. He is met with a chorus of "Hey hey hey, *language!*" from the surrounding parents.

"Here we go!" Like the cavalry, Franny breezes in from nowhere carrying a big bowl of normal batter. "Let's get these cookin', girls."

"I'm sorry, I refuse to cook something that will likely cause cancer years from now . . ."

Franny gives me a frightened look.

"Okay, Vivs, enough." I go behind the griddle and bump her out of the way. "You're relieved of your duties." I look at Laura. "Will you be cooking with me or joining Norma Rae here in protest?"

She looks at Vivs then back at me and makes the wise decision to side with her sister. She knows *I'll* forgive her eventually.

I look at Franny, who has joined me behind the griddle.

"I'm so sorry for this."

She shakes her head as she pours batter on the electric griddle. "Don't worry. That's why we always have backup batter. I tried those green ones, and I'll tell you what, I don't think I've ever had a gritty pancake before."

Once people are happily eating regular pancakes (no toppings because the girls only brought walnuts, which are forbidden at this nut-free school), I wave Ron over to spell me and charge through the cafeteria looking for Vivs and Laura. I find them at the back sink, cleaning their mixing bowls.

"Why?" It's the only thing I can think of to ask them.

"Laura makes these for Maude all the time and she loves them."

"And you know we have to stick to our branding," her sister adds.

"What branding? No one knows who the hell you guys are yet. And now, if they see *that* logo again"—I point to their T-shirts—"they're going to run in the opposite direction."

"You know what?" Vivs turns to me. "Just say thank you." She sounds more like me than I care to admit. "We gave up our Saturday morning for you and this is what we get? That one guy called our food shit."

"Well, I thought they were great." A deep voice interrupts our discourse. A man who I now know is Coach D (which stands for Dana) approaches us. I can't help but blush when I see him because he is so ridiculously good-looking. He's easily six feet tall, dark skin and short dark hair, and has electric blue eyes. He reminds me of the hot guy from *Bridgerton*, but instead of period clothing, he's dressed in blue track pants and a blue-and-white sweatshirt with the school's logo on it.

"Hi, Coach. I'm sorry about all the drama this morning." I look down because I just can't make eye contact with someone this gorgeous.

"Are you kidding me? Those pancakes are the superfood I've been looking for to fuel my team. I had six!"

"You're going to have a hell of a poop in about two hours." Laura steps into the conversation. I can tell she's smitten, too.

"These are the ladies responsible," I say proudly. "My daughters, Vivs and Laura."

"Hi" they say in unison, and then Laura adds, "We're Max's sisters from other misters."

Coach D laughs, but Vivs is horrified.

"God, Laura!" she snaps. "Hi, I'm Vivs." She reaches out to shake Coach D's hand. She's the only one keeping her wits about her. "I'm glad you liked them."

"It's my own recipe," Laura leans in, wanting to take his focus back.

"Well, I came over to find out what kind of fish oil you used."

"It's an omega-3, but it has a bit of a lime flavor to it," Laura whispers as though she's giving the nuclear launch codes.

Coach Dana nods thoughtfully. "Do you do any baked goods with the same kind of ingredients?"

"I've been experimenting with a cranberry muffin," she tells him enthusiastically.

"Since when?" Vivs scowls. She is not pleased to be sidelined by all this talk of ingredients.

"We've just started the business, Dana, is it?" She smiles at him.

"Yes, but everyone just calls me Coach D." He smiles back.

"It's called Good Clean Grub . . ."

"Great name," he interjects.

"I thought of it." Laura jumps in and is rewarded with a scowl from Vivs.

"Trust me, it was a group effort." Vivs's fake laugh is probably only obvious to me. "Anyway, we make all organic and healthy sandwiches and salads that we sell at workout venues across the city . . ."

Well, that's a bit of a stretch, I think to myself.

". . . but our goal is to open a café."

"Is that your logo?" Dana asks pointing to Laura's chest, which is easily twice as big as Vivs's.

"Yes. What do you think?" Laura sticks her boobs out enthusiastically.

He nods. "It's really fresh."

I'm standing to the side, a mere observer to this mini flirt session. I've never really seen my daughters in the wild like this—peacocking and flinging their poo at this hopefully eligible man.

"Well, I'd love to talk to you guys about maybe doing snacks for my wrestling team."

At this I decide to go back into the cafeteria, where I'm happy to see it is a lot calmer. Ron is performing at the griddle by flipping pancakes behind his back and catching them on a plate for an audience of kids. When he sees me, he winks, and I can't help but admire his capacity to rebound.

5

"Big stretch overhead, then bring your hands to your heart." I take a deep breath as does my whole spin class. "Great job, everyone."

I get a nice round of applause and people start to file out. Lynnie something-or-other pauses by my bike, wiping her face with a pink towel.

"Are we still on?" she asks.

"You bet. I'll see you at the juice bar in five."

And so it begins. Lynnie is my first foray into getting to know my riders. I thought she was a good place to start because she never seems in too much of a hurry to leave, so I have to believe she has time for a chat. I haven't yet figured out what to do about the people who run off before they stretch.

I towel off and put on a dry T-shirt before I meet Lynnie, who is already sitting at a table that faces the front desk. I grab a green juice and join her.

"So what's up?" Her big brown eyes seem to be taking in every inch of my face plus everything around us at the same time.

"Not much. I just see you in my class a lot and I realized I don't know anything about you."

She lights up like a Christmas tree.

"Well, I'm twenty-eight, single, and I'm the assistant night manager at the Marriott by the airport, but I'm hoping to get transferred to a better location—maybe like Reno. I grew up in Wamego, Kansas, . . . I know, kill me now, right? All that *Wizard of Oz* stuff? I've been forced to sit through that movie like a *billion* times." She shudders and continues before I can even react. "Well, I got the hell out of there as soon as I could and went to Highland Community College to study human services, but that was a bust. They were trying to get me to be a parole officer, and I was like umm, no thank you. I'm never going to meet a guy if I'm stuck with criminals all day. My mother went postal when I quit and moved to KC—the 'big city'"—she uses air quotes to punctuate her point. "She told me I'd get off the bus and someone would poke me in the ass with a needle full of marijuana and I'd be hooked. Needless to say, *that* didn't happen."

As Lynnie rambles on about the various jobs she held before landing on her chosen career as assistant night manager, all those internet jokes about Gen X versus millennials start to make sense. This chick is from a different planet. I need to extract myself from this one-woman show. I mean, all I said was I didn't know anything about her. What if I were to actually ask her a question?

When she finally pauses to take a sip of her juice, I seize the moment and have every intention of wrapping things up, but instead and for reasons I will never understand, I ask if she has a boyfriend.

"I think I mentioned I'm single, but I am *not* looking right now. I've had the worst luck. First, there was this guy, Grant. I met him on Tinder. All he wanted was to hook up a couple of times. By the way, that's all anyone on Tinder wants. I found that out pretty quick. Brad, Denny, and Cooper. They just wanted booty calls. So I stopped going on Tinder, and a couple of weeks later I met a guy named George at a flower shop. He hit on me while he was buying flowers for another girl, can you believe it? That should have been my first clue, right? But he was so hot! We went out for like a month and then he ghosted me. Whatever. He wasn't the smartest bulb in the drawer, if you know what I mean. There's a guy at work that I kind of like, but I'm thinking I may not want to get tied down, especially if I'm going to move to another Marriott. They let you do that, you know. You can go all over the world if you speak a different language. But I only speak American . . . so Reno it is! Or maybe even Orlando. There's just so many opportunities."

I smile at her optimism. And at the pause in conversation before she starts again.

"I love your spin class because you play all the music my mom did when I was growing up. I came in by accident one day. I thought Patrick was teaching. But you were there, and I was going to leave, but then I was like how bad can it be? And it wasn't at all. I'm really glad I stayed."

"Thanks for saying that. You're a really strong rider."

She nods because, apparently, she knows this. "I ran track in high school. Made all-county my senior year. That was also the year they made me play the Tin Man in *The Wizard of Oz*. I wanted to be Dorothy so bad, but so did Gina Delvechio, and of course she had the dark hair and didn't need a wig."

"Oh gosh, I didn't realize what time it is! I have to go pick up my father," I lie and stand up.

"Oh, bummer! This was so fun. We should totally do it like every week."

"That would be fun, except I'm trying to get to know *all* my students a bit better. Maybe we can do a catch-up in a few months."

"Cool! If you get to talk to the bald guy who always sits in the back, ask him if he's single. He's got that ugly/sexy thing going on, like Vin Diesel."

"Sure," I tell her and grab my sports bag before she can launch into a story about why *xXx* was his best role, or something equally ludicrous.

✦ ✦ ✦

Later that day I make my way to the PMS gym for Max's first wrestling match. I'm both nervous and excited because, honest to God, I really don't know what to expect. The only thing I know for sure is that when he comes home from practice, his gym bag smells like the seventh circle of hell. He used to just drop it by the back door, but now I make him take it down to the basement and throw everything into the washing machine. I was expecting some pushback, but surprisingly, he doesn't seem to mind.

In the past month I've seen a marked difference in Max's general behavior and specifically his attention to his body. He showers two to three times a day, for which I'm grateful (see the gym bag reference), and now seems very aware of his hair growth *down there*. He proudly told Ron the other day he now has four. And this morning I caught him shining his cell phone flashlight on his underarms to count the hairs there—ten on the left, eleven on the right, in case you're interested. I don't remember the girls obsessing about their hair growth, but maybe they just didn't share it with me. I'll have to ask Vivs.

Today our PMS BlueHawks are facing the Hawthorne Hornets, from a middle school about five miles away. When I walk into the gym, I see a large wrestling mat has been placed right in the center of the floor—a blue mat with a huge blue-and-white BlueHawks logo smack-dab in the middle. Hawthorne's colors are gold and white, so it's a very colorful group.

The boys are warming up, I think. They are milling around in their singlets, doing somersaults and cartwheels and what I'm guessing are different kinds of wrestling moves. I spot Max talking to Coach D. He looks nervous, and I want to go give him a hug, but I shudder at what the fallout would be from that kind of faux pas.

"Where's your T-shirt?" Franny sneaks up on me from behind. She is all decked out in her mat moms T-shirt, BlueHawks hat, and (what else?) yoga pants. I cringe because I never actually ordered my T-shirt. I could make the case that I just forgot (which seems to happen a lot lately), but, truthfully, I didn't want to wear one. Blue doesn't really look good on me. I had my colors done once at the mall when I was in my early thirties, and the woman at the counter told me my season was "rainy."

"Oh gosh, you know, mine hasn't come yet," I lie.

"Yes, it did!" Franny presents me with one. "I noticed you didn't order one so I got one for you."

"Oh, thank you." I try to smile as I take the T-shirt and hold it up against me. "That was really thoughtful."

She waves me off. "That's my job! You owe me twenty-five dollars. You can Venmo me. I put Max's name on the back."

I turn the shirt around and indeed it says *Get Off Your Back Max!* Franny nods her head and smiles at me, but the look on her face says, *You didn't think you'd get away with not wearing a T-shirt, did you?* I'm beginning to see her genius. What she lacks in personality, she makes up for in single-minded relentlessness.

"Just put it on over your shirt. Come on, we're all sitting together over here."

We walk toward the far side of the gym where a blue wave of color is standing by the bleachers and looking quite impressive, if I'm being honest. I take my jacket off and as I'm following Franny, I defeatedly put the mat moms shirt over the white T-shirt I am currently wearing. I spot Maria and Georgina, the two I connected with at the Donut Hole meeting, and I join them.

"First match?" Georgina asks. She is the taller of the two but not by much. Her hair is dirty blond and doesn't seem to see the business end of a brush very often, but she keeps it clipped back.

"Yup. Anything I should know?"

"Whatever you do, don't cry," Maria tells me. "The kids really hate that."

"At some point, you're going to want to punch a kid . . . we all go through it. But don't. It doesn't help, and you just end up going viral on the internet," Georgina adds.

While I ponder any scenario that would lead me to cry or punch a child, I notice a tall and very athletic woman striding through the gym doors wearing a Hawthorne Hornets warm-up jacket and matching pants. Her curly red hair is in a messy bun. I can only assume it's the coach of the team until the murmuring starts amongst our mat moms.

"Oh shit, here we go," Maria says out of the side of her mouth.

"I didn't know she had a kid at Hawthorne," a mat mom behind us whispers.

"She didn't until this year," Franny informs those of us within earshot. "I think she wore out her welcome at Singleton."

"Who is she?" I ask after realizing I'm the only one who doesn't know.

"That's Mimi Melon," Maria says ominously, and I start to laugh. She frowns at me. "Why are you laughing?"

"Because it sounds like a stripper name."

They stare at me blankly.

"You know, when you put together your first pet's name and the last thing you ate, it's your stripper name."

"I always thought it was your pet and the street you grew up on," Maria said.

"Well, that would make me Tinkles 110th Street," Georgie groused. "I think I like Jen's better." She pauses and puts her hands up like she's seeing it on a marquee.

"Tinkles Gummybear," she says proudly and we all laugh.

"Jupiter Yogurt," Maria adds.

"Chirpie Turkey," I say in honor of the budgie bird I had when I was five.

"Chewie Sandwich," Franny announces.

We all crack up at this and Georgie says, "I wonder what Mimi Melon's *real* stripper name would be?"

"Probably something boring like Cathy Burger," I say, and Franny cackles.

"Watch out for this one. She's a jokester."

A jokester *and* a funster. Not sure I can live up to both. I better dust off some knock-knock jokes.

But then she leans closer and whispers, "Don't *ever* say that outside of this group. Mimi will ruin you."

I want to ask exactly how a woman I don't know whose kid goes to another school could do anything to me, but I don't. Mimi is sitting with her crew, and they seem entranced with her banter.

As a whistle blows and the teams form a circle, I see Ron rushing

across the gym wearing a BlueHawks hat and searching the crowd
for me. I wave him over and introduce him to the mat moms
around me.

"Did I miss anything?" he asks, settling in.

"Not yet."

"Do you know what Max weighed in at?"

Max has been hoping to wrestle in the 120-pound weight class,
but as of yesterday he was still 113.

"I don't. But he's been eating like a monster."

"Ya, but he's growing, too." Ron shakes his head like this is some
kind of problem we will have to overcome.

My attention is pulled to the center ring where two wrestlers are
shaking hands. They look to be in a much lighter weight class than
Max—they are both shorter and skinnier—as if neither has reached
puberty yet. They are wearing their singlets and headgear. The Hornets have made the interesting choice to wrestle in white uniforms
that leave very little to the imagination.

Once they start, there is a lot of circling each other in a crouched
position, then our guy (his name is Chet judging by the woman
who is yelling encouragements to him) gets put in a headlock by the
Hawthorne kid (named Shawn). This is when all hell breaks loose.
Parents are screaming, coaches are yelling, and kids are cheering. I
can't imagine how the wrestlers know who to listen to, but Coach
D's voice is distinctively deep, so when he yells, "Break, break,
break!" Chet seems to do just that.

"These little guys are scrappy." Ron laughs, really enjoying
himself.

I wish I could tell you I understood what I was watching, but
that would be a lie. To my layman's eye there is a lot of hugging and
grabbing and rubbing and touching—pretty much behavior that
would get you kicked out of the local Denny's—and before I know
it, Shawn from the Hornets is declared the "winner by points." All
the mat moms yell, "Good try, Chet!" and "Way to hang in there!"
but Chet's mom isn't having any of it and goes to have an animated
chat with Coach D.

The first few matches are in lighter weight classes and go pretty much the way of the first one. As Ron and I watch I ask him about his day at the yoga studio.

He rolls his eyes. "I'll tell you later."

"Tell me now!"

The crowd erupts at whatever is happening on the mat.

"The girls had a screwup with their lunch stuff."

"What happened?"

He looks across the gym and points to the door where I see both girls walking in, but not walking together. "Maybe I'll let them tell you."

"Oh, that's so sweet, they've come to watch Max."

Ron lets out a huff. "I don't think it's Max they've come to see."

Both girls make sure to catch Coach D's attention before they take seats on opposite ends of the same bleacher.

"So what happened today?" I press Ron.

"Well, you know they haven't really been getting along since the pancake breakfast."

"Uh-huh." They've been sniping at each other over, of all people, Coach D. I guess they both took a shine to him and have been arguing over who he likes better. I think I can safely say this is the first time they have ever fought over a guy. They have such polar opposite tastes.

"So I guess Vivs said something about Laura's cooking, so Laura refused to make the food for today, which left Vivs to do it."

"Oh shit." I put my hands to my face. The noise around me drops away as I recall what happens when Vivs cooks pretty much *anything*.

Ron sighs and scratches his head. "I guess the recipe called for paprika, but she accidentally used cayenne pepper."

"No!"

Ron nods and gives a grim laugh. "Yeah."

"How bad?"

"Nine calls. People burned their mouths, and one had an allergic reaction."

"Oh no!"

"Not a bad one, but Benadryl-worthy, or so I was told. I spent a good part of the day doing damage control and then talking to the girls about professionalism and responsibility and keeping their personal life out of the business. They agreed to refund everyone and write personal apologies to the customers."

"They got off easy."

"Not that easy. I really laid into them."

I glance over at my daughters. They both have game faces on.

"Good. I will too, later."

"I wouldn't," Ron cautions me. "I spoke to them as a business partner, not a father. If you chime in, they'll take it less seriously."

While I mull over the insinuation that my *chiming in* wouldn't be taken seriously (after all, I'm a business partner too, albeit a silent one), Max is called to the ring. I sit up and squeeze Ron's knee.

"It's time!" I lightly squeal as we see our son stride to the middle of the mat.

Max is all business, as he should be. I thought I might get a wave, but he stares straight ahead at his opponent, named Kyle, who looks a bit heavy to be in Max's weight class, but what the hell do I know? They shake hands, and when the whistle blows, they crouch and start to circle each other like a couple of feral cats. Then out of nowhere, Kyle takes Max down by the knees in one stealth move. Max is on his back faster than you can say, *Don't hurt my baby!* He tries to scramble up, but Kyle has him pinned by the shoulders using his whole torso. The ref declares Kyle the winner. The other team goes crazy, but Max looks like he's going to cry. My heart aches and I grab Ron, so I won't get up and run to him.

"Beginners nerves," he mumbles and gives my shoulder a hug.

The ref raises Kyle's arm in victory, then his coach hands him what looks like the safety pins they used on diapers in the olden days. Kyle seems thrilled and runs to his teammates for a high five.

"Why did he get a diaper pin?" I ask.

"If you win your match by pinning someone, you get a pin," Franny tells me. "Most kids wear them on their warm-up jackets."

I look around and see many of the kids have two, three, or in some cases more pins on their jackets, like medals won in battle. I wonder if Max will ever get one. I see him standing, listening to Coach D and nodding.

By this time, I'm getting the hang of what is going on and start counting how many kids are left to wrestle before I can get Max home and give him a hug. The next match is called, and something happens that makes me pay attention. Two boys make their way to the center of the ring, and as they do, Mimi Melon steps down from her perch in the bleachers and stands ringside.

"Are we supposed to do that?" I whisper to Ron. He shrugs.

"She *always* does that," says Georgina, who is sitting on the other side of me shaking her head. "I don't think the refs like it, but technically it isn't illegal."

Mimi cuts quite an intimidating figure as she rocks side to side waiting for the whistle to blow and the match to get underway. When it finally does, she takes mat mom participation to a new level. Mimi starts screaming instructions from her place ringside, and let me tell you, hers is the only voice any of us can hear.

"Come on, Conner, bring it! Get him down! You got this. Come on, Conner! Lift! Lift!" And, impressively, Conner is doing exactly what he is told. The boys—Conner and Josh—are very evenly matched, and it seems like nothing is happening for a long time. Once they start mixing it up, they end up out of bounds sometimes and other times rolling around on the floor. Ultimately, Mimi's son Conner is declared the winner by points, and Mimi gives an arrogant nod and strides back to the bleachers. Our side is not happy.

"There's no way," Josh's mother says to Franny. "I'm going to look at the scorecard." And she marches to the side where the scorekeepers sit.

Just when I think the last of them have wrestled, I notice one of the original kids is back at the center mat and wrestling someone new.

"What the hell?" I whisper to Ron. "That kid already went."

"I know. They have three matches each."

"What?" I say much more loudly than I mean to. "Max has to wrestle two more times?"

Ron nods and I groan and settle in for a long afternoon.

Max's second match is against a boy about the same height and weight as him. In this one they start circling each other and do their little dance for about thirty seconds. But then suddenly Max gets his opponent around the top of his legs and brings him down to his back. The boy (Marcus, judging by all the yelling) quickly scrambles to his knees and they are locked in a battle of wills—neither wants to give an inch. Ron is yelling so loudly he is going hoarse. My heart is in my throat, and I can't catch my breath. The boys are now on their sides and look like they are spooning until Max throws his leg over Marcus and forces him onto his stomach.

"Nelson, nelson!" screams Coach D, and Max somehow gets his arm under the boy's arm and grabs the back of his neck. The ref is now down on the mat with the boys and looking for something.

"What's he doing?" I ask Ron.

"He's trying to see if Max is pinning the kid's shoulders to the mat. They need to be there for a solid second."

I didn't know one second could be so long! Marcus is wriggling and thrusting and doing anything he can to get Max off his back. At one point he goes still for a moment, and I think it's over, but then he thrusts his body up with all his might and manages to escape Max's hold. They set up again, and this time they start with Max on his hands and knees and Marcus beside him. As the whistle blows to start, Marcus flips Max onto his back and throws his body over Max's torso, effectively pinning his shoulders to the ground, but not for long! Max thrusts his way out of the hold and they are standing up again. Coach D is yelling, and the wrestlers and mat moms are cheering. Honest to God, I don't know how much more of this I can take. Sitting here watching my only son, my baby, expend every last ounce of energy he has trying to defeat Marcus seems barbaric and reckless and in no way something I want to do ever again, let alone twice a week for the next three months. The match seems to go on forever, but finally the whistle blows, and

Marcus is declared the winner by points. Max looks crushed and exhausted as he walks off the mat, and before I know it, I'm crying like a baby. I feel so helpless just sitting here watching him get the crap kicked out of him.

I decide to run to the bathroom, so I don't make a spectacle of myself. As I pass Maria on the bleachers, she frowns and mouths *No crying* to me. I stick my tongue out at her and pick up my pace. When I reach the girls' bathroom, which is right outside the gym, I'm reminded why I don't like using public toilets. The smell in this one is a weird combo of poop, sweat, BO, and lip gloss. While I pee, I blow my nose and breathe through my mouth. I entertain myself by reading the stall graffiti. Apparently, Becca is a ho, and Mr. Gilcrest sucks balls. I can hear the cheers of the match taking place on the other side of the walls, and I wonder what mood Max is going to be in after his two losses. A part of me hopes he'll want to quit because right now I know I do.

As I'm washing my hands with the disgusting-smelling soap, Laura walks in.

"Hey Mom," she says casually.

"Hi sweets. I'm surprised to see you here."

"I had to come," she tells me, wide-eyed. "I knew Vivs was coming, and I can't let her see Dana more than I do."

"*That's* why you came?"

She looks confused. "Why else would I come to a middle school wrestling match?" She goes into the stall I just came out of.

"To see your little brother compete in his first match."

"Well, that too, obviously," I hear her say. She flushes the toilet and comes out. "Did Ron tell you what happened today?"

"Yes. I can't say I'm happy about it."

"Me neither! It was all Vivs's fault."

"Because she said something about your cooking." I want to confirm the lunacy.

"Yes! I knew she'd screw up. It serves her right."

"Laura! Don't you understand that not only did you cost your company money today, but people got hurt, too. It could have been so much worse."

"Mom, we already got the lecture from Ron. I'm sorry it happened, but Vivs needed to learn a lesson."

"I hope you both learned a lesson . . ." I start in, but Laura heads toward the door.

"I've got to get back." And she walks out, leaving me at a loss for words.

Back in the gym I watch a few more fights and can't help but feel like I'm in some kind of *Groundhog Day* situation. Finally, Max is called for his third match, and God help us it's against Mimi Melon's son Conner.

"How did we get so lucky?" I murmur.

The boys meet and shake hands, and as they do, Mimi once again takes her place beside the mat. On impulse I stand up to make my own way down there, but Ron pulls me back down by the back of my yoga pants and says "No," like he's telling Maude not to pick her nose.

The match starts and Conner is on the offensive immediately. Even though he is shorter, he lifts Max up and has him down on his back within twenty seconds.

"Get off your back, Max!" Ron stands up and yells as though he's reading the back of my T-shirt, but Max is struggling under Connor's weight. Suddenly, Mimi is down on the ground in a pose that I strike only when I have to look for something under the sofa. She is less than five feet from the boys, on her hands and knees with her butt in the air, telling Conner to pin him. Max struggles, and we are all yelling for him to get off his back, which he does, but I can tell his strength is giving out, and after a few more go-rounds, Conner does indeed pin him.

"Winner, by pin," the referee yells and raises Conner's arm as Max shakes his hand with no enthusiasm and trudges off to the side with his head down. My heart sinks.

The Hornets coach then hands Conner a pin as expected. But what happens next is a real dick punch to everyone in the gym, especially Max. Conner runs over to his mother, who has just put her warm-up jacket on, and hands her the pin.

"Oh, you're going to love this." Franny's voice is dripping with sarcasm.

"Jesus, she still does it?" Georgina sounds disgusted.

As I watch, Mimi hands the pin back to her son ceremoniously and turns her back to him. I gasp when I see the back of her Hornets jacket is *covered* in pins. It looks like hundreds of them adorn the back of the jacket, yet Conner is able to find a place for one more. The Hornets go crazy, while mother and son smile and take a small bow.

"Cripes almighty, seriously?" Ron says. "Why do they have to make such a show of it?"

"What the hell?" I finally find my voice. It all happened so quickly my mind is still trying to catch up.

"I've never seen anything like that," Ron grouses.

"But aren't they new to that school? How does she have so many pins?"

"She's been collecting them for years. All four of her sons are wrestlers," Franny explains.

"They must be really good at it." I'm a bit in awe.

Franny rolls her eyes. "They should be. It's all they do."

Maria chimes in, "She starts them when they're like five and they wrestle year-round."

"Wow. Aren't the dads usually the ones who push the kids?" I give Ron the side-eye.

"Oh, her husband is worse. He was banned from tournaments a couple of years ago after he walked out onto the mat and tried to intimidate a kid who had pinned his son in a previous match. Remember, Franny?" Maria asks.

Franny nods, not taking her eyes off the action on the mat.

"It worked," she says grimly. "Jason purposely took a dive that day."

"It was her middle son," Maria whispers to me, then rolls her eyes. She mouths, *It was bad!*

I've had enough. I know the match isn't over, but this is excruciating. I tell Ron I'm going home to start dinner. I kiss his cheek and make my way to the gym exit without a backwards glance. I'm going to make Max his favorite meal, spaghetti and meatballs with garlic bread. And for me, it'll be a nice big glass of cooking wine (so named because it's the wine I drink when I cook). I'm so preoccupied that when I head for the door, I don't even notice Mimi Melon until I bump into her on her way to the soda machine.

"Man, does your kid need work!" she says, laughing and sticking out her hand. "Hi, I'm Mimi Melon."

"Jen Dixon," I answer. "And not as much as your kid is going to need therapy." I mime a mic drop and walk out the door.

6

To: Asami Chang + 25 more
From: Jen Dixon
Re: A Monster Bash!
Date: October 21

TO BE SUNG TO THE TUNE OF THE ADDAMS FAMILY

Halloween's here (snap snap)
Halloween's here (snap snap)

We're throwing a big party
We hope you won't be tardy
Costumes should be bizarre-dee
Yes, it's that time of year!

Halloween's here (snap snap)
Halloween's here (snap snap)

Greeting Parents of Ghouls and Goblins!
Your seventh grader is formally invited to a Halloween Party
On Saturday October 31, 7–10 at the Dixon residence.
5330 Levon Court, Overland Park

RSVP to this email

I know what you're thinking, . . . and you're right. I'm the last person who should be throwing a Halloween party since I have never hidden my contempt for the stupid holiday. However, I find myself more in the minority than ever these days now that Maude is full on into it. So when Max, a few days after his crushing loss at his first wrestling match, asked us if he could please, please, *please* have a Halloween party, there was no way I was going to say no. At first I suggested it just be a party—aka no costumes. But I was shouted down by everyone at the dinner table, which included my parents and Maude and Vivs. Laura was supposed to have been with us as well, because it was our weekly Sunday dinner, but she had mysteriously backed out at the last minute.

"Is this because you guys are still fighting?" I asked Vivs.

"No, this is because she's a pouty little baby," she countered.

I frowned. "I thought you guys had called a truce after the cayenne pepper incident?"

"We have. Or we had until Dana called me yesterday and asked me out." Vivs is unsuccessfully trying to hide a self-satisfied smirk.

"You're going out with Coach D?" I guess I needed this verified.

"Coach D asked you out?" Max gave an alarmed yell from the other end of the table and came marching toward us.

"Can we stop calling him that?" Vivs was annoyed. "And yes, we are going on a date this Wednesday. Mom, can you babysit?"

"I don't need a babysitter," Maude informed the table matter-of-factly.

"Well maybe we can just hang out," I suggested, which seemed to please her. To Vivs I said, "I thought you both agreed he was off limits."

"I never agreed to that. She's just pissed off that Dana didn't ask her out. She could have come tonight. She's just being a jerk."

"Sissy, don't go out with Coach D." Max was now standing by Vivs's chair.

"Why not?" Vivs asked.

"Because he's my coach, and I don't want you to be mean to him like you are to Raj."

Oh boy.

"I'm not mean to Raj!"

"You used to be," Max countered. I'd never really given much thought to how the Raj/Vivs romance played out in Max's head. I wasn't sure he had noticed any of it, but clearly he had.

"What's going on down there?" My mother shouted from the other end of the table. She had been locked in a debate with Ron about our new mayor, but Max's moving seats caught her attention.

"Vivs is going on a date with my coach, and I don't want her to," he informed his grandmother, who then glared at Vivs.

"Well, he's right, you know. Never fish off the company dock. That's what I always say."

"Nana, I'm not fishing anywhere!" Vivs retorted. "I said yes to a date with a really nice, seemingly normal guy." She turned to Max. "I'm sorry you don't like it."

"Oh, why don't you just go back with Raj?" My mother has always had a hard time accepting that they are no longer together.

"You want to know why, Nana?" Vivs snapped. "Because he has a girlfriend."

We were all shocked by this piece of gossip.

"Really? Who is she?" I asked.

"Some mother he met at the playground, of all freaking places." Vivs suddenly realized her daughter was sitting right beside her and seemed embarrassed to have been talking so openly about it.

"Daddy's girlfriend is named Janine," Maude informed us. "She smells like oranges."

"You've met her?" I was surprised.

Maude nodded. "She's Drew's mommy."

There was no reaction because none of us knew who Drew was.

"Anyway"—Vivs decided to move the conversation along—"Raj is happy, and now I'm going to be happy, too. With Dana."

Max shook his head and asked to be excused.

"Do you have homework?"

"I did it. I just want to practice some holds with Dwayne." And off he went to his room.

"Who's Dwayne?" Vivs asked. "Is he on the team?"

"That's what he named his grappling dummy—after The Rock."

"I love Dwayne." Maude sighed.

"You're not supposed to play with him," I reminded her.

"I know! But Max lets me touch him sometimes."

That sounded creepy, but I didn't say anything. I was watching my dad sitting quietly at the other end of the table. I miss his input into the dinner conversation. Plus, he could always keep my mother in check. Without his loving reproach of "*Now Kay . . .*" my mother is just a gushing faucet of unfiltered thoughts.

Anyway, despite Max's objections and whatever thoughts of impropriety I may have had, the big date happened last night, and by all accounts it went "fine," which is pretty much all I got from Vivs when she came to pick up Maude, although when I asked if he showed her any wrestling moves, she answered, "Who's to say I didn't show *him* a few?"

Right now, I'd love to start making a to-do list for this Halloween party we are apparently throwing, but I must scoot to pick up my parents. I'm taking them to Max's wrestling match. It's an away game at Osage Middle School. I missed the second match, against the Singleton school, but Ron said I was lucky because our boys got pillaged and it was brutal to watch. I guess that school is known for its wrestling program and consistently goes to the state championship. I think I remember Franny mentioning that some of Mimi Melon's boys went there. Max came home with his ear looking red and swollen, which Ron says could be a precursor to cauliflower ear—one of the many disgusting things I can look forward to as a mat mom. I guess there had to be a few downsides since the rest is all parades and spa days.

My parents are waiting for me in the lobby of their condo, wearing matching blue velour jogging suits. *It's come to this?* is all I can think as my mom opens the car door for my dad.

"Hello, you," he says as he sits beside me in the front seat.

"Hi Dad. How's it going?"

"Okay, I guess. Where are we going?"

"Ray, I already told you we're going to see Max wrestle someone. Sweetheart, will there be a place to sit?"

"Probably on the bleachers, Mom. If not, I'll find you guys some chairs."

And off we go. While Ray reads the road signs, my mother updates me with the goings-on at the church and at Riverview Assisted Living, her newfound home away from home.

". . . And Janine has a brand-new granddaughter! You remember Janine, don't you? She's hoping her son will bring her by soon, but that woman he's married to is worried about germs. She's acting like she's the first and only woman to ever have a baby!"

"New moms are always like that," I remind her.

"Oh please! I took you everywhere when you were a baby. Sammy Leighton told me Janine is just devastated she might not meet the baby for a few weeks."

"And how's Sammy?" I ask my mother with a sideways glance at my dad.

"What's that supposed to mean?" Apparently, I had asked it with a "tone."

"Nothing at all. Just wondering if you have seen him."

"Well of course I have. I see him every time I go. I've told you his children never visit."

I nod. "Have you gone out for lunch again?" I wonder if my father is paying any attention to our conversation.

"Just a few times," she says nonchalantly. "He likes to get out, you know." I can tell she's getting defensive, and I'm kind of glad. She shouldn't be getting a free pass on gallivanting around with another man every week.

"Osage Middle School," my father announces as I turn into the parking lot. The PMS wrestling bus is already here so I know Max will be warming up.

I walk my parents into the school and am directed to the gym by a security guard. I find seats on the bleachers right near the gym floor, so we settle in with a really good view of the action.

"Where is your mat mom T-shirt, Jen?" Franny, of course, is standing in front of me in full PMS gear.

"Right here," I tell her as I rip open my jacket like Superman and reveal the logo.

"We're thinking of doing sweatshirts for November and December," she informs me with a smile. I give her a thumbs-up and introduce my parents.

"That's so nice of you to come to your grandson's game," Franny says in a raised voice. I suppress a smile, but my mother isn't amused.

"There's no need to shout. I have two working ears. And why are you both announcing to the world that you have PMS?" Kay barks. Franny opens her mouth to answer but nothing comes out. Luckily a whistle blows, and the teams form a circle on the mat.

Our BlueHawks look very serious today, especially Coach D, who only breaks his game face for two seconds when he smiles and waves to me. I'm flattered to be singled out. He must really like Vivs.

As the fight begins, the teams seem very evenly matched to my layman's eye, and their mat moms are equally as spirited as ours, so you can imagine there's a lot of yelling going on. I glance at my parents and find Kay with her hands over her ears and Ray sitting quietly beside her.

That all changes when Max strides to the center of the mat and starts his match.

"Here's Max," I tell them as the match begins, and out of nowhere, my father stands up and starts shouting, "Come on, Max! Get him down! Sweep!"

My mother and I are stunned. It's been so long since Ray has even acknowledged his surroundings and now he is completely present and going all out, cheering for his grandson.

"What the heck?" I say to Kay. But she is just staring at him with her mouth open. Ray continues his cheering with the umph of a man half his age, and when Max finally loses on points, my dad sits down and winks at me. *He winks at me!*

The pattern continues through Max's other two matches—Ray comes alive when his grandson hits the mat; otherwise he sits quietly. I need to ask his doctor about this.

Once Max leaves the mat, in defeat for the third time, Ray tells my mother he wants to go. I consider trying to convince him to stay for the last few matches, but I can see he is tired, so I ask Franny to make sure my son knows I had to take his grandparents home, then I shuffle them out to the car.

"What did you think?" I ask them once we are on our way.

"About what?" my father asks.

"About Max's wrestling match."

"It was fun!" Kay enthuses. "Our Max has some moves, doesn't he, Ray?"

"I guess so," says my father. I think he's only pretending to know what we're talking about because about five seconds later, he starts reading road signs again.

"Does that happen a lot, Mom?" I glance at her in my rearview mirror.

"No. I haven't seen him that excited in I don't know how long."

I steal a glance at my father and see the fog of his dementia has mercilessly settled over his face again. The now familiar ache hits my heart, and I take a deep breath to manage the relentless fear I feel from not knowing if or when he will be back.

7

To: Asami Chang +25

From: Jen Dixon

Re: A Monster Bash Part Deux

Date: October 29

Hi,

Thanks so much for all the speedy RSVPs. I can't believe how many of you are so eager to get the kids out of your hair for a few hours on a Friday night. You're welcome!

Just a reminder that pickup is at 10:00, and for the love of God don't be late. I don't care how many beers you've had.

Thanks in advance for your complete cooperation!

Jen Dixon

Best mom EVER according to her son. If you ask her daughters, you might get a different answer.

I don't want to jinx it, but I'm totally on top of this party. I'm keeping the food simple—pizza and soda, and we are clearing out most of the living room, so the kids have a place to hang out without destroying anything. I'm repurposing decorations from years gone by and creating a kind of haunted hallway complete with weird mirrors and bowls full of eyeballs and intestines aka peeled grapes and cooked spaghetti. Ron hung a bunch of those fake lit candles from the ceiling à la the Harry Potter dining hall, using chicken wire. And at the very end I hung a black piece of fabric and wrote *TURN BACK NOW* with glow-in-the-dark spray paint. I have to say the effect is pretty cool. All this doesn't mean that I now like Halloween, but my slumbering DIY monster has definitely been awakened.

And it's all done a day early! I knew I had to teach spin tomorrow morning, and I have another meet and greet with one of my students right afterward. Yup, I'm still at it even though the last two were less than ideal.

My second outing was with the bald guy Lynnie referenced in our tête-à-tête. I'm not really into the bald look, but I have to say, Reg definitely has the ugly/sexy thing going on. He's got a great smile, nice brown eyes, and a decent, albeit stocky, body. We met after class at the juice bar last week—Lynnie gave me the eye on her way out and then mimed *Call me*.

Reg was happy to have a get-to-know-you drink with me. He told me a lot about his day job as a dog groomer, and his night job as a DJ at a party space in KC, Missouri. I found out he's forty-two and has never been married (two things that are sure to be like catnip for Lynnie).

"So tell me about you," he said, leaning in and giving me a full showing of his teeth.

For some reason, "I'm a grandmother" was the first thing that popped out of my mouth. I assumed he already knew this because I talk about my life to my riders quite a bit. But Reg's face couldn't quite hide his shock.

"Wait, seriously?"

"Yup. She's four."

"Are you married?" he asked warily.

"I am. His name is Ron."

Reg's mouth stayed open as he took in this info and then he scowled.

"So what are we doing here?"

"Sorry?"

"What are we doing here?" he repeated. "This little getting-to-know-you thing that you invited me to."

"We're getting to know each other," I said plainly.

"So you're not hitting on me?"

I nearly spit out my juice. "No! God no. Why would you think that?"

He raised his two hands in an *I give up* gesture. "I mean, you're friendly and you asked me if I was single . . ."

I swear on my children I never thought an invitation to have juice would be construed as a come-on.

"I'm doing this with all my regular riders."

Reg looked at his hands and started to laugh.

"Wow, I'm really glad I didn't go into a spiel about how much grandmothers turn me on."

"Ew!" I started to laugh along with him. "I could be your . . . much older sister."

"Listen, if a guy thinks he can get laid, he's willing to make a lot of accommodations." He continued to cackle as he rubbed his bald head. "Man, this is embarrassing!"

I thought about Lynnie and if I should mention she has eyes for him, but I decided not to, although I would give her a heads-up that he's single and looking.

My next juice date was with Alex, a rider who looked like a no-nonsense woman with straight black hair, a razor-thin body, and a prominent nose. I long ago nicknamed her "superbitch" in my head because she rarely smiles and does the bare minimum in terms of interacting with me. I had high hopes for this one because, let's face it, I needed a win.

"So how can I help you?" she asked matter-of-factly as we settled in at the juice bar.

I smiled. "Oh, I don't need help. I just see you in my class a lot and I don't know anything about you, so I thought it might be fun to get to know you a bit." I took a swig of my sweet greens and leaned forward on the table.

Alex looked confused. "What do you want to know?"

Such a good question.

"What do you do for a living?" I lobbed out there.

"I'm a gynecologist," she said, stone-faced.

"So I guess you're at my cervix," I joked. I'd seen that once on a T-shirt and thought it was funny. Dr. Alex did not, so I moved on.

"Are you married?"

She stared at me for a long moment and then her face crumbled, and she let out a sound that reminded me of a car that can't start.

"Why would you ask me that?"

Oh, for the love of . . .

"I'm so sorry."

She shook her head and wiped her eyes with a napkin. The strange little noise continued for what seemed like an eternity before she spoke again.

"I was supposed to get married this Saturday . . ." She welled up again and had to stop.

I took another swig of green juice and wondered why she would be at spin class with this going on in her life. If it was me, I'd be in the bathtub for the next three months.

"Did something happen to your fiancé?" I finally asked.

She nodded and took a couple of deep breaths before answering. This time, the noise was gone, and she was in complete control.

"The asshole ran off with my best friend."

I didn't even know what to say because this truly is the cheapest shot in the dating world. What kind of friend and boyfriend would do that to someone?

"Well, they deserve each other." It was a meek offering, but it was all I could come up with.

Alex blew her nose. "I know that, but it's gonna take me a minute to get there. I just can't believe I didn't see it coming."

We talked for another ten minutes, then she abruptly stood up and thanked me.

"That was the best cry I've had in years. See you on Friday."

In years? I cry like that because it's Tuesday.

She grabbed her sports bag and off she went, shoulders back and her resting bitch face firmly back in place.

I'm heading to Om Sweet Om this morning to take a yoga class and spy on my daughters. I haven't seen either of them in a few days, and I want to see how their business is going.

I haven't been to the Overland Park studio for a while, so I'm pleasantly surprised when I walk in to see Good Clean Grub has taken over a full wall of the lobby in such a cheerful way. The girls have put up a large vinyl banner with their logo, and beneath it a chalkboard where their daily offerings are spelled out in colorful script. One of each of the items is on display on a table, and a big cooler sits behind it holding all the fresh food. I see Laura crouching beside the cooler and Vivs standing at the table looking at her phone.

"Oh my gosh, girls! This looks great!" I smile and hug them both.

"Is this the first time you're seeing it?" Vivs sounds surprised.

"I don't get here as much as I used to," I tell her. "How's business?"

"Good," they say together without looking up.

"Between the three locations, we're doing about forty meals a day," Vivs informs me.

"Who runs the other two places?" I ask. Ron opened two Om Sweet Om franchises last year, and the girls are now selling food at those studios as well.

"I'm headed over to Lee's Summit now." Laura stands up and brushes her hands on her pants. "And we leave a small cooler at Independence that the staff sells for us."

"You may have to hire someone if you get much busier," I tell them.

Neither reply, but Laura gives me a quick hug and says, "I'm off," and is out the door. I frown as I look after her.

"Don't tell me you guys are still fighting over Coach D," I say to Vivs.

"Can you please call him Dana? And I'm not fighting with anyone. Laura's just pissy all the time these days."

"Any idea why?"

Vivs throws up her hands. "Who the hell knows with her?"

I think I need to spend some time with my younger daughter. I've been so involved with the mat moms and my spin classes and my parents that I haven't been paying any attention to her. Lunch and a Target shopping spree should do the trick. Right after Halloween.

"I'm going to take Carmen's restorative class." I look at my watch and am glad to see I'll be a bit early. "Will I see you after?" I ask Vivs.

"Probably."

"Okay. Good luck with your sales."

"Thanks," she says dismissively as she types on her phone.

Carmen, the yogini leading the class, was my favorite spin instructor when she was at Fusion, and she's the woman who made me want to become a teacher. She doesn't do the bike anymore, but I find her yoga classes just as inspiring. I have nicknamed her restorative class "old lady yoga" because it's basically an hour of deep breathing and Shavasana. If nothing else, I get a good nap in.

"How are you?" she greets me warmly, and I hope it isn't just because I'm the boss's wife.

"I'm good!" I give her a hug. We chat briefly, then I ask her if she's heard that Bob Nolan died.

"No! I didn't. How?"

"Dropped dead of a heart attack while running."

Carmen puts her hand to her mouth. "Oh my God, that's terrible." She shakes her head. "He was such a great rider. That's crazy. Were you close to him?"

"You know, I barely knew him. But I called his family and heard what an extraordinary life he had."

"Really?"

"He was in the Olympics for cycling, he fought in a war, had a child he raised alone after his wife died of cancer . . ."

"Wow. You really got into it," Carmen says but with a little less enthusiasm than I would have expected.

"Well, like I said, I called his family."

She nods, so I decide to go on.

"I felt terrible that I didn't know anything about him. So now I'm trying to get to know all my regulars by spending time with them outside of class."

Carmen's eyes widen, but all she says is "And how's that going?"

I think about my efforts so far and decide to fudge the truth. "Really well," I tell her.

"Well, good," she says without any gusto.

"What am I missing?" I ask her because her lack of enthusiasm is very apparent.

"Just be careful," she warns as other students file in and start to set up.

"Be careful about what?" I want to know, but we've been interrupted by someone asking about bolsters, so I grab my mat and get myself ready for a snooze.

+ + +

As I'm leaving class, I'm surprised to see Lynnie in the lobby chatting with Vivs.

"Lynnie? I didn't know you came here."

"I do now!" She greets me with a voracious hug. Over her shoulder I see Vivs give me a raised eyebrow.

"And I just met your daughter who's older than me! I can't believe it." She turns to Vivs. "You and I should talk! I can't imagine having this one as a mother." She slaps me on the back.

"It isn't without its challenges," Vivs says dryly.

"Are you here to take a class?" I ask her.

"I'm just checking the place out since you talk about it in class so much." To Vivs she says, "Your mom is, like, my hero."

Before Vivs can slip in a snide remark, I tell Lynnie I will have the front desk give her a free pass to try it out.

"Thanks! Your mom is the GOAT," she tells Vivs using the acronym for "greatest of all time."

"Yes, we call her that all the time," Vivs assures her.

I leave them to swap stories about me, and head home to take a much-needed shower. Max has a match after school and it's my turn to go. Ron and I have agreed to split our attendance, so we each have to go only once a week. Not that it isn't the delight of my life to be there cheering my son on, but I wish he could wrestle three times in a row so I could leave sooner. The only thing tougher than watching your baby fight is having to watch twelve other kids do the same thing.

Today is extra special because it's the ninth match for the team, and that means it's my turn to bring home and wash the uniforms! Huzzah! I'm very happy to do my part, but I'm not looking forward to putting that laundry bag in my car.

I wanted to bring my father again, but I had brought him to a match last week, excited to see him come alive and start cheering Max. Sadly, he didn't have the same magical reaction to seeing his grandson wrestle that he'd had before. Instead, he just sat in his seat and read the signs on the gym walls like *Book Club Meets Every Thursday in the Quad* or *Remember to lock your lockers!* I guess you can't make lightning strike twice.

It's a home meet, thank goodness, so I know my way around and what to expect. Maria and Georgina are waiting for me in full mat mom regalia. I'm getting to know more of the moms on the team, but so far these two and Franny are my posse. It's interesting to note that every mom seems to bring a little something different to the table. Maria is kind of the 411 of the group. She has *all* the info *all* the time. And I'm not talking about gossip, although she's pretty good at that, too. I'm talking about stats and past matches and who is who and what happened when. She can recall things from years past when her older son wrestled, but she also studies the rosters and just kind of knows who is playing where and when. It's impressive. I would have to care so much more than I do now to have any of this stay with me.

Franny is the boss and the mother hen of the group, always reminding everyone what they need to do. And she's just quirky enough to keep me interested. She would have made a great class mom.

Georgina's specialty is high tech. She is like the Stephen Spielberg of the team. She shoots every match and sends the recordings to all the mat moms, which is incredibly generous of her.

The only match she doesn't shoot is that of her own son, Tyler. I think she was hoping I'd be her go-to cameraman, but I'm really bad at filming anything. First, my eyes are getting worse by the day, but I'm just too vain to wear my glasses in public. Second, something happens to me when I'm handed a smart phone and asked to film. I crack under the pressure and always blow it. When Georgie first asked me if I would shoot Tyler's match, I told her that I'm all thumbs and basically blind, but she insisted. Let me just say, it wasn't *my* fault her phone was in selfie mode when she handed it to me. I just pointed it and pushed record. She basically got three minutes of me squinting and has never asked me again.

"Got your T-shirt on?" Franny gives me her standard greeting.

"Yup!" I smile and show her the bit of blue sticking up from my sweater. "When are you getting the sweatshirts? T-shirt weather is way over."

"I know. They should be coming any day."

As I take a seat with our group, I ask Maria about the team we are wrestling against.

"North Shore is the worst in the league. I always feel bad for them. I don't think their sports program gets any support. They like to say, 'We're mathletes, not athletes.'"

"That's catchy," I tell her. "So are you telling me Max might actually win a match today?"

"I'll be surprised if he doesn't, but we don't know who they have this year." Maria shrugs.

"Are you all set for the party tomorrow night?" Georgina asks as she sits down beside me.

"I think so!"

"You're a better woman than I am," she tells me. "Tyler is really excited. He's been trying to find the right costume for weeks."

"What did he end up with?"

"It's between a policeman and Mr. Peanut."

We both laugh out loud, but then Franny shushes us as the teams take to the mat.

I wish I could tell you Max was victorious in his matches, but sadly he was not. I guess North Shore got an influx of sporty kids from a nearby primary school and they are competitive for the first time in years. Now they can say they are mathletes *and* athletes.

Afterward I have to wait around for the boys to get out of their singlets and put them in the laundry bag. When Coach D hands it to me, I'm expecting it to be somewhat noisome, but nothing could have prepared me for the stench wafting from the mesh bag. I refuse to put it in the car and spend another ten minutes strapping it to the top of the Palisade using some bungy cords that Ron left in there.

"I stink," Max grouses on the way home.

"That's just the laundry," I assure him.

"No, Mom. I mean at wrestling. I suck."

"You don't suck. You're still learning. Most of these kids have wrestled for a long time. I think you get better every time I see you."

He doesn't respond, and I can tell meek platitudes from his mother are not going to make him feel better. I decide to change the subject.

"Are you excited about tomorrow night?"

He gives me a one-shoulder shrug, but a glance in the rearview mirror shows me a slight grin on his face.

"Your costume is so great."

I know this will get a smile out of him. He's going as classic wrestler Hulk Hogan. Ron helped him fill a skin-colored body suit with lots of muscles, and I shaved the top of a blond wig to give him that half-balding look. We used the shaved hair to make a handlebar mustache, and Laura just finished crafting a WWF world championship belt.

"It's going to be epic," he proclaims.

Oh God, I hope not is all I can think.

8

"Such a good class today," Mary Willy enthuses as we sit down at the juice bar, and she shakes out her thin and sweaty hair. "Where do you get your ideas for music?"

"Lots of 80s on 8," I tell her. "And even 70s on 7. Satellite radio is my best friend."

"Remember when we had to wait for the DJ to play the song we wanted to hear?" She laughs.

"Please. I remember eight-track tapes."

"Me, too! Everything is so much easier now with streaming."

I wonder just how old Mary Willy is. She doesn't look old enough to remember the good old days.

I look toward the gym and see Lynnie staring at me with a dumbfounded look on her face. I wave and she waves back and then turns toward the locker room.

"So, Mary, you're an author . . ." I begin, but I'm interrupted with an eye roll from her and a sigh.

I frown. "You are, aren't you?"

"Well obviously you know I am." She seems irritated. "But I can't tell you anything about what's happening with Greta Johansen.

"Who's Greta Johansen?" I ask.

Mary Willy laughs. "Yeah right. And I suppose you'd ask J. K. Rowling who Harry Potter is."

"Well, actually, I wouldn't. Is Greta a character in one of your books? I'm sorry that I don't know. I'm not much of a reader."

She takes a moment to size me up and then starts to laugh.

"Oh my God, you really don't know?"

I shake my head and shrug. Is Greta Johansen the new age Nancy Drew or Clarice Starling that I'm not hip to? It wouldn't be the first time. As I get older, I'm more and more pop culture challenged. I saw an *Us Weekly* magazine at the grocery store the other day, and for the first time ever I had absolutely no idea who was on the cover.

Mary puts her hands over her face and groans. "I'm so embarrassed! I thought you asked me to have juice so you could pump me for info on my next book."

"Well, now I'm going to!" I assure her. "Who the heck is Greta Johansen?"

"She's the female protagonist in a series of books I have written."

"What are the books about?"

She pauses to consider her words. "It's sort of a coming-of-age series about a girl in her twenties leaving home for the first time."

"Is it one of those young adult series?" I remember Laura getting totally hooked on some books about a girl in a dystopian society.

"Uh, no. Definitely not for teens. Greta's journey is kind of a sexual awakening."

She lets that linger between us as an invitation for me to ask more, so I do.

"Oh, I see. So she's trying to find the love of her life?"

"More like she's trying to find the best sex of her life," Mary corrects me.

"Is it dirty?" I can't think of a better way to ask that question, unfortunately.

"I prefer erotic rather than dirty. And yes, it's very erotic."

Well color me shocked. Meek and mild Mary Willy writes mommy porn for a living!

"How many books are there?"

"I'm writing the fifth one now. The fourth book had quite a cliff-hanger, so I'm being stalked by my fans to find out how it turns out." She looks sheepishly at me. "I'm so sorry I accused you of doing that."

"Please! I'm embarrassed that I didn't know about this series!"

She waves me off. "Don't be. But it's called *Wanderlust* if you want to check it out."

As much as I want to ask her more, I decide to switch topics. I find out that she is happily married with no children (her husband has slow swimmers), and she was an editor-at-large for a fancy décor magazine before trying her hand at writing fiction. She was born in Boston, lived in New York for a while, and followed her husband to Kansas when he invested in commercial real estate here.

"It was a tough adjustment moving here, but your spin class really helped. I love singing along when I exercise."

"I'm so glad. It's all about the music for me."

We chat for a while about our husbands and where we like to vacation, and as we're wrapping things up, Mary asks why I asked her to join me for a juice in the first place if it wasn't to pump her for info.

"I'm trying to get to know my regular riders. I realize I see some of you guys like three times a week, but I don't know much about you. Case in point!" I gesture to her.

Mary Willy laughs. "Well, if you read my books, you might find out more than you want to!"

✦ ✦ ✦

Back home, I'm happy to see everything is pulling together for the party. Ron has been doing final touches on some of the more complicated decorations (that is, anything that needs to be plugged in). He greets me in the front yard with: "Your mother called. She's bringing Ray over."

"Are you kidding me? Why?"

"In her words, 'Tell Jennifer I just need to pop out for a little while, and I know what a busy day this is for her, so I'll bring Dad there instead of asking her to come here.'"

I have to say, Ron does a pretty good Kay impression.

"Alright, well I hope she won't be gone long."

"He'll be fine. I'll get him to help with the lawn."

"What's happening on the lawn?"

"I found more ghouls and goblins to put out."

My mother shows up half an hour later dressed as Dorothy from *The Wizard of Oz*. It's a bit off-putting to see a septuagenarian in that getup—what with the pigtails and short dress. She has spray-painted a pair of flats red for her ruby slippers and she is holding a stuffed dog.

"Wow, Mom, you're really getting into the spirit this year."

"I know! I can't believe this fits me. This was your costume, wasn't it?"

"I think it was Laura's."

"Well, they're having a party over at Riverview and everyone has to dress up."

My father is standing in the doorway behind her dressed in khakis and a T-shirt with a bomber jacket on top.

"Looking good, Dad!" I give him a hello hug.

"Hello, you." He smiles.

"Mom, why don't you take Dad to the party with you?"

"Well, I would, sweetheart, but it's only for residents."

"You do know *you're* not a resident, right?"

"Of course, I know! I'm a guest."

"I really don't see why Dad couldn't be a guest, too," I mutter.

"I'll be back later." She waves and is off. And Toto, too.

I look at my father and shrug. "What do you feel like doing?" I ask him.

"Oh well, I dunno."

"Ray, can you help me in the front yard?" Ron strides in to save the day. Now I have a chance to do all my final checks. Lots of candy? Check. Is the haunted hallway scary enough? Check. I call to make sure the pizza is going to be on time at seven-thirty and check the garage fridge to see that we have more than enough flavored waters and soda for the kids. I do believe I am ready.

✦ ✦ ✦

It's eight o'clock and I'm in a complete flop sweat.

First of all, every kid showed up at 7:05, which I guess is a twelve-year-old's idea of fashionably late. So instead of people trickling in and enjoying the haunted hallway a few at a time, we were slammed all at once, much like when a cruise ship docks in the Bahamas for a few hours. The kids swarmed the hallway leaving a path of destruction behind them, including the remnants of the floating candles, which they tore from the ceiling.

The girls all look adorable, if not a bit risqué for their age. Or maybe I'm a prude. There are two nurses, a queen of hearts, a policewoman and firefighter, and a few animals like mice and cats and even a puppy. But every costume consists of the same thing—a short skirt or shorts, a skimpy, tight top, and then one thing to make it look like a costume . . . like a badge or a headband with ears, or in the case of one of the nurses, a stethoscope. Some of the girls haven't reached puberty yet, but others look like they could be waitressing at Hooters, so the effect is varying.

I only mention the girls' costumes because of what happened to poor Max. He was standing in the living room, all decked out in his Hulk Hogan outfit, when he saw the girls piling into the house. I think it was one of the nurses that put him over the edge. I caught sight of him staring at her with his mouth open, and unfortunately, the thin bottom part of his costume left no doubt of his admiration for her. About half the kids noticed before Max finally did, and he's been in his room for the past half hour. Ron is trying to talk him off the ledge.

Meanwhile, my mother, as Dorothy, has been circulating with her stuffed dog, complaining about the food (*Only pizza, Jennifer?*) and the kids' costumes (*What nurse would wear a skirt that short?*

Or, *Whatever happened to dressing like cowboys and Indians?*) while my dad sits at the kitchen table and reads the newspaper for the umpteenth time.

I didn't really expect my parents to stay. I mean, a tween rave isn't exactly their scene, but Kay came back from her party at Riverview Assisted Living in such a festive mood that she said she wanted to stay and "help out," which is currently code for opening a bottle of white wine for herself and complaining to me.

At least the kids are having fun. The music is pumping in the living room, and from what I can see, the boys are doing wrestling moves and the girls are watching and taking pictures and cheering them on.

Ron and I take a seat in the dining room, away from the action and yet close enough to hear if anything goes awry.

"Seems like more than twenty-six kids in there." He frowns.

"Max asked if he could invite a few kids from outside school, but I thought it was only like four."

We spend the next little while talking about Vivs and Laura's business and what the next steps are now that they are up and running.

"I've been looking at investing in a display fridge to put in the lobby of the Overland Park studio," Ron tells me. "I'm just worried it's going to spoil the aesthetics of the place. It has such a noncommercial, low-key vibe right now."

I try to think of ways to make it not look like a fridge. I run into the kitchen to grab my laptop so I can get an idea of what he's dealing with, and I'm just in time to see Batman and the Hulk running out the other side of the kitchen, giggling. My father is sitting at the very messy table reading and yawning.

"Were those boys bothering you, Dad?"

"What boys?"

"Never mind."

I tidy the mess around him by throwing away some used paper plates and napkins and put Kay's now empty bottle of wine in the recycling bin. I then grab my laptop and go back to the dining room where Ron and I look at commercial refrigerated display cases, because hey, it's Friday night and I know how to have a good time.

The dull roar from the living room gives me peace of mind. Silence is where the trouble starts.

My mother comes in to announce they are leaving.

"Good-bye, sweetheart. Do you need me to come in the morning and help you clean up?"

I don't burst out laughing immediately because in her mind she actually *does* help.

"No thanks, Mom. I think we've got it covered. Um, are you okay to drive?"

"Why wouldn't I be?"

"Because you drank a whole bottle of wine by yourself."

"I did no such thing! I only had one glass, Jennifer, and I'll thank you to stop policing my alcohol consumption."

Ron gives me a confused look.

"I'm not," I assure him. To my mother I say, "I was in the kitchen fifteen minutes ago and I saw the empty bottle. I don't care if you drink *six* bottles. I just want to make sure you aren't too tipsy to get behind the wheel."

Ron jumps in. "Kay, why don't you let me drive you and Ray home?"

"No need. I'm fine." She marches into the kitchen, and I follow her. I pull the offending bottle out of the recycling bin.

"See, Mom? It's empty."

Kay shrugs as if this is no concern of hers. "Ray, are you ready to go?" My dad looks up and gives her a thumbs-up.

I can tell my mother is angry by the amount of slamming she's doing as she packs up to leave. On her way out she delivers a classic Kay parting shot.

"To be judged by *you* of all people about my drinking is just beyond the pale, Jennifer. Physician, heal thyself!" And with that she is out the door, my dad in tow, and Ron and I watch from the window as they get into the car and drive away.

"She seems fine." He puts his arm around me and gives me a reassuring half hug.

"I know. It's just strange."

The mystery is solved about twenty minutes later when Max runs in and excitedly tells us two of his friends are throwing up on the front lawn.

"All you can see is chunks of pizza," he informs us as Ron and I go racing to the front door. "Do you think they were poisoned?"

"Of course not," Ron assures him. When we reach the lawn, I'm not at all surprised to see Batman and the Hulk lying on their sides. I'm also not surprised to see that I don't recognize either boy, thanks to their masks.

"Who are they, Max?" I ask while Ron checks on them.

"It's Kyle and Conner from wrestling."

I scan what's left of my memory for those two names and come up empty.

"Have I met them?"

He shakes his head.

"They go to a different school."

As the realization of who this is comes over me like a frozen blanket, I inadvertently shiver.

"Is that Conner *Melon*?"

"Ya. I saw him and Kyle at the mall last week. I told you I was inviting them, remember?"

"I do," I answer him absently. My mind is currently wondering what the hell I'm going to do about Mimi Melon's son being three sheets to the wind on my lawn.

9

To: Jen Dixon
From: Mimi Melon
Re: Your Halloween Party
Date: November 2

Jen,

    My husband insists I apologize for what I said to you Friday night.
    I take back my threat to have you arrested for serving alcohol to minors. I now understand that Conner was coerced into drinking the wine you unwisely left out on your counter, unattended. I hope this was a good wake-up call for you and your husband. No legal action will be taken by us.

                    Mimi Melon

Nice apology. I click reply.

To: Mimi Melon
From: Jen Dixon
Re: Your Halloween Party
Date: November 2

Mimi,

Thank you for your note, but let's not call it an apology since the words "I'm sorry" were nowhere to be found. However, I am glad to hear your threats to sue us were just that.

And yes, we did learn a valuable lesson about leaving a bottle of wine on the counter: some kids were never taught boundaries and have no self-control.

Jen

The scene on the lawn when Kyle's and Conner's mothers arrived had not been pretty. I called them after a lot of cajoling on my part to get the boys to give me their mothers' phone numbers, and a lot of begging on their part for me not to call them.

Mimi showed up first, wearing a Cat Woman costume, which, I have to admit, she wore very well. Her husband, John, dressed as Batman, waited in the car, but Mimi beelined it up our driveway seeming pretty unhinged for a mother of four boys. Surely this couldn't be her first overindulging incident. But as she lit into Ron and me about what terrible parents we are and how we'd be hearing from the police and her lawyer, it sure seemed like these were uncharted waters for her.

"Who leaves alcohol out for just anyone to drink? Do you have any idea how much harm you've done? Conner may never wrestle again."

I was grateful when Kyle's mother showed up. I couldn't tell if she was dressed as an old housewife complete with robe and slippers and curlers, or if that was a real outfit, but it didn't matter because she was so nice.

"Are you Jen?" she asked as she approached me, smiling.

"Yes, hi Irene," I responded with a smile back. "I'm so sorry about this."

She waved me off and rolled her eyes. "Please. I'm the one who should apologize."

By now pretty much the entire party was on the front lawn, and we'd drawn a crowd along the sidewalk, too. Kids and parents in costumes were rubbernecking or just outright staring at the goings-on at 5330 Levon Court. I could have made a mint selling tickets.

As Irene walked over to her son Kyle, still lying on the front lawn, Mimi went charging over to her, practically dragging a wretched-looking Conner by the arm.

"You!" She sneered. "Why is it every time Conner is in trouble, he's with *your son?*"

"When you think about it, I could say the same thing," Irene answered calmly.

This stopped Mimi for a moment as she pondered whether Irene was blaming Conner.

"This is the last time. I mean it! These two are finished as friends."

"Mom, no." Conner whined in a way that reminded me of Max in third grade.

"Shut up, Conner. It's for your own good. I have half a mind to make you wrestle one of your brothers when you get home. That'll teach you."

Five minutes ago, he might never wrestle again. It was a Halloween miracle that he had bounced back so quickly!

"Take it easy, Mimi," Irene chided her. "The way he's going to feel tomorrow will be punishment enough."

"I don't need any parenting advice from you, Irene."

Irene shrugged and helped Kyle to his feet.

"Don't throw up in the car," she ordered him.

I handed both mothers a bottle of water and only one of them said thank you, if you can believe it. The other told me I hadn't heard the last of this and half carried her son to the car.

It was still thirty minutes until the other parents were due to pick up their kids, so I led them all back into the living room and they played a few rounds of Heads Up! with their phones until moms and dads started trickling in. Of course, they all had to share the drama of the evening with their parents, so Ron and I ended up standing around answering questions until almost midnight. Max stayed with us because I guess he wanted some questions answered himself.

"So they drank Nana's wine?"

"Yes. You know why that was wrong, right?"

He nods. "Why doesn't Nana or you or Dad get sick when you drink wine?"

"Because alcohol is for much older people," Ron told him.

"So, if I drink it, will I get sick?"

"Yes," we answered in unison, and that seemed good enough for my son.

So, with the threat of a lawsuit no longer hanging over our heads, I can get on with my exciting day of cleaning and shopping. I whisk through my chores then get ready to meet Laura for lunch and Target.

We meet at a place called the Salad Scene, a huge salad bar restaurant on the way to Target, and I notice immediately that Laura doesn't have the usual spring in her step. If I had to describe my youngest daughter, I would sum her up this way: She is the smartest person I know who doesn't have a clue. The things she does know, she knows very well. But she has a side to her that is completely oblivious to the more practical things in life. Case in point, she shows up for lunch having forgotten her phone and her wallet. Who the hell does that? I personally never leave the house without singing my own version of "Head, Shoulders, Knees and Toes," which is "Keys, Wallet, Glasses, Phone." But when I ask her how in the world she could leave two of life's essentials at home, she just shrugs and says, "I do it all the time."

"So, how's Good Clean Grub doing?" I ask, after we have helped ourselves and found a table by the window.

"It's good! We sell out every day."

"That's terrific."

"I know, right? The only problem is Riverview is getting a little annoyed by the amount of food I have to bring in to make our stuff. And sometimes Graham"—her prep cook—"offers to help me. When they found that out, they kind of freaked out. I may have to find another kitchen."

"What are your options?" I pop a tomato covered in ranch dressing into my mouth.

"Right now, I don't have any." She pauses, looking at her salad. "Do you think they wash their lettuce properly here?"

I shrug. "I have to believe that they do."

"At Riverview, we clean ours in a washing machine on a rinse and spin cycle." She takes a reluctant bite of romaine.

"How are you and Vivs getting along?"

"Fine," she says dismissively. "I barely see her. She's always off doing something."

"With Coach Dana?" I ask.

"I don't ask." She looks away.

I'm about to change the subject when she blurts out, "I don't know why he likes her."

"Well, Vivs has an impressive presence—" I start.

"I know that. But he has so much more in common with me."

I'm not sure if that's even true, but I nod in sympathy.

"Is he over a lot?" I'm thinking how hard that would be on Laura to have to see them together in her own home.

"Barely ever. I'm guessing they meet at his place."

She sighs and leans in. "If I tell you something, can you promise you won't run back to her and say it?"

"I rarely run anywhere these days."

"Mom, I'm serious!"

"Okay!" I zip my lip for effect.

"It's just, I feel like she doesn't really *do* anything for the business."

"What do you mean? Of course, she does."

"I knew you'd take her side."

"I'm not taking a side! But you can't tell me she doesn't do *anything*."

"I mean, she handles the money stuff, but I do all the manual labor. I think up the recipes, I *make* the food, and I feel like all the real creative stuff comes from me. All she really does is buy the groceries and deliver them to me at Riverview. I'm working like a hundred hours a day."

I ignore the exaggeration and try to give a practical answer.

"Well, I'd say that's your part of the partnership. We both know Vivs is *not* a creative person. My God, don't you remember when she was doing arts and crafts with Maude, and we couldn't tell who had done which glitter glue project?"

Laura giggles.

"Listen, you got all the creative genes. But don't pooh-pooh the money stuff. Vivs does all the paperwork so you don't have to, and that's a big part of the business."

"But why does she have to make me feel stupid every time I open my mouth? Like with Dana. All I said was he was going to have a big poop after eating six of my pancakes, and she jumped all over me."

I try, unsuccessfully, not to smile. "I'm sure he didn't think any less of you."

I could easily describe both Vivs and Laura as frank, tell-it-like-it-is women. But they deliver their truths in polar opposite ways. When Laura says something, it comes across as both honest and innocent at the same time. Kind of like being hit really hard with a soft pillow. Vivs's comments, on the other hand, are delivered about as gently as a sledgehammer through butter.

I reach across the table and take her hand. "Listen, my girl. Hang in there. You guys have a great thing going, and it looks like it's only going to get bigger. And as for Coach D, you need to move on. I refuse to watch you girls fight over a guy."

"But he's such a *great* guy." Laura sighs. "I can't remember the last time I liked someone."

"I know, baby girl. But don't worry, it just means something better is on its way."

✦ ✦ ✦

As we wander through Target an hour later, my phone rings. I'm surprised to see it's Peetsa because I know she's working today.

"Hi," I answer.

"Do you know someone named Lynnie?" she asks right out of the gate.

"Yes. She's one of my riders. Why?"

"She came in today, asked for me, and claimed she wanted to buy a car."

"Did you help her out?" I ask while trying to remember when I had ever mentioned P to her.

"I did. Spent a good two hours with her, fielded a lot of questions about *you*, which I didn't answer, and then she left saying we should get together for lunch."

"That's random."

"It is. Are you guys friends?"

"Friendly, but not friends." I can't imagine why Lynnie would seek out Peetsa. "Sorry if she bothered you."

"She didn't. I just wanted you to know."

"Thanks. I'm at Target. Do you need anything?"

"Nope. Wait, yes. Can you grab me some of that body wash you turned me on to?"

"You got it. Talk to you later."

I immediately text Lynnie:

> Hi. My friend Peetsa just told me she met you. How did you know we were friends?

I get the three dots for a nano second.

I overheard you and Tour de France Jeff talking about her.

Oh. Are you looking to buy a car?

 No.

I sigh. This girl is so strange.

I push my cart along the Target aisle trying to recall the six things my mother said she needed me to get for her. The only thing I can really come up with is that I said I didn't need to write it down because I would totally remember. One of the many lies I tell myself in a day. Another is that the diet starts Monday.

"Cinnamon gum!" I say out loud, not realizing that Laura had wandered off. I turn to head to the candy aisle and who do I bump into? None other than Mimi Melon and three beefy, redheaded teenage boys I can only assume are her sons. Six months ago I would have passed this group in Target without a second thought, except maybe how cool it would be to have red hair. But today the sight of them sends my anxiety level into the stratosphere.

"Hi" is all I can think of to say.

"Hi," Mimi says back.

So now I'm thinking this could go one of two ways. We could exchange pleasantries and be on our merry way, or we could end up in a YouTube viral video entitled *Karen on Karen Smackdown at Target*. Luckily Laura arrives at my side and a third option is put on the table.

"Hi, I'm Laura, Jen's daughter," she says with a friendly smile because she knows not to whom she is speaking.

"Hey," says the shortest son, who is probably a junior in high school judging by his facial hair.

"Hey," say the other two gingers by his side. They all seem to be appreciating her long blond hair and tight blue jeans.

"How do you guys know each other?" Laura asks Mimi and me.

"Wrestling," we both answer without looking at each other.

As I'm about to move on, thinking that was easy enough, Mimi tells her sons, "That's the house where Conner got drunk."

The three boys' eyes bug out.

"No way!"

"Way," I say, because again, I don't have any other words.

"That was your son?" Laura directs her comment right to Mimi with a laugh. "Wow, I hope he learned his lesson! I remember the first time I got drunk, it was on gin and blue Gatorade. Oh my God was I sick . . ."

She goes on to tell a story I know all too well of passing out in her friend's parents' bedroom and how she can't even smell gin without gagging to this very day.

"Who gave you the gin?" Mimi asks, looking directly at me.

Oblivious to the innuendo, Laura answers honestly, "My friend stole it from her mom's stash."

"Well, her mom should have done a better job keeping her booze under lock and key," Mimi says pointedly.

"*Or*, Laura should have known not to take something that didn't belong to her." As it comes out, I realize I'm blaming myself for Laura's binge, but it's a shot at Mimi, too. I hope she catches it.

"Well, we'd better go get Nana's gum," I say by way of extracting ourselves from the conversation.

"See you on the mat," Mimi says, but somehow it sounds like a threat.

"They were nice" is Laura's takeaway. Ignorance really is bliss.

✦ ✦ ✦

I stop to drop my parents' Target items at their apartment and find my mother happier to see me than usual. Since Halloween she has been greeting me like I'm the tax collector, but today she's all smiles.

"Sweetheart! You're a lifesaver. I've just got a call to be a fourth for bridge this afternoon. You can stay with Dad for a bit, can't you?"

I look over and my dad is sitting in front of the TV watching an infomercial about the Bowflex machine.

"What is he watching?" I ask her.

"Oh, who knows? But it keeps him happy for a few hours when I'm trying to get things done. You can just leave him there . . ."

"No! Mom, he needs stimulation."

"Jennifer, he doesn't want to do anything. He likes just sitting and being quiet. So . . . I'll only be gone a couple of hours."

As it happens, I don't have any big plans this afternoon, but she doesn't know that.

"Really, Mom? Weren't you just there yesterday?"

"Well, I didn't know you were keeping track," she snaps back at me.

"I only know because Amelia told me you asked her to stay with Dad for a few hours."

"Well, that's because I took a bunch of the ladies to the mall. And why is Amelia talking to you about anything? She's *my* cleaning lady."

"I bumped into her at Gus's Chicken, and I asked her." God, the last thing I need is for my mother to turn on Amelia.

"Well, today I'm not being a chauffeur to a bunch of little old ladies—it's something fun for *me*—but if you don't think I deserve a little bit of fun in my life I understand."

I overly exaggerate my eye roll. "Yes, Mom, that's exactly how I feel. I'm glad it's finally out in the open."

"There's no need to be bold," she admonishes me. "Are you going to stay or not?"

"I'll stay." I match her tone.

"Well, thank you for your sacrifice." Her voice drips with a sarcasm that I really don't think is called for in this situation.

"You know, you catch a lot more flies with honey than you do with vinegar," I remind her.

"Yes, well, I'm not in the market for flies today," she answers as she grabs her purse, kisses my dad on the head, and walks out of the apartment with nary a wave at me.

✦ ✦ ✦

Tonight, as we get ready for bed, I talk to Ron about my parents.

"I just don't get how my mother feels she can just waltz out anytime she wants. And even when she's home, I don't think she really does anything with him."

"You don't know that for sure," Ron reminds me.

"I know, but even she says she plunks him in front of the TV for hours at a time."

"Listen, you don't walk in her shoes. It has to be hard having no one to talk to all day. I mean, she has basically lost her life partner."

"But you'd think she'd want to spend all her time with him."

"I think that would be very lonely for her." Ugh. Ron is just so empathetic.

"What did you and Ray do?"

"I took him out for a walk." I sigh.

"Did you talk?"

"Not really. He read some street signs and asked me where we were going like nine thousand times. I guess I can understand why my mother wants to get away."

"So." He stretches. "Do you have any time for your man?" he asks in his trying-to-be-sexy voice. This is the fourth time he has asked, and I want so much to say yes, but even if I did, my vagina is so dry I've nicknamed it Gobi. So I tell him I'm tired and he goes to sleep without saying good night.

10

Text from Lynnie:

> Hey girl! Saw you having juice with Tamera today. I totally could have joined you! She's my girl! I tried to make eye contact again but you didn't see me. Let's make a plan!!

I sigh and put my phone down. Lynnie has made herself quite present on my DMs and in my life in the past few weeks. I don't think she understands the concept of my getting to know my riders—plural—and not just her. She now comes to spin class in a replica of the outfit I tend to wear—a black-and-white ensemble I got at Target—and yells "twins!" every time.

I went out for lunch with her a couple of weeks ago because, just like with Ron, I can say no only so many times. Anyway, it pretty much went the way of our juice date, but I was able to follow along a bit better because I'm now familiar with the players in her life.

"Lynnie, do your parents live nearby?" I asked after we had settled into a booth at her favorite sandwich place.

"No, thank God. They're still in Wamego. They never go anywhere. My brother is there too, but he's a senior in high school and plays varsity sports, so he at least has an excuse. It's like they have no idea there's a whole world outside of there. I do go see them every other weekend though, mostly to get my laundry done. My mom is like a laundry wizard. I'm not kidding. One time I got grape soda and throw-up on my favorite white sweater. Someone told me you couldn't get drunk on grape soda and vodka—that like the two canceled each other out—but, let me tell you, they didn't. I got so freakin' sick all over my sweater. But my mom got it out. I don't know what she uses—soap or something—but my laundry is always clean. Anyway, that's why I go back to Wamego. And I hook up with my ex-boyfriend from high school too, if I'm not seeing anyone else. He's cute but he's kind of a nerd. He's a nurse." She cackled at the lunacy of this fact. I seized upon the pause in her diatribe to jump in.

"Nursing is a wonderful profession," I told her. "He will always have a job."

She looked confused. "Yeah, but he'll never be a doctor."

"I'm sure he could be if he wanted to."

"Whatever. He's good for sex if I want it."

"Did you ever go out with Reg?" I asked her about the stocky bald guy she thought was cute. I hadn't seen him in class for a while.

Her mouth pursed. "We went out once." It was an uncharacteristically short answer from her.

"And?"

"He ghosted me." Again, with the short answer.

I wanted to ask, "What did you do wrong?" but I didn't. Instead, I asked, "Where did you go on your date?"

"He took me horseback riding, can you believe it? It was so whack. Plus, he was an asshole when I told him I hated horses. He was like"—she lowered her voice for effect—"'How can you live in Kansas and hate horses?' And I was like, 'How can you be so short and *like* horses?' I mean, he looked ridiculous on it."

I tried my best not to laugh.

"That sounds pretty bad."

"It was! I could barely get through the sex afterward."

"You had *sex?*"

"Of course. I didn't want the entire date to be a waste."

Honest to God, as long as I live, I will never understand this generation's attitude about sex. Plus, I'm guessing that's why Reg hasn't been to class. He's obviously steering clear of this particular crazy train.

Which makes me wonder about Tamera, the seemingly normal twenty-something I had juice with this morning after class. If she and Lynnie are "buds," then Tamera might have a little more edge to her than I thought. I decide not to answer Lynnie immediately as I know there will be another text later.

I'm picking Maude up from preschool today and taking her to Max's wrestling match because Vivs is busy. (That's the answer I got when I asked why she couldn't make it to pickup.) It's the last match before Thanksgiving and the eighth from the last for the season, but who's counting? I wanted to take my dad too, just to see what happens, but he has a cold and isn't feeling up to it. I asked his doctor about it, and he told me sometimes dementia patients are triggered by something traumatic, but it usually worsens their symptoms, not the opposite.

Now that it's wrapping up, I can grudgingly admit I've actually enjoyed my time as a mat mom. I've made some new friends, gotten to know more than I ever wanted to about jock itch, ringworm, and impetigo, and I've watched my son go from being a sore loser to a gracious loser all in a matter of months. Max still hasn't won a match, but he seems pretty okay with it. A lot has to do with Coach D and his incredible coaching style. The support he gives his players, whether they win or lose, is inspiring. He always tells Max how much he believes in him and how advanced he is for someone so new to the sport. Miraculously, Max gets less despondent and more determined with every loss. Plus, he and Ron now have a nightly routine after dinner to work on moves and holds until they both smell worse than Dwayne. All in all, it has been a very positive experience for all of us, and I can't wait 'til it's over.

Maude's preschool is called Rosy Day Kinder Care and it's just about the cutest place I've ever seen. Miss Dawson, Maude's teacher, has a real flare for decorating her classroom using the kids' artwork along with twinkle lights and colorful beanbag chairs. One part of the room is called the Enchanted Forest, and the children are encouraged to sit there and dream about how they can make someone else's day a little nicer. No surprise, Miss Dawson herself is the recipient of most of the good deeds that come out of there.

I wait outside the classroom and fool myself into thinking I'm blending with the gaggle of teen moms (at least they look like teens). I'm looking at my phone to give the impression that I'm very busy when I notice another text from Lynnie.

> Tamera says she had a great time with you. Maybe we can all have drinks after work this week?

My God, I forgot drinks after work was even a thing! Being young is so awesome. You work a full day, then have tons of energy to go out with your friends and get buzzed. Maybe shove some deep-fried calamari or nachos in your face and call it a night. I had so little of that. My parents were never that thrilled when I left the girls with them and went out to have anything resembling fun.

"You had your fun," my mother would helpfully remind me. But once every few months she would offer to give the girls dinner and I would go out with one of my co-workers from the insurance company I worked for and try to remember what it was like to be responsibility-free.

"Gee Gee!" Maude's voice cuts through my reminiscing.

"Well, hello, my girl! How are you?" I hug her and notice Miss Dawson standing behind her.

"Hi," I say, smiling. "How was she today?"

"She was great. Maude, tell your grandma what you learned today."

"The Pledge of Allegiance," she says proudly.

"Wow! That's a lot of words to remember."

"It's no problem for me," she boasts. But a glance at Miss Dawson tells me she's getting a bit ahead of herself. I give her a nod.

"Say good-bye to Miss Dawson."

She turns and shakes Miss Dawson's hand.

"Thank you for today. See you tomorrow," she says earnestly. The school trains all the kids to do this. In the morning it's a handshake and "Good morning. Nice to see you today." It's a little formal. I mean, even Max got hugs from his crazy kindergarten teacher, Miss Ward. But I guess hugging isn't encouraged anymore, even though I happen to know Maude needs at least a few squeezes every day to make her feel good in her own skin. Apparently, she asked Miss Dawson for a hug on the first day of school, and Miss Dawson said she couldn't. That, quite honestly, nearly broke my heart. For a child to ask for a hug and be given a handshake is just sad.

"Are you excited to see Max wrestle?" I ask as we settle in the Palisade.

"Yes! Will Dwayne be there?"

Maude has a real thing for Max's grappling dummy.

"No, sweetie. He's just for practicing."

"Do you think he gets lonely in Max's room all day? I could bring him to school with me," she suggests.

"I think he's safer at home," I tell her, and she seems satisfied.

We have about an hour before the match, so I break all the rules and take her to McDonald's to teach her the joy of dipping a French fry into a milkshake. The look of pure euphoria on my granddaughter's face will make Vivs's inevitable wrath worth it.

✦ ✦ ✦

The match today is against Hawthorne again—Mimi Melon's school, in case you forgot; I wish I could. It's the last time the Blue-Hawks will face the Hornets this season, and I'm relieved. Not that it hasn't been entertaining to see Mimi coach from the sidelines and contort herself into a variety of impressive pretzel-like positions when she's down on the ground beside the mat. But the pin ceremony has gotten really old, and I'm amazed her fellow parents still cheer like it's the first time they're seeing it. I liken them to hostages enabling their captor.

Today the Hornets' bench is packed with students and parents alike because unbeknownst to us, the coach is handing out superlatives before the match. So we mat moms from PMS are treated to the bestowing of awards for best this or best that on members of the opposing team.

"This seems weird," I say to Franny as Maude and I settle into the stands. Franny is shaking her head.

"Unbelievable." She seems genuinely shocked. "I've never seen a school do this."

"Probably Mimi's idea," Maria says knowingly. "So her kid will have a big audience when he wins an award."

"And to intimidate us," Franny adds with a scowl.

We listen to a brief speech from the coach about what a great season it has been, even though it isn't over yet, and how these boys have earned his admiration. Then he gets to the awards. To his credit, he tries to get through it quickly, but every time he announces a category, the crowd yells out names of possible winners and he has to wait for quiet to announce the name. While he goes through most improved (ZAC COURIC! BILLY STERN! SANDY KULOCK!), hardest worker (CONNER MELON! ZAC COURIC! KYLE BLISS!), and best sportsmanship (ZAC COURIC! JESSE GILES!), I amuse myself by yelling names too, but stupid ones like Jim Nasium, Ben Dover, and Herbie Hind. Franny elbows me to stop, but even she is laughing.

Then the coach sets up the final category—something called the hard-core award. As he explains it, this is the team member who dominates in the ring—the person with the never-say-die attitude, who does whatever it takes. Kids start yelling out names one last time, but even they are getting weary, so the Greek chorus fades sooner than expected, and I am caught screaming "Mimi Melon" into a silent room.

Some people burst out laughing (okay, two), and the rest give a low rumble of dissent at my inappropriate outburst . . . including Franny, who tries to put some physical distance between us by leaning away from me. I guess she doesn't see the fun or the joke in it. Maude giggles, so I know she'll still love me. Kudos to their coach for rolling with it and saying, "No, but close! It's *Conner* Melon!" Everyone cheers as Conner accepts his trophy, and I wonder if he's going to pin it on his mother's back. I look over and see Mimi giving me a death glare that has me contemplating if she counts cold-blooded murder among her many talents. I was warned at the beginning of the season that she would ruin me if I crossed her. Well, do your worst, Mimi, this is our last match against you, and I don't much care what your worshippers at Hawthorne think of me.

The matches play out like most others except when Max meets Conner in the second round and Conner inevitably wins—it's on points, instead of the dreaded pinning. I know Max will consider this a victory, and when I look at Mimi, I can tell she is disappointed.

When Maude starts loudly asking if we can leave, I slip out the side door of the gym and put her in the car, knowing that Max will want to take the bus home with his buddies.

Maude gives a big yawn and settles into her movie. I'll be a little early dropping her at Vivs's place, but it's okay. I'll just wait for her to get home.

Vivs and Laura's apartment is an interesting mesh of their styles. Vivs has always been a minimalist—little to no color and only the most necessary furniture. Add to that Laura's shabby chic sensibility and their living room is reminiscent of a flowery kill room. But somehow they make it work, and Maude's room is, thank goodness, very much her own. Ever since she could talk, Maude has had an opinion about everything, including her favorite color (green), her choice of décor (Peppa Pig), and her fondness for sparkles. She lets everyone know her room is *dee-lite-ful*, and you know what? It really is. I have no problem spending time in there while waiting for Vivs to get home.

While I hang up some of her clothes and make the bed, Maude asks Siri to play the *Mary Poppins* soundtrack and plays in the tent my mother gave her for her fourth birthday. It's a piece of white gauze with stars on it that hangs from the ceiling and spreads out at the bottom to accommodate a bunch of green and pink pillows. She absolutely loves it, and I don't blame her one bit. We could all use a pretty hangout like this.

Vivs wanders in about half an hour later, dressed in workout clothes.

"Hi!" She gets down on her knees and kisses Maude. "How was your day, kiddo?"

"Good." Maude yawns.

"She liked watching Max wrestle," I tell my daughter.

"Oh right. Thanks for taking her. Did Dana say anything to you?"

"No. Was he supposed to?"

Vivs looks relieved. "No."

"He never talks during the matches. He barely waves even if I catch his eye." I pause. "Everything okay between you?"

"Uh-huh." Vivs avoids eye contact by pretending to busy herself with one of Maude's puzzles.

"What were you up to today?" I ask as casually as I can.

"Work," she answers as per usual. This time I decide to pry.

"Good Clean Grub work?"

Vivs looks at me and scowls. "That's the only work I have, Mom."

"Right, I know. I just thought you did most of your work at home."

She shrugs. "Sometimes I'm more productive if I work somewhere else."

"Like where?" I ask, even though I know I'm on shaky ground.

"Like, anywhere I can plug in my computer. Why all the questions?"

"No questions," I tell her, then add, "Okay, here's a question. Why couldn't you pick Maude up today . . . really?"

As I try to read Vivs's reaction to my query, a little voice from the tent upsets the whole balance of power.

"Mama! Gee Gee and I went to McDonald's and had French fries and milkshakes."

It should come as no surprise that I never did get an answer to my question. But I certainly got an earful about something else.

11

To: Mat Moms
From: Franny Watson
Re: Thank-You Dinner
Date: December 5

Hello ladies,

I want to invite you, your partners, and your wrestlers to a
season-end potluck dinner at Trent's and my house on December 15 at
6 p.m. That's the night after our final match. Please bring your favorite
entrée—enough to feed at least ten people—and whatever you'd like to
drink. We will supply the rest.

See you on the mat!

Franny

She's brave is my first thought. By my calculation that's a lot of
people to have at your house. And right before Christmas! Yeesh. I
RSVP yes, and in the notes tell her I will bring skillet tacos. It's my

easiest go-to recipe, and you can make it for two or twenty in pretty much the same amount of time.

My mother and I are taking my dad to the neurologist later today for a six-month follow-up to see if his memory is getting worse. Kay insists he's exactly the same, and it's a waste of time, but I'm glad we have the appointment scheduled.

I dash off to spin class like a woman on a mission. I enjoyed myself a little too much over the Thanksgiving holiday and am trying to take off the extra poundage before I inevitably do the same thing at Christmas.

Thanksgiving was pretty much a win as far as I'm concerned, because no one got sick, nothing broke, and it was relatively drama-free. Everyone came to our house as usual except for my best friend Nina and her husband, Garth, who couldn't make the trip from Memphis because Garth's mother, Yvette, wasn't able to travel. We missed their energy at the table—especially Kay, who is fascinated by Yvette's spirit guides that predict the future. I used to roll my eyes at just the thought of taking her seriously until two years ago when her guides sent me a message that really helped with the school fundraiser I was put in charge of. Since then, I'm always the first to ask if Yvette has any messages for me from the guides. I was thrilled when Nina told me over the phone that she did.

"Yvette wants you to get into shape."

"I'd like to think I am in shape."

"Don't shoot the messenger."

"Did she say anything else?" I asked, hoping for something a little more thought provoking.

Nina sighed. "Her exact words were 'Tell Jen the guides say she needs to get into shape. She's going to need all her strength in May.'"

"What's in May?" I ask, as if Nina would know.

I ended the call asking her to keep pumping Yvette for more information. In the meantime, I made a mental note to up my strength training.

Without Nina and Garth and Yvette and Nina's daughter, Chyna, we had lots of extra room, so Vivs brought Coach Dana to fill a chair. It made me a bit nervous because I didn't want it to ruin Laura's holiday, but I should have known Vivs would make it about herself.

"I probably shouldn't have asked him," she muttered as she beat up the mashed potatoes on Thanksgiving Day.

"I'm glad you did," I told her. "Max is thrilled."

"Well, as long as Max is happy . . ." She rolled her eyes.

"Are you guys not getting along?" I cautiously dipped my toe into the river of Vivs's personal life because she can be less than appreciative of my curiosity.

"We're fine. It's just"—she glanced at her sister who was opening cans of cranberry sauce by the sink, and lowered her voice— "sometimes he says things that are . . . well, stupid."

"Stupid?" I queried.

"Yeah, just like clueless. It makes me think he doesn't really understand what's going on," she whispered

"I can't believe he's stupid, Vivs. The man is a teacher."

"Yes, but he teaches PE." She seemed to think this was significant.

Laura looked over.

"If you're whispering about Coach D, don't bother. I'm over it."

I raised my eyebrows at Vivs, and she shrugged.

"So what has he said that you consider 'stupid'?" I use air quotes.

"Well, he told me that Elton John is his favorite Beatle."

I laughed in spite of myself. "That's not stupid. It's just misinformed."

"Mom, please." Vivs is exasperated.

Not surprisingly, Laura leapt to his defense.

"You know, just because he doesn't know all the names of some random band from the olden days doesn't mean he's stupid."

"Ya, well, when we were watching this movie set in Russia the other night, he asked why so many of the characters were named Conrad."

I laughed, more at Vivs's bulging eyes than at what she had said.

"Again, just misinformed," I told her. "Not everyone is as worldly as you are, my dear."

To make up for Vivs's obvious annoyance at his presence, I found myself spending much of the evening being extra nice to Dana, when I could pry him away from Max and Dwayne, that is. I could tell Laura felt bad for him too, and we made sure to sit beside him at dinner.

Raj ended up leaving early, to go spend time with his girlfriend and her kids, but not before he and Vivs had what looked like an argument in the driveway. I only saw them because I walked in on Maude and Laura watching from the kitchen window.

"What are they fighting about?" I whispered to my youngest daughter.

"Who knows?" she said, sighing.

My parents also left early, my mother not wanting to "be on the road with a bunch of drunks." She's convinced that on every holiday the roads are just one big demolition derby of people who drink too much. And finally, after a successful cleanup, I sent Vivs, Coach D, Laura, and Maude home with a bunch of leftovers. I knew the girls had an early day the next morning what with all the after-the-turkey workouts. I had to teach a double myself.

✦ ✦ ✦

My après spin juice date today is with Donna, another of my long-time riders who always comes to class ten minutes late. It used to bother me, but now it's so much a part of the class routine that if she started coming on time, I really believe it would throw me off. She looks to be about my age with short salt-and-pepper hair, a kind face, and, in true fifty-something form, she carries a few extra pounds around her middle even though she spins at least three times a week.

I'm curious to know why she always comes late, so it's the first thing I ask her when we sit down.

"Oh, I know. And I'm sorry. Honestly, I didn't think you noticed!"

"Not in a bad way, but I always wondered if you know when class actually starts." I try to keep it light because I can see I have distressed her.

"I do know, and I only live five minutes away, but my mother's aide doesn't arrive until eight, and I have to wait for her before I can leave. I'm really sorry." She pronounces "sorry" like it rhymes with "Lori," and I wonder where she is from.

"Truly, I don't mind at all. I'm always just glad to see you. Is your mother ill?"

"She has ALS," Donna says without meeting my gaze.

"Oh gosh, that's awful. How long has she had it?"

"This is her nineteenth month. It's really starting to take a toll on her. She can barely move, and her speech is getting slurry."

All I can think of to say is "I'm sorry." It tastes hollow on my tongue.

"Do you have any siblings?" I ask.

"No. It's been just Mom and me for pretty much my whole life. I even moved her here with me from Bismarck when I got a job. I took care of her as long as I could, but she needs full-time attention now. That's why we have an aide come in during the day."

"What's your job?"

"I'm the creative director for the performing arts center."

"The *Kauffmann* performing arts center?"

She smiles. "Yup. That's the one."

"That is such a cool job! You must get to see everything."

"That's definitely one of the perks."

We finish our drinks chatting about shows we are binge-watching on Netflix and what our favorite books are.

As I'm driving home, I smile at the realization that she is the first rider I could see being friends with. She carries her heavy life load with such grace and good humor, and I'd love to spend more time in her company.

As if to mock my thoughts, my phone buzzes and I glance down quickly to see that it's another text from Lynnie. It can definitely wait 'til I get home.

✦ ✦ ✦

"I need to find a bathroom," my mother announces and walks out, leaving my father and me sitting alone in front of Dr. Mithat's pristine desk in his roomy office. He's finished doing the cognitive tests on my father and we are waiting to hear his thoughts.

"Want to go for lunch after this, Dad?"

"Okay," he answers, but I'm not sure he even heard the question. He seems tired after the testing—I think it stresses him out to be asked so many questions.

Kay was borderline ridiculous with her interference during the testing. Dr. Mithat said we could stay if we sat quietly on the sidelines. Seems that was too many instructions for Kay, who sat beside me and did her best to either answer the question being asked of my father, or try to explain why he didn't know something like "Who throws the ball in a football game?"

"He's more of a baseball man," she lobbed out when my father hesitated.

Dr. Mithat and my mother return about the same time and we all wait anxiously to hear what he has to say. He is a short, round man of about forty with a toothy smile, and as far as I'm concerned the patience of a saint for the way he deals with my mother.

Before he says anything, as if on cue a nurse pokes her head in the doorway and asks my father to go with her, saying, "Mr. Howard, we are going to need a urine sample from you."

"Okay," he says and goes with her. She closes the door behind him.

"I think it's important we talk in private," Dr. Mithat begins. "I do see some regression since our last visit. I'd like to increase Ray's medication and see if it slows things down a bit. But I think the most important element in fighting this dementia is keeping him in a positive frame of mind."

In that moment it hits me like a sucker punch that my father is not going to get better. The man I've gone to for advice my whole life will never be able to give it to me again. I didn't realize until this minute that I had quietly been living with the assumption that Dr. Mithat would ultimately cure him. An unfamiliar panic rises in my chest that is so overwhelming I have to bite down on my cheek to stop myself from screaming out loud.

"What do you mean?" Kay asks, a bit aggressively. "Ray's always happy."

How can you tell? I think but don't say.

"I'm sure he is." The doctor tries to smile at my mother. "Just make sure he doesn't feel bad about repeating himself and forgetting things."

"He barely says anything," my mother points out. "But he's certainly not *un*happy. He just likes to sit quietly and read or watch TV."

"How do you know that, Mom?" I surprise myself and everyone else with this outburst. "What indication has he ever given that he likes just sitting?"

"Jennifer, what the devil are you talking about?" Kay shoots a glance at Dr. Mithat.

"Mom, how do you know that he wouldn't rather take a walk or a ride in the car, or dance in the kitchen?" I'm getting very ramped up.

"Dance in the . . . what in God's closet are you talking about? We've never danced in the kitchen in our whole lives. You sound like a crazy person." My mother's voice has elevated to match mine.

"Ladies, please," Dr. Mithat interrupts us calmly. He doesn't seem fazed by our exchange, so I'm guessing we aren't the first to blow off a little steam in this room. He continues.

"Kay, I think Ray needs as much stimulation as possible."

"What does that mean? He doesn't talk. How am I supposed to stimulate him?"

"You can try to play simple games with him, take him with you when you go places, just keep him included. The more time he spends inside his own head, the sooner you're going to lose him."

That sentence drops like mud in the air. I look at my mother. She sighs and nods.

"Okay, I get it. Do more with him."

"We'll all help, Mom," I tell her. If I'm being honest, I do let my dad sit and read a lot of the time I'm with him, while I either cook or answer emails or make my spin class playlists. I take him out too, but not enough. The guilt settles on me like a wet blanket.

"Want to have some lunch?" I ask as we all head to my car.

"Oh, let's just stop by LaMar's," Kay answers, looking at her watch. "It's too close to dinner."

I nod and we find our way to LaMar's Donuts and Coffee. They only do takeout, so I guess we'll be eating in the car. While Kay goes in to get us all a snack, I sit with Ray and check my phone. I find a text from Max asking for whoever comes to his meet to bring him his headgear. That would be Ron today, so I send him a reminder text with the request.

I look over at my father, who has been staring out the window this whole time.

"Oh, Dad," I sigh. "I wish this wasn't happening to you." I start to tear up and put my head on the steering wheel. "I miss you so much."

There is a long pause and then I hear a voice say, "I'm still here, Jennifer." I look up to find him staring out the window, but he has put his hand on my leg. I don't know what to do, so I let my instincts take over and just hug him and continue to cry on his shoulder. It is only a moment, but he is truly there with me, his daughter. I don't know if that will ever happen again.

The back door opens and my mother plops down with two bags—one with coffee, and one with doughnuts—mid-sentence, as though she's been talking to herself.

". . . pay with cash anymore? The kid at the register looked like I'd handed him anthrax. And then he couldn't count the change. Do they not teach kids math . . . wait, what's happening in here?"

She has finally noticed that Ray and I are hugging. I wipe the wetness from my cheeks.

"Nothing. Just having a hug."

My mother hands my father his coffee and a maple glazed doughnut with walnuts, and me my tea and apple fritter.

"Now watch you don't spill, Ray. Although it's not like you'd be ruining anything." Kay looks around my somewhat messy vehicle with disapproval.

"Sorry, Mom, I've been driving Max and his friends a lot lately, and they're pigs."

"They're only pigs because you let them be pigs," she informs me, her mouth half-full of a powdered jelly doughnut. She's not wrong. Lately, I've been letting some things slide with Max, mostly his behavior with his friends, because I know he's been feeling his wrestling losses. The last thing he needs is for his mom to be nagging him in front of his buddies about chip crumbs and food wrappers in the car.

We finish our snack in relative quiet—my father reading the three signs that he can see from the window, over and over again, and my mother letting out an audible sigh every few minutes. I debate telling her that Dad actually spoke to me, but something makes me want to keep that moment to myself. It has left a warm glow around my heart, and I just want to hang on to it for a little while longer.

12

Text from Lynnie:

> Did I just see you leaving Mud Pie with
> Donna from class? I thought you said you
> had to do something for your son's school.
> When can we meet for cocktails?

Okay, this is getting weird. Lynnie's texting has become a little much. It used to be cute that she'd check in every few days trying to make plans. But lately she texts every day—if she sees me having juice with another rider, and if she doesn't see me having juice with another rider. The never-ending stream of questions like where I got my yoga pants, what do I think of her outfit, did I see her latest TikTok, which Bachelorette do I hate the most, etc. . . . Yesterday, she asked me out for lunch again, and, truth be told, I just wasn't up for her millennial monologue. But I did want to ask always late Donna about how she found care for her mother. I think I finally have Kay convinced to get someone to come in to help with my dad.

> Hi. I was just having a quick coffee with
> her before my son's final wrestling match.

What did you guys talk about? Where is the wrestling match?

None of your damn business.

Just some stuff about our parents.

What stuff? Are your parents okay?

Yes, we were just discussing eldercare.

Oh, okay. Want me to come to the wrestling? I know a lot about it.

No, that's okay.

Well, let's hang tomorrow. I've already told Tamera you were down for getting a drink or something.

While I'm flattered that a couple of twenty-something girls want to "hang" with me, I can't think of even a moment in my schedule tomorrow that would allow for such a thing.

Can we set something up for later this month? Maybe the 22nd. We could go to TGI Friday's for happy hour.

Yay!

See you then.

Dude, you'll literally see me like three times
before that!

I'm not sure if I'm enabling Lynnie's weird obsession with me, but I honestly don't know how to keep putting her off. Maybe I'll ask Laura to come with us to get her perspective. I mean, they're almost the same age, so she may have a better take on the situation.

I bundle up before I get out of the Palisade. It hasn't snowed yet this season, but the weather is bitterly cold today. The song "No More Drama" by Mary J. Blige pops into my head. I think of it as an homage to my delight that this is Max's final wrestling match.

"No more pain, no more pain." I'm probably singing a bit too loudly for the school parking lot, but I can't help it. This is a happy day.

Listen, I'm glad he did it—wrestling has been a wonderful focus for his energy. Max is more organized, more prompt, and more driven in all parts of his life, even his schoolwork. But watching your son get beat up every week ain't for sissies. So I'm looking forward to having my son around more and hoping he holds on to all the habits he has acquired even if he doesn't have Coach Dana in his ear every day encouraging good behaviors.

A good crowd has turned out for the last match of the season. Lots of boys and girls sporting the school colors and chanting, "Let's Go BlueHawks!," all the mat moms and most of the mat dads including Ron who I see has already taken a seat by Maria and Georgie.

I wonder yet again if I should have brought my father to this final match, to possibly recapture the magic of the first time I brought him and Kay, but then I remember my mother's determination to take him with her to play cards at Riverview today.

"Sweetheart, it's perfect. He can sit and listen to some woman play the piano while I'm with the girls."

Her words are innocent enough, but her attitude smacks of vindictiveness.

Ever since our visit with Dr. Mithat, she has dragged my father out daily, insisting he go everywhere with her. At first glance it looks like she really took the doctor's advice to heart, but I get the feeling she's overdoing it to show all of us who doubted her that she is on the job.

I wave to Coach Dana, and he nods back, his game face perfectly in place. I haven't seen him since Thanksgiving, but I assume he and Vivs are still dating since I haven't heard otherwise.

The BlueHawks and the Overland Park Raiders are ready to rumble, so I take a seat in the bleachers beside my crew and give Ron a swift kiss.

"Hi girls. Big, big day!"

"Hey, Jen," they say in unison.

"I don't know about you guys, but I thought this day would never come."

"It hasn't been that bad, has it?" Georgie chides me.

I pause before I answer. I want to give her question real thought. "Yes, yes it has."

They both laugh just as the ref blows the whistle for the first match.

"Here we go," I say to no one in particular, as I pull a LaCroix lime seltzer from my pocket and pop it open.

As we watch the first match, Maria leans into me and asks if I have signed up for something yet.

"Hmm?" I'm barely listening because I have my eye on Max and am trying to send him a psychic message to stop scratching his privates. God, I hope he doesn't have scabies again.

"Did you sign up for City League?" she repeats. "It's the winter wrestling league."

"The what?" I raise my voice over the cheering crowd.

"City League!" she yells in my ear. "It's where the boys wrestle in the off-season."

"Yeah, right." I laugh.

"You should do it soon so Max can stay with the other boys."

I look directly at Maria. "I can't tell if you're kidding or not."

"Kidding about what?" Ron leans in to join our conversation.

She furrows her brow. "Why would I be kidding? You should have gotten an email from the City League like two weeks ago."

"What's City League?" Ron asks, and I really wish everyone would stop saying "City League."

"It's the off-season wrestling league," Maria tells him.

As the pit of my stomach meets my bowels, I turn to Georgie. "Georgie," I yell. "City League?"

"Definitely!" she yells back and gives me a thumbs-up.

I turn back to Maria and Ron, who are now in deep discussion. "Max has never mentioned this to me," I tell them.

"Oh, you know boys." She shrugs.

The cheering crowd sounds like distant thunder in my ears. I can't wrap my head around this new development.

"Maybe he doesn't want to join," Maria adds casually without realizing what a lifeline she has thrown me. A burst of hope hits my heart. Yes, absolutely that's what it is. He doesn't want to keep wrestling. Otherwise he would have told me about it.

"We should get on that," Ron informs me, and I know that when he says "we" he means "*me.*"

"I don't think there's any rush. I mean, Max hasn't said anything about it," I repeat.

"Well, we should at least ask him."

Now this to me is just crazy talk. If Max hasn't brought it up, it's probably because he doesn't want to disappoint us by telling us that he doesn't want to wrestle anymore.

"I think we just wait until he mentions it. We don't want him to feel pressured."

I look over at my son, who is on deck to wrestle. He is having an intense consult with Coach D. As he's called to the mat, the two shake hands and Max strides to the center of the ring.

"Let's go, Max!" Ron's velvet voice booms.

The two boys, the other named Arjen judging by the yelling, start circling each other, and almost immediately Max has him in a headlock and brings him down to the mat.

"Nice move, Max!" Ron bellows out. Coach D is standing as close as he can to the side of the ring without stepping in, and yelling encouragements to our son.

"Hold strong! Hold strong! Don't let his shoulder up." His baritone voice cuts through the noise. Max seems to be struggling to keep his hold, but to my genuine shock the ref blows his whistle and declares Max the winner by pin.

The whole team erupts into cheers because they all know this is Max's first win and first pin. Ron is on his feet furiously clapping. I'm clapping too, but am I a bad mom for also having a sinking feeling that even if Max didn't want to wrestle anymore, this might change his mind? One glance at my son and the joy on his face and I'm pretty sure my fate is now sealed. I'm going to be watching this rodeo for years to come.

✦ ✦ ✦

The car ride home is a blur. Max ended up winning two of his three matches, and he and Ron go over every second of each match.

"Buddy, when I saw you take that second kid down, I thought it was going to be another pin."

"Ya, but he was squirmy. I knew I'd get him on points, though. His form sucked. Mom, what's for dinner?"

"What?" I say only because my name cuts through the din of their conversation.

"What's for dinner?"

"Why don't we go out for dinner and celebrate?" Ron suggests. "Let's go home so Max can shower, and I'll see if I can get us into J. Gilbert's."

"Cool!" Max enthuses. "I've never been there!"

"Well, it's a special day." Ron looks at me curiously. "Sound good to you, sweetie?"

I don't answer immediately. I feel like I'm in some kind of alternate universe where everything is predestined to work against me.

"Uh, sure," I say as I pull in the driveway. I'm hoping against hope that this high Max is on will be the perfect ending to his wrestling career. And then he says the words I've been dreading.

"Can I sign up for City League? I wasn't going to do it, but I made a deal with Coach D that if I won a match today, I would."

"Sure," Ron says. "I'll take care of it tomorrow," and he nods at me with a grin.

I nod back with a small smile on my face, and I'm sure Ron sees it as a stamp of approval on this whole plan. Little does he know that I'm already thinking how I'm going to exact my revenge on Coach D for making that deal with my son.

13

"What are their names again?" Ron asks his usual question just before we ring the doorbell.

"Trent and Franny. You've never met Trent," I reply while I shift my Tupperware full of skillet tacos from my left arm to my right. Ron is carrying two bottles of wine, and we are both dressed in our holiday best. I have my favorite dressy yoga pants on along with a long gray sweater and high-heeled boots, and Ron has put on a jacket and tie for the first time in I don't know how long. When you run yoga studios, you basically live in athleisure wear, so I had forgotten how nice he can look all dolled up. I'm hoping my warm thoughts toward him will turn into a desire to fool around when we get home tonight. Ron has stopped asking, so I feel like I'd better initiate at least once before the year is over.

The Watsons live in a very nice modern barn-style home with more emphasis on barn than modern. You walk into a high-ceilinged great room that has exposed beams and a big echo. It's already uncomfortably loud because of all the parents and kids talking over each other.

"I'm ready to go whenever you are," I say to Ron out of the corner of my mouth as Franny approaches us carrying two beers.

"Merry Christmas!" she says loudly. "Food goes in the kitchen. Want a beer?"

"Sure," Ron says and relieves her of one of the bottles.

"I'll wait for wine," I tell her, then add, "Are you okay?"

"Oh, I'm just terrific," she says brightly. "I mean, I have absolutely no idea who is going to show up and if we're going to have enough food." She takes a large swig of the beer in her hand. "But it's a party so I've got my happy face on!"

I hold up my Tupperware. "Skillet tacos for twenty," I tell her. "Is there anything else I can do?"

"Just have a good time and don't eat too much." As she walks away, she says, "But *drink* as much as you want. We've got loads of booze."

I tell Ron to mingle, so he makes a beeline to the other side of the room where Coach D is holding court with a bunch of wrestling team fathers. I head in the other direction to the open-style kitchen, which is visible from the front door. I put my dish beside the others and see why Franny is concerned. I hope more people are bringing food, or dinner is going to consist of skillet tacos, olive tapenade, and scalloped potatoes.

I grab a glass of red wine for myself and scan the room for Max. He had come earlier to hang out with Franny's sons and more than likely go a few rounds on the mat they've had in their basement for like ten years. He's nowhere to be found, so I take my glass and join a gaggle of the mat moms sitting on the sofa.

"What's up, girls?" I ask them. Maria and Georgie are there, as are three other familiar faces from the team.

"Just talking about what we're getting the boys for Christmas," an eighth-grade mat mom named Janice informs me.

"Anything good?"

"The usual," she says, shrugging, and I can relate to the ennui she is obviously feeling. There is nothing all that exciting about shopping for boys. It's basically sports equipment or electronics. Thankfully, this year Max needs a new phone so that's what he's getting. I tell them as much.

"Well, wouldn't you get that for him even if it wasn't Christmas?" one of the women I don't know asks. "I mean, if you say he needs it."

"I guess so," I say.

"Then why would you make it a gift? That seems mean." I detect a slur in her words.

"What's mean about giving him a new phone?"

"But you're cheating him out of a good gift by giving him something he needs."

I'm not following her logic at all, and I don't like this feeling of being in the hot seat so early into my glass of wine.

"Have we met before?" I ask her sweetly.

"Not officially, but I've seen you at a few matches."

I turn a quizzical eye to Georgie, who says, "Charmaine's son wrestles for Hawthorne."

It takes me a minute to put two and two together. She's from Hawthorne, so she is a fellow mat mom with Mimi Melon. Jeez, are they all hostile at that school?

"Well, he's also getting sneakers and he really doesn't need them if that makes you feel any better," I tell Charmaine and walk away. Lovely start to my evening.

I make a beeline for Franny, who is in the kitchen, to ask why a Hawthorne mat mom would be at a BlueHawks team party.

"Oh that was all Trent." Her cheerful chirp has a bit of an edge to it. "We were at a birthday party last night, and after a few tequilas he just started inviting anyone within earshot to come tonight." She laughs, then gestures grandly at the growing crowd to show the results of his conviviality.

"So you're okay with a rival mat mom being here?" I sound like a new wife asking why the ex-wife gets to be here, too.

"There are actually several here, and no, I don't mind because the season is over, and now"—she sighs—"we're all on the same team again."

"Ya right. What team is that?"

"The City League."

"I thought the City League is where our boys play in the off-season."

"Our boys, their boys, all the boys in Overland Park. We merge and we play, as a team, against other cities. I can't believe you don't know this."

My mind is playing catch-up with her words. The rivalries are over and now we're all one big happy family?

"Even Mimi Melon?" I whisper.

As if to answer my question, she nods toward the door. I turn and see the redheaded devil herself (with a blue dress on, if you can believe it) striding toward us with a bottle of wine in hand.

"Hey ladies!" She smiles broadly and hands the bottle of wine to Franny.

"Oh goody, more booze," she says with a forced smile.

Mimi pours herself a glass of already opened wine and turns to toast us.

"Here's to being on the same team again!" We all drink, and then she adds, "Until next year, that is, when we'll once again crush you like the bugs that you are." She laughs at her own joke.

"That's the spirit!" I say not quite under my breath. It's a passive-aggressive move, I know, but I'm past worrying if I offend her.

Mimi's green eyes stare me down. "I heard your son finally won a match."

"He's won two actually." I try to mirror her glare but fail miserably.

"Well, good for him. Maybe now he won't bring the rest of the team down so much." She laughs again, clearly amusing herself with her cruelty.

Franny has been silently drinking her beer but sees it's probably time to jump in.

"He's going to be great. They're all going to be great," she enthuses.

"Hope you've nipped Conner's drinking problem in the bud." I smile.

"I didn't have to. I just had to keep him away from your house."

"Ooh, good one." I'm dripping sarcasm at this point and wondering how this conversation escalated so quickly. I usually don't let anyone work me up like this, but there is something about this woman that just rubs me the wrong way.

"Okay, you two, this is a party." Franny's nervous giggle sounds like a plea. In that moment I feel contrite.

"Sorry, Franny, you're right." I turn to Mimi. "Let's start fresh. Put all the crap behind us." I stick out my hand.

"I don't really know what *crap* you're talking about, but sure. I like to be friends with everyone." She shakes my hand, pulls me close enough that I can smell the wine on her breath, and says meaningfully, "*You and me, for the smell of it.*" The fact that she's a head taller than me is the least disturbing thing about this. I'm not sure what to say, so I just grin and toast her with my now empty glass of wine.

For the smell of it? What the hell does that mean? I walk away in search of Ron and find that he has cornered Coach D and is having an animated one-on-one discussion with him.

"Have you seen Max?" I ask them.

"Not yet," my husband answers. "But Coach and I were talking about City League."

I choose not to say something snarky and instead ask, "What about it?"

"I think Max will make giant leaps in his fighting technique if he wrestles all winter," Coach D enthuses in his soothing baritone voice.

"Yes, thanks a lot for making that deal with Max so I can continue watching him get beat up in the new year," I say as dryly as I can.

Coach D beams. "You're welcome!"

Was I not sarcastic enough? Or is gorgeous Coach Dana really *not* that sharp? Maybe Vivs was right. I ask Dana why she isn't here with him tonight.

"She said she had to work." He looks disappointed.

"Is everything okay with you guys?" I ask tentatively.

"I think so." He scratches his head. "She's hard to read sometimes, you know?"

I nod. Yes, indeed I do know. This poor sweet guy is probably getting put through the ringer by my bossy firstborn. Laura would definitely have been a much better match for him. But Vivs was the one he called, so it is what it is. I guess he prefers brunettes.

"Anyway . . ." He changes the subject back to wrestling. "Just so you know, Max will be around some of the best in his weight class in the league, so he can practice with kids like Toby Colby and Conner Melon."

I roll my eyes at the mention of that name.

"What, no love for Conner?" he says, smirking, and I wonder if he's heard about Halloween.

"No real problem with Conner," I tell him, then lean in and whisper, "but that *mother*!"

"Who, Staff Sergeant Pin Me?" Coach D laughs.

"Is that what people call her?" I can't hide how thrilled I am.

"Just the coaches. The pin thing is a bit much, but I have to say she raises some amazing wrestlers."

I give Coach D a face fart, so Ron jumps in. "Mimi made the fatal mistake of criticizing Max's wrestling and has been on Jen's shit list ever since."

"It was his first match!" I try to justify my grudge. "I literally just tried to make a fresh start with her. She shook my hand and then said, 'You and me, for the smell of it.'" I try to make my voice sound as menacing as hers did.

"Oh crap, really?" Coach D giggles.

"Why 'oh crap'? What does it mean?"

He puts his hands up as if to stop the question from reaching him.

"Nope. Not gonna be me. I don't want to be the buyer of bad news."

I'm about to ask him if he meant to say *bearer* of bad news, but Max jumps into our conversation circle and asks if he can sleep over.

"Here?" I ask. Franny has four sons, but none of them are Max's age. The closest is Jon, who is in eighth grade.

"Yeah. A bunch of the guys are staying. Please???"

"But you don't even have your toothbrush."

I get eye rolls from all three males, so I tell him he can.

"Yes!! Hey Coach, want to come and see me do a sit out escape?"

"Sure!" Coach D seems happy to get away from us. I had wanted to ask him more about him and Vivs, but he's gone before I can get to it.

"Having fun?" Ron asks.

"Absolutely," I tell him with overexaggerated umph. "Did you happen to ask Dana if he's coming for Christmas dinner? Even though Vivs will be away, I wanted him to know he's welcome."

"Well, I hate to be the *buyer* of bad news, but he said he's going home for Christmas."

"Ha ha."

"Are you hungry?"

"No, but I could use some more wine."

We make our way back through the crowd toward the place where the wine bottles have congregated, and I pour myself a glass of what looks like a decent Shiraz. Ron spots a client from Om Sweet Om and says he'll be right back.

The party is now in full swing. Franny has decorated her living space very tastefully for the holidays—I wouldn't have pegged her as a minimalist but the subtle white lights on the tree and packages wrapped with brown paper and red ribbon underneath tell me she likes to keep her home simple. I tend to overdo my Christmas decorations because I feel it's the prettiest time of year—lots of garland and lights and way more poinsettias than necessary. Not as over the top as my mom, who used to adorn the lawn with a six-foot lit-up sign that said *Happy Birthday Jesus!* and an extra-large nativity scene. People used to drive by the house just to see it.

Christmas is going to be smaller than usual this year. Raj and Vivs are taking Maude to India for ten days so that Grandma Varsha can get at least one goddamned holiday with her granddaughter (that's a direct quote from the lady herself!), and Laura is spending Christmas in Florida with a friend she met when she was taking a class on gluten-free baking at the Culinary Center. Not the greatest decision for their business, which they are shutting down for two weeks, but probably the best decision for their souls. So it will just be me and Ron and Max and my parents—the quietest one we've had in years.

When I told my best friend Nina on the phone last week, she suggested we spend a few days in Memphis with her and Garth and her daughter, Chyna, but I didn't want to leave my parents alone.

"You can bring them," she offered.

"I'm not sure how well Ray travels these days—especially a seven-hour car ride." I didn't mention I'd need sedation to get through seven hours of road signs being read to me.

"Well, if you change your mind, we've got lots of room," Nina said, then added that Garth's mother insisted that she remind me to get in shape for May.

"On it," I told her. I've decided she means don't let yourself go to pot over the holidays, which I won't.

Franny starts to clink her glass to get everyone's attention, and when that doesn't work, Coach D gives a piercing whistle using his index finger and thumb, which I happen to think is one of the most useful skills a person can have.

Not surprising, the boys all come running like the whistle is a call to arms, and they plop themselves down on the rug in the living room while the adults slow their conversation to a murmur.

"Thanks, Coach," Franny says gratefully, then consults a piece of paper in front of her. "I just want to welcome everyone and thank all the parents for the amazing support you have shown for our BlueHawks this season."

The room erupts with applause, and the boys start whooping and hollering. When they calm down, Franny reads on, giving it about as much pizzazz as dictating a grocery list.

"Of course, none of it would have been possible without

our wonderful Coach Dana. Thank you so much, Coach." More applause and Coach D waves bashfully.

Franny scans the crowd and for the first time seems to be going off script. "I'd also like to thank those of you from opposing teams who have made our season so tough. You made us a better team."

Mimi Melon lets out a resounding "*woo-hoo*," which is followed by boos from the boys. I thought Franny might reprimand the kids, but to my delight she just laughs and shrugs. "Might as well get over it, boys. We're all on the same team now." She goes back to her paper, and I wonder why she doesn't ad-lib more often.

"The weekly pancake breakfasts raised almost six hundred dollars for the team, which means we are that much closer to getting new mats and headgear for the school."

Again, applause stops her for a good thirty seconds. She smiles gratefully, accepting the appreciation of her fellow parents.

"So merry Christmas, everyone. I hope you have a great holiday and, fellas, you better be ready for City League in January!"

She folds her piece of paper as more whooping and hollering comes from the kids and some shouts of "We love you, Franny" and "Great job, mat mom" as the party resumes.

Georgie and Maria make a beeline toward me.

"We just heard," Georgie tells me excitedly.

"Heard what?" I try to match her enthusiasm.

"About you and Mimi and 'for the smell of it.'"

"Ya, what is that? She said it to me earlier."

They look at each other and burst out laughing.

"You're kidding, right?"

"I never kid," I deadpan.

"It's the City League fundraiser. They have it every year."

"Oh. Okay." My inner voice is thinking, *Oh, great, another fundraiser.* "So, what is it? More pancakes?"

"No! It's just one big night at the end of May. Hundreds of people pay to come and watch."

"Watch what?"

"Watch the mat moms wrestle."

"I'm sorry, what?"

"The mat moms wrestle each other. It's hilarious," Georgie assures me.

I'm still trying to process what they are telling me. "So the moms wrestle," I confirm. "Do you *have to* wrestle?"

"Well, you don't have to, but everyone does unless they physically can't."

Oh shit.

"And Mimi just told a bunch of us that she challenged you," Maria says excitedly. When she sees what I'm sure is a look of horror on my face, she laughs. "Don't worry. It's all for fun."

"Ya." Georgie snorts. "Unless you wrestle Mimi. Jen, I know you teach spinning, but wrestling is totally different. You better get in fighting shape for May. You're going to need all your strength."

I look to the heavens and shake my head.

Right again, Yvette.

14

To: City League, Overland Park
From: Jen Dixon
Re: This and That
Date: January 4

Hello CLOP!

My name is Jen Dixon, and it is my dubious honor to be your representative for the West Kansas division of City League Wrestling where our motto is I'd rather throw ya than know ya!

Yes, indeed, the inmate is now running the asylum.

Practices start this Tuesday and Thursday, 4 p.m. to 6 p.m., and Saturday, 8 a.m. to noon, at the Pardee Community Center gym. Charmaine Grimes has volunteered to be snack mom for the first week, but I'll be expecting all of you to take a turn, so do yourselves a favor and hit the sign-up sheet that will be posted in the gym toot sweet unless you want me to give you a verbal haranguing in front of everyone. And if you think I'm bluffing, I refer you to anyone who had me as a class mom at William Taft Elementary.

*The coaches are asking for healthy snacks, so good luck finding something that will please both them and the kids, but my daughter Laura is happy to help you for a nominal fee. You can find her at **laura @goodcleangrub.com.***

Same old rules apply—shower often, do your laundry, don't share equipment, and for the love of God, buy extra strong deodorant for your wrestler.

Nothing more for now, but you can look forward to hearing from me often now that I'm in charge. Prepare for me to be drunk with my power and very difficult to deal with.

Go forth and keep it clean.

Jen "I volunteered for this" Dixon

Honestly, I always wondered what it would actually take to get me back in a volunteer position where I'd have to deal with other parents, but, apparently, City League was the magic bean. I figure, with Mimi Melon in the mix, I want to be on top of all the things happening with the Comanches, which is the name our Overland Park wrestling team is saddled with. Franny was going to do it "yet again," as she said, but I told her I'd be happy to take the reins. I really enjoyed her shock and awe at my stepping up. Plus, now that I have been challenged to a fight by that momster Mimi, I need to get a clear picture of what exactly happens at this Just for the Smell of It Fundraiser. Knowledge is power. In fact, it's the only power I'm going to have over her because she has a good six inches and about twelve pounds on me. I'll have to ask Georgie if she has video from last year.

I'm comfy sitting at my kitchen counter office and I really don't want to get up, but I must because today is the day I take down the Christmas tree, period, full stop. I've been dreading it since the day we brought it home from Bierman's Christmas Tree Farm in mid-December. How can something that goes up with such joy and anticipation become the chore of the century to take down?

I haul out the boxes from the garage and start the arduous process of taking off the ornaments and wrapping them up, then unraveling the garland, which is looking a bit anemic, so I throw it out and make a note to hit the after-Christmas sales to get some for next year.

As I put the lights away, I reflect on the quiet Christmas that was. The lack of holiday week craziness left Ron and me time to reconnect and have a really good heart-to-heart about our sex life. He seemed very determined to help me fix it. I wish he could show even half as much zeal when I ask him to fix the toilet, which has been running for the better part of a month. He suggested a little light porn and a trip to the Moonlight Adult Boutique, which I must say is one of the more tasteful sex toy establishments in the greater Overland area. And he even said he'd be willing to go to a marriage counselor to talk things out. But I explained to him that my absent libido has nothing to do with him but is really all about me and my hormones. So we agreed that I would go see my doctor in the new year. Oh, and we had sex, which put him in such a good mood that I couldn't begrudge the fact that it did nothing for me.

My own gynecologist, Dr. Clit (I'm kidding; it's actually Dr. Clint), is on maternity leave, and I don't much like the fresh-out-of-med-school twelve-year-old who is taking her place in the interim, so I asked if Dr. Alex (the heartbroken superbitch from my spin class) would see me for a consult. She kindly said she could fit me in at two o'clock today, so that's where I'm headed after I finish the Mount Olympus of chores.

Once the tree is naked as the day we brought it home, I drag it out of the house and down the driveway, where it will sit until the city picks it up. Overland Park is great about recycling used trees. Then I vacuum up the telltale trail of pine needles and put the now full boxes of decorations back in the garage. I'm freaking exhausted but also exhilarated that it's done. I wonder how long it will take Ron and Max to even notice the tree is gone.

I happen to like January, when everyone gets back to their busy lives and things get back to normal for me. Vivs and Laura are home from their trips and coming for dinner tonight. I can't wait to see Maude. I've never gone two weeks without her. I wanted my parents to come too, but my mother was noncommittal.

"Oh, sweetheart, I just don't know how we're going to feel. Dad gets really tired after a day out."

And by a day out, she means a day spent either at Riverview watching Kay play bridge or out and about in the car taking people to doctor's appointments. My mother rarely asks anyone to watch my dad anymore. She is doggedly determined to take care of him herself even if it means dragging him hither and yon.

I'm dying to hear from Vivs about how she and Raj did together for two weeks in India. It couldn't have been easy—they've been fighting on and off since Thanksgiving. About what is anyone's guess.

I clean up for my trip to the gyno as one does if one has any consideration, and I head downtown to Dr. Alex's office. After weeks of having Max either home or wanting to be driven somewhere, it's liberating to have all this time to myself. I've gotten really used to being the boss of my own day, and I missed it over the holidays.

Dr. Alex Shatner's office is at College Park, so I guess she's the real deal what with all the other doctors who work there. I walk into her empty reception area and am greeted by a young, seemingly efficient woman with her short brown hair pulled back from her face with a plastic headband. Even though I tell her I am only there for a consult, I still have to fill out ten forms that all pretty much ask the same questions. Whatever. If Dr. Alex can give me some insight into how I can get my groove back, it's worth it.

Before I even finish with my paperwork, a nurse comes out and asks me to follow her. As we walk down a hallway, I notice none of the exam rooms are in use. She explains to me that Dr. Shatner doesn't usually see patients on Tuesday, but she has made an exception for me. She doesn't say it, but her tone implies that I should feel flattered. She takes me to an exam room and tells me to undress from the waist down, but I can keep my socks on, for which I'm grateful. January has hit hard in KC. Once I've changed into a gown, she comes back to weigh me (ugh, six pounds up since the beginning of December), takes my blood pressure, and even checks my height, which I'm happy to report is holding steady at five feet four inches.

Dr. Alex comes in about five minutes later. She says hello without looking at me, but instead reads a file that I have to assume is my unfinished paperwork. Her superbitch face is firmly in place, and I begin to regret coming to her when what I probably need is someone a little more, well, nice. But then she looks up and something unexpected happened. She smiles and asks me how I'm doing.

"Pretty good, thanks. Glad the holidays are over."

She purses her lips but doesn't comment.

"So what brings you here today?"

"Well, I'm concerned that I don't want to have sex with my husband anymore."

She consults her notes. "You're what, fifty-five?"

"Yes."

She goes on to ask about my health history, and a ton of questions about the medicine I'm taking, the food I eat, my relationship with Ron, my daily stresses, how I'm feeling about my age, if I've tried any hormone replacement therapies, and on and on. She writes notes furiously in my file, then suddenly stops and asks me to lie back and put my feet in the stirrups. While she examines me *down there* she tells me how much she enjoyed class yesterday.

"I never knew I could get such a rush from riding to a Rick Astley song."

"Uh well, I like to keep people surprised."

"You should play more ABBA." This as she replaces the spreader thing with her own two fingers and presses my stomach. I tell her I will bust out the *Mamma Mia!* soundtrack just for her.

"Great." She pulls her fingers out and snaps off her gloves. "My favorite is *Voulez-Vous*. You can sit up."

Dr. Alex continues to write notes with such zeal that she kind of looks like a mad scientist. Finally, she lets out a sigh and looks at me directly.

"Well, Jen, I hate to tell you this, but barring anything unusual in your blood work, it would seem that you're totally normal."

She laughs, and I join her although I'm not sure what I'm laughing at.

"I'm sure you know you are perimenopausal; your hormones are going crazy, you're gaining weight, and your libido is taking a nosedive. All things you'd expect at fifty-five."

"Great. So this is the rest of my life?"

"Pretty much," she deadpans, then starts to laugh. "No, this is just a phase like puberty, only longer. You'll get through it. Normally I would recommend a healthy diet and exercise, but you seem to have that covered."

"I'm really just worried about my sex drive," I remind her.

"I know. Have you tried a vibrator to get things going?"

I'm not sure why, but vibrators have never done anything for me. I tell her as much and she grunts.

"I'm going to prescribe you a suppository to stimulate your vagina, which should help, but may I also suggest some light porn?"

I laugh nervously. I find this funny coming from a doctor.

"My go-to porn hasn't really been doing it for me," I confess.

"What's your go-to?" she asks curiously.

"Umm . . ." I start to blush.

"No judgment," she promises. Jeez, I would hope not.

"Well, pretty much any variation of a domineering man being brought to his knees by love used to do it for me."

She nodded. "Like *Fifty Shades*?"

"More like bad-boy pirate or tough-guy rancher."

"But not anymore?"

"Nope."

"Have you read any of Mary Willy's books?"

I start to laugh. "No. You know I didn't even know she was a famous writer until I had juice after class with her."

"Her books are a pretty good aphrodisiac. Her girl-on-girl stuff gets the job done for me."

"Really?"

"Oh yes." She smiles.

I've never thought about lesbian porn, but I'm willing to try anything. I thank Dr. Alex and promise her a good ABBA fest for the next class.

It may not surprise you to know that I stop by Rainy Day Books on my way home and buy the first in Mary's Wanderlust series, titled *Leaving Las Vilas*. I am humbled to see her other three books on the shelf and wonder where I was when this series became a thing. I open it to the middle and the first thing I read is . . .

She slowly eased my plain white panties over my quivering ass and slid them down my legs, her tongue following and creating a moist path to my ankles.

Suddenly, I feel an unexpected jolt of energy *down there*. Wow. Way to be a stereotype, Jen. I slam the book shut and look around to make sure no one had seen me reading a dirty book!! And then I went back into Rainy Day to buy her other three books.

✦ ✦ ✦

To: Jen Dixon

From: Mimi Melon

Re: This and That

Date: January 4

Jen,

I just wanted to let you know that I won't be buying any of your daughter's "snacks." Nice grift you've got going. Is that why you volunteered to rep Overland Park in the City League? And by the way, NO ONE calls it CLOP.

Mimi

I smile as I read this at my kitchen counter office. Well, if I can annoy just one person, my work here is done. It's just a bonus that it happens to be Mimi. I get up from my chair and glance at my family, who are all in the kitchen, minus my parents. They were too tired to come to dinner.

"Thanks for making the chicken, sweetie," I tell Laura. It's her own recipe involving chickpeas, Mediterranean spices, and a little bit of yogurt. She serves it over quinoa, and it is outstanding. She makes a version of it for Good Clean Grub and serves it cold over lettuce. Either way, it's delicious.

I swear Maude grew three inches while she was in India. She came back with bangs and a penchant for saying "*baap re*," which I guess means "oh my God!" It's hilarious and disturbing all at the same time.

"Gee Gee, I drank tea!" she informs me as we're catching up.

My eyebrows go up and I glance at Vivs, who gives a disapproving shake of her head.

"Did you like it?"

She nods excitedly. "Can I have some here?"

"I think that'll just be a special treat when you see Daadee."

"Oh *baap re*," Maude says dramatically and puts her head down on the table.

Over dinner we hear all about Laura's trip to Fort Lauderdale and how weird she found it to walk through the mall in shorts and listen to Christmas carols. She got an impressive tan over her ten-day trip and has come back happy and refreshed. I think the separation from Vivs did them both a world of good. They are back to talking *to* each other instead of *at* each other, which is a nice change.

Vivs gives us details about their trip to India—it's the second time she's gone, and she really likes it. Well, most of it. Raj's mother is still a bit of a challenge sometimes, but Vivs has learned to go with the flow. And she stays at Raj's aunt's house instead of with Varsha. That way she isn't asked to chop onions every day.

"How did you and Raj get along?" I ask.

"Fine" is the breezy response I get.

She tells us she spent a lot of her time in Mumbai coming up with a new business plan for Good Clean Grub—expanding to their own storefront and hiring at least two people. She explains they don't need a seating area—just a place with a kitchen in the back, and a counter out front. "So we'll need to start looking at real estate," she says excitedly.

As she's telling us this, I realize that she will need more seed money, and I'm hoping Ron will agree to invest in them. As if he was reading my mind, he tells them he thinks this next step is an excellent idea and offers to bankroll the initial changes.

"Umm, thank you, but we already have another investor," Vivs says quietly.

"We do?" Laura is as shocked as I am. "Who?"

"Raj."

"WHAT?" Laura and I yell together.

Vivs growls, "Can you not? He wants to get involved for Maude's sake."

"Why didn't I know about this?" Laura is both hurt and angry.

"I was going to tell you," Vivs defends herself. "We literally just decided."

"You do know I'm part of this too, right? You can't just decide things without talking to me."

Vivs looks bored by the direction of the conversation.

"You make menu changes without talking to me," she points out.

"Because you don't care!" Laura practically screams. Max and Maude visibly jump at the unexpected outburst.

"Alright, let's calm down," I say. "Max, can you take Maude to your room? She can watch *Dora* on the iPad."

He jumps up and takes Maude's hand, probably realizing that this task will get him out of any cleanup duty. As soon as they are out of earshot, Vivs lets loose.

"I don't care? *I* don't care?? All I do is care. I'm trying to build this business."

"And this business is the food that I create. There's no business without me," Laura counters.

"Well, without me, you'd be just a sandwich maker. When we started this, we agreed that I would be the brains and you would be the brawn."

"I never agreed to that! I said I would be the creative one and you would be the nuts and bolts."

"Exactly. And money is nuts and bolts. I don't bitch when you try a new kind of lettuce."

"That's just rude. You make it sound like that's all I do."

It's hard for me to stay silent, but Ron's hand on my leg tells me I shouldn't interrupt. I'm guessing this fight has been brewing for a while.

"How can you bring Raj into our business without even asking me? Who's next, Dana?"

"Jesus Christ, is that what this is about? You'll be happy to know we broke up."

"You did?" I'm surprised. "Why?"

"It was never going to work out. We're too different, and the malaprops were driving me crazy. I'm not sure why he asked me out in the first place."

"I know why," Laura lobs in.

"Oh really, why?" Vivs is still annoyed.

"Because he mixed up our names."

We all look at her, and Vivs says what we're all thinking.

"What the hell are you talking about?"

Laura takes a breath. "He thought he was calling me, but he called you. He didn't realize his mistake until he came to pick you up."

At this Ron starts to laugh.

"Well, why the hell didn't he say anything?" Vivs wants to know.

"I think he was embarrassed. And then you guys had sex that night, so he couldn't just blow you off and call me."

"How do you know all this?" Vivs takes the words right out of my mouth.

"I don't. But it makes sense, don't you think?" Laura is at her most sincere.

Vivs stares at her sister in disbelief. "Wait, you just made all that up?"

Laura shrugs.

"Oh my God, you're unbelievable!" She looks at me. "Why did you have her?"

"Hey!" Laura barks. "Mom told you not to say that anymore."

Vivs shakes her head. "You can have him. Be my guest. He was too goofy for me anyway."

"He is not!" Laura jumps to his defense. "*You're* goofy."

This makes everyone laugh including Laura. Vivs is a lot of things, but goofy isn't one of them.

"Is he upset that you broke up?" she asks.

"Why don't you call and ask him?" Vivs rolls her eyes.

I'm surprised when Ron interrupts.

"It sounds like you guys really needed to have this out—and not just because Raj is now in the mix."

"Ya think?" Vivs snipes.

Ron ignores her tone. "Can I suggest you go to neutral corners for now and schedule a time and place to discuss it as adults and business partners and not feuding sisters? I'd be happy to be there to moderate."

They both nod their agreement, and for about the nine thousandth time, I thank God that I married this man.

"Now, how about we end the night on a good note?" He winks and prompts me to regale the girls with my adventure going out with Lynnie and Tamera from spin class. As much as I'd like to forget about that whole night, I know the story will make them laugh so I give them the broad strokes.

As promised, I met them for drinks after work a few days before Christmas. Among the things I had forgotten about "drinks with the girls" is that it's not just a drink or two and then you leave. It's drink Mexican Mules all night long with nary a potato chip in sight to keep the alcohol from impairing your judgment. How else can

I explain my slurry phone call to my husband at one-thirty in the morning asking him to pick me up at the Bare Fax All-Male Review out on highway 69?

"Oh God, Mom, you didn't go there, did you?"

"I can only confirm that I was picked up from there. I don't remember anything about being inside, if I even was."

"Oh, you were inside." Ron chuckles. "You showed me all those books of matches you swiped from the hostess station."

I groan. I haven't been that hungover in years. Not even Tylenol and Burger King could make me feel better. I still dry-heave when I think about drinking anything with tequila.

Although it took me three days to feel like myself again, Lynnie and Tamera bounced back with the resilience that only a twenty-something has. Lynnie texted me that we absolutely had to do that again, but maybe next time without Tamera "'cuz she was a buzz kill."

Actually, from what I can remember, Tamera was the only thing that made the night tolerable. She told me all about the night courses she is taking at KC community college to become an eldercare advisor. According to her, it's the fastest growing field in health care, and chances are she will get a job almost immediately and pretty much have one for life. She seems like such a bright, delightful girl. I'll never understand why she hangs out with Lynnie, who by the way was in rare form that night—telling us all kinds of stories about her life, then transitioning to her opinions about everything from why *The Real Housewives of New Jersey* is the best reality TV show ever, to how just about everyone over thirty is an idiot (excluding me, of course) and that's why she doesn't want to get "old." Tamera at least tried to argue her own views on the matter, but no one filibusters like Lynnie. I'm thinking that's why the drinks got away from me. I was just trying to dull the noise coming from her.

Anyway, lesson learned, and I have decided to press pause on any further outings with Lynnie. And as for the owners of Good Clean Grub, they left laughing and set up a meeting with Ron for tomorrow.

15

To: City League Overland Park Parents
From: Jen Dixon
Re: Comanche Gear
Date: January 24

Hello Clippity CLOPpers!

Three weeks in and may I say you guys are a cut above any other parent group I've worked with (although the bar was set pretty low at William Taft).

Snacks are covered for the entire season, so well done! And thanks to those who asked my daughter to bake for them. Now she can finally afford that expensive nail polish she has been eyeing.

Now on to the important task of making our Comanches the fiercest-looking group of middle schoolers in the league.

Last year's Just for the Smell of It Fundraiser enabled the team to purchase new singlets, and may I say they are the cat's pajamas in all their gold-and-black grandness. You will be able to pick up your gear this Thursday, just ahead of our first match on Saturday against the Ottawa Orioles. It's an 8 a.m. home game so you know where to be.

I'm here for you.

Jen

Done and done. I take a final swig of coffee (let's not call it back-wash, okay?) and jump to my feet. I'm in fighting form today, I tell you. My Monday spinners better gird their loins. Jenny's comin' in hot this morning!

To what do I owe this newfound spring in my step? That would be the wily words of one Mary Willy. The exploits of Greta Johansen have given me my mojo back in a big way. Turns out Mary writes the kind of mommy porn I like—dirty, not raunchy, and with a compelling story at the heart of it. I'm only halfway through the first book and my my my, that Greta is a busy and curious lady. She is not unlike a young Jen Howard (me) who slept her way across Europe in search of love. I just hope Greta is smart enough to use birth control. Lord knows Jen wasn't.

Needless to say, the return of my libido has made it a happy new year indeed for Ron. Or it was until he put together that my horniness coincided with the nights I read before bed. This led to questions about what I've been reading, and instead of lying, I foolishly told him the truth. At first, he laughed, but that's because he thought I was kidding.

"Wait, really?" He frowned. "Lesbian porn is what's turning you on?"

"Well, it's not *all* girl on girl, but I know it's crazy, right?"

He moved to the other side of the bed and glared at me.

"So when we're having sex, you're thinking about women?"

"No!" I laughed nervously and scooted over to bridge the distance he had created between us. "It just gets the motor running. When we're doing it, it's all you." It was a little white lie, which was totally acceptable in this situation.

He was weird about it for a couple of days, but then I walked in on him reading *Leaving Las Vilas* before bed, and since then he's all in. Now we read it together. Is that weird?

Ron's meeting with the girls went about as expected. They each had a grocery list of grievances, most of which were legit, and only some were, shall we say, petty girl shit. After the fireworks the other week I was worried Good Clean Grub would fizzle out before it even got off the ground. But Ron has always been a good negotiator for them, even when they were little and fighting over who got to pick the TV show. I think the biggest takeaway from their summit was to keep personal things out of any argument about the business. And also to respect each other's input (something I had talked to Laura about months ago, by the way).

They are tentatively going forward with Raj as a third partner and are now busy looking for a storefront.

✦ ✦ ✦

"Good morning eight a.m.!" I tell my spin class, and as always wait to hear Bob call out a time check to me. I wonder if that will ever stop.

I start the class with Elton John's "Love Lies Bleeding," and as I'm adjusting my bike, I take a peek at who is in class. The new year always brings a new crop of people with the best of intentions, and it's fun to see who sticks with it and who gives up after a few weeks.

Lots of regulars, which is nice, and a few new but familiar faces with whom I will have to connect after class to see where I know them from.

Lynnie is on her usual front-row bike and gives me a big wave. I involuntarily gag at the memory of our night out together. Oh my God, what if I gag every time I see her from now on? That's going to be inconvenient to say the least.

After class, she runs up to me and gives me a sweaty hug.

"Oh my God! How are you? You haven't answered any of my texts. I thought you were going to die that night!"

"I'm fine now, but it took a few days." I give her a weak smile.

"That night was sick! I hooked up with the guy dressed like a sailor, remember him? He had those huge biceps. He was so hot, but he had a small dick. I couldn't believe it. He must have stuffed his boy shorts."

I glance around to see if anyone is listening and am mortified to see a woman standing behind me waiting to talk to me.

"Well, have a good one, Lynnie." I steer her toward an exit in our conversation, but she doesn't take the bait.

"Was your husband pissed that you were hammered?" she asks a bit too loudly. "Sorry I had to leave you in the parking lot, but my sailor boy was ready to go."

"Not a problem," I assure her and turn away.

"Is this who you're having juice with today?" she calls after me.

This shit has to stop. I turn, walk right up to her and lower my voice.

"Lynnie, excuse me but there are other people in the class besides you. This constant need for my attention is getting ridiculous. And I'd appreciate you not talking about my personal life so loudly."

I turn away but not before I see the shocked and hurt look on her face, which pisses me off even more. I take a deep breath and approach the woman with the familiar face who has been waiting to talk to me.

"Hi, where do I know you from?"

"Hi. Wrestling. My son is in City League with yours," she tells me. "I'm Teddy's mom, Charmaine. We met at Franny's party. Your class was great!"

When she says her name, I remember her as the mom from Hawthorne who gave me shit for buying Max a phone for Christmas. But that person is a far cry from the friendly face in front of me.

"Oh right. We talked about Christmas gifts for our boys."

She immediately looks chagrined. "Oh, you remember that, huh? I guess I should apologize. We had just come from my husband's office party, and I was already pretty lit."

I nod, not sure whether to believe that alcohol had anything to do with her bitchiness, but I'm willing to give her the benefit of the doubt, especially since she came to my class.

Looking at Charmaine now, sweaty, makeup-free, hair matted up under a bandana, she seems pretty harmless.

"Ya, well, we've all had one too many at one time or another." I smile.

"Sounds like you did with that other rider!" She laughs, but I don't. I'm irritated that she heard Lynnie's comments, so I change the subject.

"Is this your first spin class?"

"No, I used to spin at the JKC"—which is the Jewish Community Center of Kansas City for those of you not in the know—"but I heard about your class from some of the league moms, so I decided to try it. You're great. I love your music and the vibe you give off."

"Thanks. I'm a work in progress." I tell her that I didn't start teaching until two years ago, and it was pretty bad at first, but I think I'm getting better.

"I didn't think I'd ever want to hear Kenny Rogers in a spin class, but you proved me wrong."

"I'm so glad. Which league moms told you about my class?"

"I think it was Mimi Melon."

Immediately my radar is on high alert. Is Mimi sending spies to my class? And if she is, why would they out themselves? Or maybe that's part of the plan—be up front and backstabbing all at the same time?

"Are you okay?" Charmaine asks, and I realize my thoughts must have been playing out on my face.

"What? Oh ya. I'm just confused because Mimi has never been to one of my classes."

"Huh, maybe she heard about it from one of her friends. Anyway, she definitely told me to check you out, and I'm glad I did. Sorry for the way we met. I hope we can start fresh because I'll definitely be back."

"Anytime," I tell her, but I'm distracted. Who could have told Mimi about my class?

As Charmaine is leaving, I ask if she can do me a favor. "Can you ask Mimi who recommended the class to her? It's always nice to thank people for new riders."

"Sure, no problem. Oh, and by the way, your league emails make my day. Even my husband reads them. You're hilarious."

And that's how I decided that Charmaine would be my very next juice date.

On my way to the car, I hear my phone ping and see a text from Lynnie. Grrrr.

> Are you mad at me?

Yes, you idiot, I scream at my phone. I want to ignore the text but she is one of my riders, a customer at Fusion and really, not a bad person. Just annoying. I text her back.

> I'm not mad, I just wasn't comfortable with you talking about our night out in front of everyone.

I hit send, and then because I'm feeling righteous and brave, I decide to type more.

> And if I'm being honest, I'm not thrilled with all the ways you have inserted yourself into my life. I think you should respect the teacher/student boundary.

I see the three dots linger on my screen for a good minute before she sends a reply.

> You were the one who asked me out for juice bitch.

Well, she's got me there. And since she just called me a bitch I decide not to feel bad for her at all.

✦ ✦ ✦

The day of the league's first match is bitterly cold. Luckily the rec center gym warms up very quickly with so many bodies inside. There's easily five times the number of kids and parents compared to a school match, and the four different rings are in constant use.

Our Overland Park Comanches look sharp in their new gold-and-black uniforms and are eager to get fighting.

It's surprisingly easy to avoid Mimi because she follows her son and I track Max. But I'm happy to see Charmaine, who came to another spin class yesterday. Because she's new she should have been at the back of the line for a juice date, but she pole-vaulted over everyone else so that I could pump her for more information. It delighted me to find her kind of a cool mom (there are so few of us). We had a lot of laughs talking about the wrestling season that was and the trials and tribulations of having a son in the sport. Turns out it's her first year too, so when I waded into Mimi Melon territory, she seemed as mystified by Mimi as I am.

"All I know is people at Hawthorne were thrilled that she transferred her son because it helped the team." She shrugged. "That and everyone is scared of her."

"Really?" I pretended to be shocked by this.

She nodded. "It's weird everyone wants to be her friend, but they all talk about her behind her back."

We've all known this person at one time in our lives. She is very charismatic and gathers people around her easily, but then she insists on being the one in charge, and if you challenge that in any way, you are iced out. At the games Mimi seemed like the most popular mom there—always surrounded by a gaggle of moms hanging on her every word. I said this to Charmaine.

"Yeah, they definitely do that. But then they say stuff about her when she's not there."

"Like what?"

Char thought for a minute. "Like how obnoxious it is that she does that whole pin thing with her son. Or that she doesn't like any plans being made without her input, or that she never lets her kids have any fun."

"She doesn't?" I thought of our Halloween party.

"No girlfriends or parties anyway. All they do is wrestle. But maybe that's not a bad thing. Her oldest is on track for a full ride to Duke."

Now that *is* impressive. Mimi just might have the secret sauce for teenage success. But at what cost?

"To an outsider like me, she just seems kind of mean," I told Charmaine.

"Only if you cross her. If you kiss the ring and play nice, she won't bother you."

"I'm not much of a ring kisser," I mumbled.

Charmaine laughed. "Neither am I, but I learned to pucker up pretty quickly."

I see her now, standing with a group of moms I don't know, and she waves me over.

"Hi! I was just talking about you!" she says and then addresses her group. "This is the spin instructor I was telling you about."

"Hi." I wave, a little embarrassed. "Only good things, I hope."

"I was talking about yesterday's ride. It was so much fun."

I had surprised my class with an '80s hair bands ride just for fun, but everyone seemed to love it.

"I'm glad you liked it."

"She plays the best music," Char gushes.

One of the moms tilts her head. "Did you used to take Carmen's class at Fusion?"

I look at her curiously. "Yes, did you?"

"I thought I recognized you. I was always there. Sadie." She reaches out her hand. "Carmen called me Shady."

I give a big guffaw. "I remember the name. She called me 'Jenny from the Block.' She was the best. She's the reason I became an instructor."

"I don't think I've taken a class since she left Fusion," Sadie says.

"Come take Jen's class with me!" Char encourages her, then looks around. "You guys all should."

"What are we doing?" comes a voice from behind me.

"Oh, hey, Mimi. We were just talking about taking Jen's spin class."

I turn around and the redheaded momster is standing there with a slight furrow in her brow.

"You're a spin instructor?" She looks amused.

"I thought you knew that. Didn't you tell Charmaine about my class?"

I think I see a quick flash of panic in her eyes, but then it's gone, and she's cool as a cucumber once again.

"Oh, that's right. I completely forgot." She shrugs.

"I'm just curious, who told you about it?"

"I think a friend mentioned it." She waves her answer away with her hand.

"What's their name? Maybe I know them." I am not letting this go.

Mimi pretends to think long and hard before she looks directly at me and says, "Actually, she has the same last name as you."

"Dixon?"

"That is your last name, isn't it?"

"The only Dixon I ever had as a rider was my . . ."

Ho-ly shit. It can't be. There's no way. This town is way too small if Mimi is friends with Ron's crazy ex-wife, Cindy.

For those of you who need a primer, let me just say Cindy is the ex-wife that makes Kate Gosselin look like spouse of the year. But we haven't heard anything from her in the past two years. She had been taking my spin class at Fusion and acting all friendly and normal so I thought she was finally past the grudge she had against me for the crime of marrying Ron, so I agreed to teach a special birthday ride for her and all her friends. Little did I know it was part of an elaborate plan to humiliate me in front of her friends and accuse me yet again of stealing her husband.

"So you're friends with Cindy Dixon?"

I can't help but notice that all has gone quiet around us—the other mat moms playing spectator in this battle of the bitches.

"New friends. But she has a lot to say about you."

Well, this explains a lot. I'd hate me too, if I saw myself through Cindy's nutty eyes.

"Well, don't feel obligated to come to the class," I tell her.

"Nonsense! If everyone's going, let's make a day of it. I'll host brunch at my house afterward."

"Wow! Great idea! You're the best." The chorus of approval from the mat moms is so loud I want to yell, "You're all a bunch of suck-ups!" But I don't. I have enough on my plate with Mimi as a nemesis.

"Sounds like a plan," I say, then add for reasons that will never be quite clear to me, "Why don't you invite Cindy?"

Mimi smiles. "I just might."

As she walks away, I picture myself taking Mimi down by the knees and pinning her with a cross-face cradle. Clearly the Just for the Smell of It Fundraiser has been looming large in my thoughts. I basically have four months to step up my strength training and learn a few trick moves so I don't embarrass myself on the way to my inevitable defeat at the hands of Mimi. I know I can't win, but I do plan to go down swinging. I started lifting weights right after New Year's, plus doing leg presses and squats—all things Garth, my former trainer, taught me years ago. But what I really need is a wrestling coach—someone who isn't affiliated with the league. I don't want anyone to know how seriously I'm taking this challenge.

I turn my attention back to the action. Max isn't on the mat right now, but it intrigues me to see there are two girls fighting . . . and not each other. I know Ron and Max told me about this, but I guess I had to see it to believe it. The Ottawa Orioles have four female wrestlers—one of whom is fully, and I mean fully, developed, so I'm curious to see how that's going to work. She isn't on the mat yet, but I'm going to keep my eye on her. Thank God she's in a higher weight class than Max.

The Comanches have one female wrestler—a cutie named Leah with long blond braided hair who fights in the lowest weight division. I'm happy to see the boys support her just as they would any team member.

Max gained weight over the holidays, but unlike me, he was thrilled about it. He's still in the gangly category of pubescent boys, but his muscle tone is really developing, and he has gone up a weight class. When he's called to ring four, I make my way over and join Ron on the sidelines.

Max's opponent is shorter but beefier than him. His headgear seems to be a bit too tight, giving his face a pug-like look that is more cute than intimidating. They take their positions and begin the dance—circling each other and waiting for an opening. Max makes the first move and has Pug Face down on his back, but not for long. They are rolling and undulating and finally wiggle their way out of the ring, so they start again. I'm no expert, but Max's technique seems so much better than before Christmas. He's been coming home from the league practices completely exhausted and hungry as a bear in springtime.

The next time Max gets Pug Face (okay, okay, his name is Graham) to the ground, he pins him in under thirty seconds. Ron and I roar our delight and watch proudly as Max's arm is thrust into the air, and he is given a pin by one of his coaches. As a spectator mom, I have to say it's a lot easier to watch your son win rather than lose. If we can keep this little streak going, I might not mind coming to matches.

The curvy girl from Ottawa (named Tinsley) has just started a match on another mat, so I gravitate over to check it out. She is wrestling a boy I have come to know as Monk—his last name is Monkowitz, and he is having quite the time of it. It can't be easy for him to go for a hold only to find himself with a face full of boobs or his hand slipping through her crotch.

"Oh, that poor kid," I say to Georgie, who has joined me ringside.

"Who, Monk? Why?"

"He has to wrestle that girl."

She looks at me like I have two heads. "Don't feel bad for him. The boys are trained for this. They're told to treat the girls as equals and not to take it easy on them. And the girls know what they signed up for."

"But it just seems like a no-win for the boys. If you win, you beat a girl, good for you. If you lose, you've been beaten by a girl. I don't care how woke we all are, neither of those scenarios is ideal."

"If you talk to the kids, they don't seem to have a problem with it." Georgie shrugs.

I'm realizing I have quite the antiquated view of this. What the hell is wrong with me? These girls are warriors. I wish I could be more like Georgie, but I just can't help feeling bad for the boys.

After Monk ultimately pins Tinsley, Georgie's son Tyler is called to the mat to wrestle Ottawa's own Samantha. They are both thin and muscular, and thankfully Samantha is as flat as a board. Unfortunately, she is also very nimble, so no matter how hard Tyler tries, he can't seem to hold her down. They reset three times, and ultimately Samantha wins on points. Tyler looks like he's about to cry.

I turn to Georgie, who is watching her son. "Do you think he's okay?"

She turns to me red-faced. "How can he be okay? He just lost to a girl!"

16

To: CLOP
From: Jen Dixon
Re: Mystery Solved!
Date: February 11

Good news CLOPpers,

I believe the mystery of the ringworm epidemic has been solved. Turns out the Leavenworth Chiefs are ground zero for the outbreak that has plagued us this week.

So no more blaming each other at practice. The boys were rubbed the wrong way at last week's match, and that is that. If anyone needs more antifungal cream, be sure to see one of the coaches. We bought a year's supply at Costco yesterday. Plus, I'm looking into filling a huge vat with Lotrimin so the boys can take a big dip after practice and matches.

Remember, we don't have a match this Saturday, but there will be practice, so make sure you're extra diligent ahead of next week's match against what I lovingly call the armpit of Kansas. (Sorry, not sorry, Wichita.)

Gina Christensen is scheduling carpools, so go bother her if you don't have a ride.

As always, you're welcome.

Jen

It's been a hell of a week and its only Thursday. Ringworm is no joke, and Max has it just about everywhere, including places where I can no longer comfortably apply the ointment for him. Thank goodness he is ridiculously diligent with his cleanliness. He uses like three towels after he showers and puts them right into the laundry along with any clothes he touches while deciding what to wear.

I have a feeling the PMS seventh-grade Valentine's "hangout" (don't call it a dance!) just might be the fuel behind his fire. Not that Max has said anything, but I heard a few tidbits when I was driving a bunch of his ringworm-infested buddies home from the match last Saturday. It was something about whether Max knew if Tanya was going to show up, and then there was some giggling and playful punching. The nice thing about tween boys is that they often forget someone is driving the car and just let loose. It's the only time I don't mind feeling invisible as a fifty-five-year-old woman.

This was also the week that the mat moms finally came, en masse, to my spin class. We had been trying to get a date on the calendar for weeks, but someone (mostly Mimi) would always have a conflict. She kept saying it wasn't a good day for her to host. Well, no one asked you to, Mimi! Way to make it all about yourself.

But it finally came together, and yesterday they all showed up to my Wednesday 8 a.m. class. Even Franny came, despite protests that she hates exercise. I was more anxious than I would like to admit that Crazy Cindy might show up to the class, but then I remembered Fusion revoked her membership after the little stunt she had pulled on me at her birthday spin. Even still, until everyone was saddled up, I would flinch every time a strawberry blonde walked in the room.

When I got to class, I noticed Lynnie standing near some of the moms. I didn't hear from her again after our text fight, so I was glad to see her back in class. But when she saw me, she made a beeline for her bike without making eye contact.

We had to add some extra bikes to accommodate everyone, and as it turns out a packed class feeds off its own energy, so it turned into an epic ride. I tailored the playlist to the average age in the room, which I took to be around forty-five, and played a lot of hits from the '70s, '80s, and '90s. Not even Mimi's bemused expression and refusal to clap along to "Saturday Night" by the Bay City Rollers could yuck this yum.

I could tell that Sadie (Shady) was a Carmen disciple because her energy was immediate and infectious. From the first lines of "Your Love" by The Outfield (*"Josie's on a vacation far away . . ."*) to the last note of Lionel Richie's "Still," the class was on fire.

I got a big round of applause at the end and had a gaggle of people waiting to talk to me, which never happens. But Mimi managed to crush the moment by gracelessly telling everyone they could talk to me later and to please head to her place for après spin snacks.

Lynnie approached me as I was walking out the door.

"I know I'm not supposed to talk to you, but I think I can help you."

"Lynnie, you can talk to me, we just need to keep it within the bounds of the spin class."

"Oh" is all she says.

"So, you say you can help me. Is it with the class?"

She looks down. "No."

"Is it about something in my personal life?"

She fidgets with her hair. "Yes."

"Then it probably isn't appropriate for us to discuss."

She looks like she's about to argue but I push past her and head to my car.

On the way to Mimi's house, I call my bestie Nina to ask how Yvette is feeling.

"About the same. Garth spends a lot of time with her. I'm bracing for the day he comes and asks if she can move in with us."

"Yikes. That's a tough one," I commiserate. "What will you say?"

"What can I say? It's his mother. She's not that bad most of the time. It's just when she talks about her guides . . ."

"Well, you know how I feel about them." I had told Nina that Yvette was right about my needing to get into shape for May.

"I know." She sighs. "And she does get a lot of things right. It's just weird. And for some reason it creeps Chyna out."

Chyna is Nina's daughter from another relationship.

"What creeps her out?"

"Yvette likes to tell her about Sid."

I physically blanche. Sid is Chyna's father whom she has never met. He left when Nina was nine months' pregnant, which makes him among the lowest of the world's lowlifes.

"What about him?"

"She says, 'The guides tell me your father is thinking about you.'"

"Eww."

"I know. It really upsets her."

"I can see why. Maybe set up some ground rules if she moves in? No unsolicited messages from Tweedledum and Tweedledee."

"I'm not sure she can stop herself. Garth and I need to hash it out."

"Well, take a bit of your own advice and stop worrying about what could go wrong."

"Oooh! Look who's wise now." She laughs.

I pull up in front of Mimi's house. "Okay, I'm here. Wish me luck!"

"I do, but you don't need it."

"Thanks, friend."

As I walk into Mimi's place, my eyes dart to every corner of the room in search of Cindy. Even after I have established that she isn't in the kitchen or living room, I can't fully relax and enjoy all the love I'm getting from my fellow mat moms. This is the first time I have had even an inkling of what Carmen must have felt every damn day, and it would have been a real ego boost if I hadn't been looking over my shoulder for an unwanted surprise.

When Mimi comes to tell me how impressed she is by my cardio stamina, I am sure she is going to have Cindy pop up from behind the couch.

"You seem distracted, Jen. Are you looking for something?"

She knows what I'm looking for, and in that moment I realize the true power of terrorism. It's not that something happened; it's the worry that something *might* happen.

"Of course, you're not going to need your breath when we have our rumble." She laughs. "I'll have you pinned long before your heart rate goes up."

"Well, you'd better step up *your* cardio, Mimi, 'cuz I plan to make you work for your win." I mimic her laugh. I want her to know that I will be going down swinging.

✦ ✦ ✦

My phone rings as I'm pulling into my driveway.

"Jen's Bean Shack."

"Sweetheart, that's just so off-putting," Kay tells me in her no-nonsense voice.

"Mom, hang up and call me again. I'll do better."

When the phone rings ten seconds later, I pick up. "Jen's House of Ill Repute!" I say with the same chirpy zeal. All I hear on the other end is a large sigh.

"What's up, Mom?"

"I just wanted to tell you that I think all the going out and about is working on your father."

"What makes you say that?"

"He just seems better."

"Does he talk to you?" I'm wondering if she has seen a bit of the old Ray coming out, like I did in the car that day.

"He always answers any question I ask. And he lets me know when he needs to use the bathroom. Plus, he sleeps like a log."

"Well, that's good. Has anyone been helping you?" My mother hasn't asked me for help since Christmas.

"No. I'm quite capable of handling things myself." Her voice is a little sharp.

"I know, but everyone needs help now and then."

"Well, Amelia is around, so she helps," she says dismissively.

"Do you guys want to come for dinner this week?"

"That would be lovely. Can you make fish? Your dad needs the omegas."

"Of course. How about tomorrow?"

"Fish on Friday. Very appropriate." I can hear my mother smiling because she thinks I'm holding to the old Catholic ritual on purpose.

"I'll see if the girls are free," I tell her.

✦ ✦ ✦

Friday turned out to be the Christmas dinner we never got to have. The girls came, along with Maude and Raj and my parents.

When Vivs left the room, I asked Laura how she and her sister were getting along.

"We're good. Well, we're fine. I still can't believe what she did."

"You mean bringing Raj into the business?"

"No! I mean breaking up with Dana."

"I thought you'd be thrilled. I mean, doesn't it open the door for you?"

"Ya, but now I have to wait for him to get over Vivs and think of me again. Then he's going to wonder if it's appropriate because Vivs is my sister and he may not want to see her if he asks me out. It's going to take forever."

"Well, the hardest test in life is having the patience to wait for the right moment."

"You sound like Nana."

She's right. It's one of my mother's favorite sayings.

"I still think my theory is right, by the way. It makes more sense that he intended to call me."

I smiled at her, but there's no way I'm going to encourage her delusion.

"I knew she didn't really like him," she continued. "It was all about beating me. I'm the one that liked him, and now it's all messed up."

I would have loved to tell her she was wrong, but I wouldn't put it past Vivs. I just feel bad that Coach Dana got caught in their crossfire.

My parents arrived ten minutes early—my mother profusely apologizing for being late. She and my dad were dressed in their usual velour track suits, and I was happy to see they both looked healthy. My mother made a fuss over everyone, especially Maude, while my father shuffled in behind her and took a seat on the sofa.

"I can smell the fish," my mother informed me. "You should probably open a window."

"The fish is still in the fridge, Mom."

"Oh" is all she had to say.

Ron tried engaging my father in conversation with questions about the weather, the Chiefs, and the state of our yard after the recent snowstorm—three things that would normally have lit up Ray's day. My father answered the questions asked without much more than a murmur of agreement and didn't have anything else to add. I could see why my mother thought he was doing fine. He does answer when asked, but he's not really there.

Maude recited the Pledge of Allegiance for us and sang "You're a Grand Old Flag" three times. I didn't know they even taught kids that song anymore. My parents loved it—even my dad clapped along to Maude's Merman-esque performance.

At one point, Max took Laura up to his room, and I found out later he wanted to run some outfits by her for the seventh-grade Valentine's hangout, which is where he is tonight.

I barely recognized him in his jeans and a new rugby-style shirt with gold-and-black stripes (the Comanche colors!) when he left for the hangout. He had put some kind of product in his hair that smelled suspiciously like Mennen Speed Stick, and I wondered if he improvised that little trick or if Ron had coached him.

The hangout ends at ten, so I'm trying to stay awake until he gets dropped off—Ron fell asleep an hour ago, after a "romantic" Valentine's dinner of hamburgers and chocolate fondue. Ron thought it would be more special if he cooked for me than if we went out. I'm not sure where the hell he got *that* idea.

To kill time, I wander into Max's room and recoil at the wall of odor that hits me. No number of showers or loads of clean laundry can suppress the native smells of a middle school boy. I'm humming a Crowded House song as I hang up his jeans and realize that Ron's going to sleep early means he and I won't be having a special Valentine's Day joint reading session, which is what I call sex these days. We are on Mary Willy's second book, *Til the Cows Come Home*, and enjoying the story almost as much as the dirty stuff. I sneak quietly into our room, grab it off my nightstand, then head back to Max's room. In this book, Greta Johansen has taken her sexual journey to the heartland, where she finds an unlikely number of farmers' daughters who are willing to widen their horizons with a drifter passing through town, especially one as hot as Greta. Reading these together has been a real game changer for Ron and me. The only thing I worry about is what happens when we run out of books.

I notice Dwayne the grappling dummy gracelessly slumped in the corner, and it reminds me yet again that I need to find someone who can teach me some moves and holds. Max has tried to teach me a few, but he gets very frustrated when I ask too many questions. I grab Dwayne and throw him on the ground—he's an easy pin. Then I go on my hands and knees and put him on my back, like he is starting on top. I thrust up, mimicking what I've seen the boys on the team do, and he falls on his back with me on top of him. It's so easy that I have to wonder how this helps Max at all. Beyond my confidence level getting a boost, I don't think it's doing anything for me. I try to pin him again, this time without touching his chest area or between his legs. It's impossible. I end up hugging Dwayne around the waist like a body pillow, grab my book, and begin to read chapter five.

✦ ✦ ✦

The dry Oklahoma breeze brushes against Greta's skin as she takes Briana by the hands and leads her to the stand of trees behind the barn. As they kneel on the dewy grass, the girl's breasts are straining the buttons of her denim shirt. Greta can tell Briana wants her to rip it off her, and she will, but . . . not yet. Briana needs to learn patience. And Greta is the one who's going to . . .

"Mom! What are you doing?"

I bolt up to see Max staring at me from the doorway. I hadn't realized that I was a bit flushed from my reading, so the combo of me on the floor with the dummy, breathing hard, does not look in any way wholesome.

"Just taking Dwayne through some moves!" I say as I hide the book under the dummy's butt. "How was the hangout?"

"Good."

"What did you do?"

"Not much."

"Was there a DJ?"

"Yeah."

"Did you dance?"

"Sometimes."

I really love how he just opens up to me.

"Mom, can I tell you something?"

I perk up. "Of course. You can tell me anything."

Oh my God, are we going to have a real moment here?

He takes a breath and I brace myself for any truth that is about to spill from my baby's lips.

"I don't like it when you come in my room."

Well, that was unexpected.

"I . . . I was just tidying up . . ." I start.

"And I don't want you practicing with Dwayne. You might wreck him."

Ouch. Insult *and* injury.

"How could I wreck Dwayne?"

"I don't know. He could rip or something. Can you just not?"

Since I don't see how it could help me anyway, I promise that I won't use him.

"However, I can't promise I'll stay out of your room when it smells like this."

"Like what?" He takes a whiff and doesn't react.

"Trust me. At least open the window during the day when you're at school, or I will, okay?"

"Okay."

As I stand up to leave, I take my book from underneath Dwayne and throw it into the laundry basket that I quickly pick up and rest on my hip. I pause at the door. "So was anyone your valentine?"

Max blushes and rolls his eyes. "Mom!"

"Good night, sweetie."

17

"Vivs! It's Mom. Call me back." I hang up my cell and text her, *Call me asap.*

As I pull out of Fusion Fitness, I'm excited to tell her what I hope will be great news. She and Raj and Laura have spent the better part of a month looking for a storefront for Good Clean Grub, but everything they've looked at is just too big, too expensive, or geographically undesirable. This on top of keeping their business going, and they have been crazy busy. But oddly enough, the stress has pulled them together rather than ripped them apart . . . for now.

I just finished having juice with one of my newer riders, Doug, and when he told me he was in commercial real estate, I think I scared him with my enthusiasm.

"Really? That's so exciting!"

Doug smiled. "Well, I usually don't get that big of a response."

"No, of course you don't. I'm sorry. It's just that my daughters are looking for a small retail space where they can make and sell food."

He frowned. "So they need a restaurant space?"

"No," I assured him. "Just a small front counter area and a kitchen in the back."

"Hmmm . . ." I can tell he's going through his listings in his head. "What kind of food is it? I only ask because I'm thinking of an ice cream shop that literally just closed. They had the most delicious ice cream, but it was right beside a dentist's office. So"—he chuckles—"they didn't stand a chance."

"Well, my daughters make really healthy sandwiches and salads, so no worries there."

"Do you know what they have budgeted for rent?"

"I don't. But I can find out."

"Tell them to give me a call." He pulls a business card out of his warm-up jacket pocket. "I'd love to help them out since their mom has helped me drop five pounds in the new year." He pats his stomach for effect.

"That's great! Good for you."

"Ya, my wife has been bugging me to try your class."

"Who is your wife?"

"Mary Willy."

I spit my juice all over the table.

Doug doesn't even blink. "Again, not the reaction I usually get."

"I'm so sorry." I wipe my chin with my hand and then grab napkins to clean up the table.

"I'm guessing you read her books."

"I'm a recent fan," I confess. "And I miss her energy in the class." Mary had told me in January that she would be taking a break from spinning in order to finish her fifth book.

"How is her writing going?" I ask Doug. I am now seeing him in a completely different light.

"She's close to finishing."

I want so much to ask him what his role is in her whole writing process. Does she try things out on him? Does he do stuff to her to see if she likes it? But I don't, and I'm proud of my restraint.

Vivs calls me back as I'm driving home.

"What's wrong?" she asks when I pick up.

"Nothing! Why?"

"My God, Mother, you called and texted like it was life or death."

"I'm sorry, it's just I have a lead on a place for Good Clean Grub."

"I'm sure we've already seen it," she grouses.

"Nope. You haven't because it's not even on the market yet."

She gives me an indulgent sigh.

"I'm going to text you the number of a guy from my spin class. He's in commercial real estate."

"Send it to Raj. I'm burned out."

"No! I told him my daughters needed help. One of you should call him."

"Fine."

"Jesus, Vivs, what's with you today?"

She's quiet for a moment, and I think she's going to actually tell me, but then she says, "Nothing. I'm sorry. I just need more sleep. Thanks for this, Mom."

"You're welcome. I hope it works out."

I hang up and text her Doug's name and number while I'm at a stoplight, which isn't really illegal, is it?

✦ ✦ ✦

My parents and I are sitting in Dr. Mithat's office waiting for him to join us. Actually, my father has dozed off again. He did it in the car on the way here as well.

"Is Dad getting enough sleep?" I whisper to Kay, so I don't wake him.

"Of course, he is," she answers at full volume. "He sleeps all through the night. We both do."

Before I can ask her how she knows that if she's sleeping as well, the doctor comes in.

Dr. Mithat doesn't smile when he sits down, which I take as a bad sign.

"Ray seems very tired." He nods toward my sleeping father. "Can you tell me what his days are like?"

"Well, we start with a good breakfast. Then we get dressed and go out to do errands," my mother informs him.

"Generally, how long are you out?" he asks her.

"Well, it depends. We usually have lunch and then I spend some time with my friends at Riverview—that's the assisted living facility where I work."

"What?" I look at Kay like she's just told us her superpower is flying. "Mom, you don't *work* there."

"I do, too! I help out. I drive people places, and I'm always available to play cards if they need a fourth.

"That's not a job," I tell her.

"Well, I didn't say it was a job. I said it was work. I work for free." She seems pleased with her rebuttal.

"What does Ray do while you're . . . working?" Dr. Mithat asks calmly.

"Oh, he's always with me, Doctor. He rides with me in the car and sits in the lobby or the card room when I'm busy visiting."

"Yes, but what does he *do*?" the doctor reiterates.

My mother shrugs. "Well, he watches me," she says simply.

"Does he sleep like he's doing now?"

"Oh yes. He sleeps all the time."

The doctor sighs and glances at me.

"Mrs. Howard, we have talked about Ray's need for stimulation . . ."

"He *is* stimulated! He's out with me all day. He doesn't watch any TV."

"Mom!" I've had enough. "You can't be this obtuse. You have to know that just hauling Dad around doesn't give him stimulation."

"Well, I talk to him, too!" She directs this to Dr. Mithat. "I ask him all kinds of questions."

"Like what?" he asks.

"I'll say, 'Are you warm?' 'Do you want to go to Riverview?' 'Are you hungry?' He always answers."

"Mom, those are yes or no questions! Let me guess. He always answers, 'I guess so.'"

"Jen, let me handle this please," the doctor says gently.

I zip my lip and listen while he explains to Kay once again that she needs to engage him, and not just with yes or no questions.

"You should be doing simple puzzle games with him and making sure he gets his whole body moving every day, not just sitting in a car or a chair. You're not giving him the help he needs. What you're doing is exhausting him."

I can tell Dr. Mithat's words are hitting my mother hard. She puts her face in her hands and starts to cry. I mean really, truly ugly, snot-bubble cry.

"I just miss him so much," she chokes out.

"Mom, why didn't you tell me." I reach over to hug her.

"No!" She pulls away. "Damn both of you," she yells. "You should walk a mile in my shoes!"

At this my father wakes up and looks at my mother.

"Hello," he croaks. This makes my mother cry harder. He reaches out his hand and puts it on her knee. I raise my eyebrows at Dr. Mithat, but he holds up his hand, so I don't say anything.

We let Kay cry it out, and when she is finally down to the occasional shudder, the doctor asks her how she's feeling.

"About ten pounds lighter," she says with a laugh/sob. "Oh, my goodness. Can I have some water?"

I run out to the waiting room and grab her a full paper cup.

"Thank you, sweetheart," she says gratefully.

"Kay, I'm glad you were able to have a good cry. You're not going through this alone, and no one expects you to, so please, lean on your family." Dr. Mithat is using his kindest voice to advise my mother. "But you may also need to cut back on your duties at Riverview. I don't think it's doing either of you any good to be there so much."

She nods. "I will. I promise. Thank you, Doctor." She looks at my father, who has fallen asleep again.

Dr. Mithat spends the next fifteen minutes showing us simple games and puzzles and exercises we can do to help stimulate Ray and strongly encouraging my mother to have some professional help come in during the day. My mother really listens for what I think is the first time and is back to her old self by the time she pats my father on the knee.

"What do you say, Lovey? Want to go home?"

My father doesn't reply, so she nudges him, and he leans further to the side, still asleep.

"Ray?" She pats his knee again. "Come on, sweetheart, we have to get going."

Dr. Mithat stands up and walks quickly to my dad's side. I'm literally frozen in my chair, unable to move as the scene plays out in front of me. He slaps my father's face and calls his name loudly. He then reaches for his stethoscope and calls for his nurse at the same time. My mother stares, stunned, as Dr. Mithat pulls Ray to the floor and starts giving him CPR. The nurse comes and he asks for the defibrillator stat. She's back in ten seconds, and I watch, horrified, as they cut open Ray's shirt and sweater and attach the pads to his chest.

"Clear!" Dr. Mithat says loudly before he pushes the button and shocks my father's heart.

Nothing.

"Clear!" he says again and pushes the button.

Nothing.

A breathless Dr. Mithat looks at us, clearly shaken.

"I'm so sorry, Kay. He's gone."

18

To: City League Parents
From: Franny Watson
Re: Jen Dixon
Date: March 10

Hello folks,

    Jen Dixon will be stepping away from her duties as liaison for the next few weeks as she has had a death in the family.

    Please refer any concerns or questions about league business to Charmaine Grimes.

    Thank you.

Franny Watson

19

Text from Jen:

> Mom, stop this nonsense and pick up your phone. We need to talk about it. I know how angry you are, and I get it. But I am, too. You can't just ignore me forever.

Text from Kay:

> I don't want to talk to you. Stop trying to call me.

I put my phone down on the kitchen table and feel my eyes start to water again. Jesus, I can't lose my father *and* my mother.

The last few weeks have been a blur of pain and anger and food. My father's death has truly tested the strength of our family bond. I don't think anyone would have guessed that Ray was the glue holding us all together. But without him we are adrift in our grief.

I've said some things to my mother that I can never take back, and, based on what she said in her text, she wants me to stop even trying.

Up until the funeral, we had all banded together in our sadness to get through the execution of Ray's final wishes. My father had left a letter with detailed arrangements, so it was easier than expected for the whole thing to come together. His lawyer told us Ray had written the letter and had it notarized ten years ago.

Ron, of course, was the captain who steered us all through the first few days of numbness, when neither my mother nor I could form a coherent sentence. He graciously accepted the dozens of casseroles and bagels sent by friends and neighbors, and answered the never-ending calls of condolence.

The girls and Max were devastated. This was the first time that a death had affected them so directly. I wish I could have done a better job of consoling them, but I was useless. My grief was all-consuming, sucking me into a void of relentless misery that was only relieved for the few hours a day I was rendered unconscious by the pills my doctor prescribed for me.

Our house became base camp for everyone while Ron liaised with the funeral home and the church. We had an open casket viewing for close friends and family the night before the funeral. This is my least favorite tradition, but I know it gives some people closure. So, on the fourth day after he died, we all traipsed to Johnson County Funeral Chapel & Memorial Gardens and greeted people for three hours while Ray lay in his casket. The funeral home had done a decent job of making him look like he was sleeping, but I still had a hard time taking more than a quick glance. Watching my mother lovingly kiss him on the forehead as we left for the night should have warmed my heart, but for some reason disgust was the only feeling that registered.

It was truly the sign of a life well lived that so many people packed the church the next day. Their entire congregation was on hand as well as his Kiwanis Club brothers, people from their condo complex, friends from their old neighborhood, a busload of those who could travel from Riverview Assisted Living, and four people from his gardening club. I know my father would have been completely bemused by all the fuss but also happy that my mother would be so well taken care of. Ron and I also had a huge turnout of friends from school and work. The mat moms were there en masse, all the Om Sweet Om staff showed up, and a crew from Fusion came, including most of my regular riders, although not Lynnie. Even Nina and Garth came from Memphis.

With all that love around me, you'd think I would have found a level of solace, but I couldn't. A quiet rage had been brewing inside me for days, the source of which was unclear until the day of the funeral when I saw Sammy Leighton from Riverview give my mother an extralong hug. Until then I'd been holding it together with a combo of pills and prayer and clutching my children close to me. But when my mother melted into the arms of her ex-flame from high school, I was triggered. All I saw was the man who had been taking my mother's attention away from where it should have been . . . on my father.

I got up from my place in the front pew and walked right over to them.

"Please leave," I said in a determined whisper.

"Jen, I'm so sorry for your loss." Sammy started to give me a hug.

"Please leave," I said a little louder as I shook off his attempted embrace.

My mother turned to me, shocked. She seemed to have shrunk in the last few days, diminished and vulnerable in her plain black shift dress and pearls. But instead of pity and love, I felt a renewed sense of fury.

"Jennifer, what has gotten into you?" she whispered.

"I want your boyfriend to leave," I told her with a calm that belied the tempest inside me.

"My boy . . . ? Sammy is my friend. There is absolutely no reason why he should leave. Now go sit down. People are looking."

The fury that suddenly filled my entire being took me by surprise. My heart rate was causing me to pant, and I was shaking.

"I want you to leave," I repeated, though this time not as quietly. "I want you to leave. I want you to leave." It was like a mantra I couldn't stop repeating.

Ron was beside me in a flash.

"Jen."

"I want him to leave." I was officially yelling now, and no part of me wanted to stop. "You killed him!" I looked at my mother. "You *both* did!"

I had a sense of floating through the church as Ron practically carried me out. I sobbed into his shoulder and repeated over and over again, "They did."

✦ ✦ ✦

"Are you okay?" Nina came into my bedroom with a glass of water and sat beside me.

"That depends on your definition of 'okay.'" I sighed and rolled onto my side.

After my meltdown at the church, Ron drove me home and put me to bed, where I promptly passed out for five hours.

"I can't believe I missed the funeral." My father's funeral. It rang hollow in my head.

"It was lovely," Nina assured me. "Kay gave an incredible speech."

I look up from taking a sip of water. "Really?" I couldn't keep the sarcasm from my tone.

"Yes. She did." She frowned at me. "What's with you?"

I shook my head. "I don't know. I really lost it when I saw that guy, Sammy."

"Lost it? You started yelling, 'You killed him.'"

I groaned. "I was hoping that was part of a nightmare I was having."

"Nope. You did it, and everyone saw it," Nina assured me as only a best friend can. "It was just so out of character for you to completely lose your shit like that."

"I know." I sighed and sat up on my bed. "I guess I've been carrying that around for a while." I paused. "Where is everyone?"

"Downstairs, hanging out and eating."

"Good. We have so much food." I rubbed my face with my hands. "Okay. Let's go face the music."

"Uh, you should probably clean up a bit." Nina was being kind. I'm sure I looked like a waterproof mascara experiment gone bad.

"Okay. I'll meet you downstairs."

After scrubbing thoroughly, I took a long look at my bare face. I remember thinking at the church that my mother looked older, and now I could see the same decline in my own face. Grief is a real motherfucker.

With that pleasant thought in my head, I went downstairs.

Everyone was in the living room, either lying on couches or on the floor. Nina and Garth were picking up dirty plates and glasses that were scattered everywhere. Max was on his phone, texting someone, Vivs was playing a game with Maude while Raj watched, and Ron looked like he was snoozing on the sofa.

"Hi Gee Gee," Maude said tentatively, and everyone looked up.

"Hi, my girl. What are you playing?" I asked as I noticed no one else wanted to make eye contact with me.

"Go Fish. Want to play?"

"Maybe in a little while." I took attendance and noticed two people missing.

"Where's Mom?" I asked the room.

"Laura drove her home," Vivs said matter-of-factly.

"She must have been tired," I muttered.

"Not really. She just didn't want to see you."

"Vivs," Raj cautioned her.

"No, she should know," Vivs countered. "You hurt Nana so much today. Why would you do that?"

"I'm hurting, too," I said as if it was any kind of an excuse. "You have no idea what it's like to lose your father."

"Thanks to you, I don't even know who my father is," she spat out.

"Luke, I'm your father," Ron lobbed in from the couch in a decent Darth Vader voice without even opening his eyes. It was his attempt at lightening the mood, but it landed like an overweight skydiver.

I grabbed my phone from my pocket and started dialing.

"Don't call her, Jen." Ron was sitting up now and looking at me.

"I need to talk to her."

"I know. But just give her a little space. Maybe try in a couple of days."

"A couple of *days*? No, we need to settle this."

"She'll be fine. We'll all be checking in on her."

"Except me apparently," I groused. Ron walked over and hugged me.

"Just a couple of days," he said and kissed my hair.

✦ ✦ ✦

That was two weeks ago. I've tried to talk to Kay every day, multiple times a day, but she won't answer. Today's text is the first contact I've had.

I've screwed up many, many times over the years, and Kay has never shunned me—not even when I showed up on her doorstep at the age of twenty-four with two kids in diapers and no money. So I can't believe she won't even get on the phone with me or answer the door when I go by the condo.

"I mean, what the hell did I say that was so bad anyway?" I ask Ron when he walks into the kitchen.

"You told her friend to leave and accused them of killing your father," he says, and not for the first time. I know he's pretty much over having this conversation with me.

"And was I lying?" I huff.

"Really?" He gives me an exasperated look. "*Murder?*"

"It was my grief talking. Can't she understand that? I mean, Jesus, shouldn't I be given a pass of some kind? My father is dead."

"And her husband is dead." He looks at me evenly. "You're going to have to adjust your thinking on this one."

I decide to move on. "Did you get the tickets?"

Ron grins. "Not in my hands, but I'm promised they are at the box office waiting."

One thing that got horribly lost in the last few weeks was Max's thirteenth birthday. It came and went with barely a mention let alone a party, and to my amazement, he only complained a bit. It's a sign he's growing up that he was able to realize that bigger things were happening. We knew we needed to do something significant to make it up to him, so Ron contacted an old friend in sports marketing and got six tickets to *WWE Raw* at the T-Mobile Center this weekend. We're telling Max that he can invite four friends, and Ron will take the bullet as chaperone.

"I really don't get why these boys like the professional wrestling. It's so different from what they do."

"Are you kidding? It's candy for them," Ron explains. "Pure entertainment. Plus, a lot of pro wrestlers come from traditional wrestling backgrounds."

For a hot minute I try to picture Max as a pro wrestler, and then I look at Ron.

"We need to get his math grades up."

20

To: CLOP
From: Jen Dixon
Re: Hello and Thank You
Date: April 1

Hey there CLOPpers,

My sincerest thanks for the wonderful outpouring of support for me and my family these past few weeks. The casseroles and baked goods and cards were so appreciated as we all dealt with the loss of my wonderful father, Ray. We truly felt loved by our community.

My thanks to Charmaine for taking the reins of CLOP. By all accounts, you didn't burn the place down, so we'll call it a win. But I'm back now, so take a break, take a breath, and take your stuff out of my office. (Kidding. I don't have an office . . . yet.)

The boys are on a winning streak that I don't want to jinx, so let's just keep everything going exactly the same way it has been going. This means nobody wash the uniforms until we lose, got it?

April Fools!

See you Saturday for the match!

Ray's daughter

Today is the first day of the rest of my life. Isn't that how the saying goes? I put everything on hold for three weeks while I indulged in my sadness, but now it's time to get back to my life. I think about Ray every day, and often I wake up thinking I need to do something for him, only to remember a moment later why I don't. I wish I could call my mother just to see if she has these same thoughts, but alas we are still not talking. Her silence has caused me to do some serious soul-searching about my breakdown at the funeral and why I took it out on my mother and Sammy. After weeks of deliberating, I have come to the conclusion that I was right. She *was* neglecting my father by going on lunch dates with that man. And I'll tell her just that if she ever agrees to talk to me again. We need to have it out and be done with it.

Today (the rest of my life) starts with my Friday 8 a.m. spin class—the first one I've taught since Ray died. I shudder. God only knows how I'm going to get through it. I know my riders are anxious to have me back, and by my riders I mean Lynnie. Vivs told me she showed up late to the funeral, and wanted to come by the house, but Vivs told her I had a nervous breakdown and needed some time for the meds to kick in.

When I walk into the spin room this morning, I am overwhelmed by the round of applause I get. Even always-late Donna is there and on a front-row bike.

"Thank you so much, guys." I tear up as I put on my spin shoes. "I missed you."

"We missed *you*!" Mary Willy hollers out.

My first song is a crowd pleaser—"You Give Love a Bad Name" by Bon Jovi—and everyone is up and ready to work, including me. The endorphins are a welcome rush through my body, and I realize how much I needed this. I'm a bit out of shape and having a hard time keeping up with my own class, but for the most part it all goes beautifully until the cool-down song. I foolishly chose "Leader of the Band" by Dan Fogelberg without thinking about the lyrics. It's all fine until I hear Dan sing, *"And, Papa, I don't think I said 'I love you' near enough."*

Wham. Devastation. I keep stretching but don't even try to hide my tears.

"We love you, Jen!" comes a voice from the back of the class.

"You've got this!" says another.

And before I know it, everyone is clapping and whooping and cheering me on. It makes me cry harder, but in a good way.

Between the sweat and the crying, I feel cleansed, but depleted. I'm not sure how I'm going to make it through the day without a snooze. I had promised myself to stop the midday depression naps on this, the first day of the rest of my life, so I figure a cold shower and a second cup of coffee are in order.

But first I catch up with some of my riders. Dr. Superbitch is anything but when she gives me a warm embrace. Mary Willy holds my hand and tells me she has just finished book five if I want to read it ahead of everyone else, and her husband, Doug, tells me he's been in contact with Raj and Vivs about a space for Good Clean Grub and understands why they haven't been able to commit to anything. I'm sad to learn that Donna has also lost a parent. Her mother finally succumbed to the ravages of ALS while I was grieving my father. We promise to get together soon for a good cry.

Lynnie has lingered 'til the end and gives me a tentative sweaty hug.

"I know I'm not supposed to get involved in your personal life, but is there anything I can do for you?" she asks kindly.

"Oh, Lynnie." I hug her back extrahard. "I'm sorry, that was a horrible thing to say to you."

Lynnie gives me a big smile. "I totally deserved it, so don't even think about it. Do you want to go for lunch or something?"

"Maybe next week. I'm still trying to get my groove back, you know?"

"I totally get it. Just text me when you want to."

As she jogs out of the spin room, I can't help but think Lynnie might just be growing up.

✦ ✦ ✦

After a good shower and a large mug of joe, I find myself in the basement taking care of the obscene amount of laundry that has piled up. After I put a load in the washer, I look around Ron's Gym and Tan, the space beside the washing machine where he keeps the treadmill. I used to spend so much time down here before I discovered spinning. This is where Garth first started training me for my ill-fated mud run eight years ago, and where I fell in love with exercise.

My phone rings and I see it's Vivs.

"Hi," I answer a bit curtly. Vivs is most definitely on team Kay when it comes to what happened at the funeral, and this has caused some tension between us.

"Can you pick up Maude today?" She gets right to the point.

"No, sorry, I can't. I have a dentist appointment."

"Well, can you switch it?"

"I don't really want to. Is there no one else? Is Raj busy?"

"Yes."

"Working?"

"Yes."

God, I hate that this is how we are now talking to each other.

"Okay. What time?"

"Two-thirty."

"I'll be there. I'll see you when you get home."

"No, just take her to your house. I'll pick her up there."

"Are you sure? I'm happy to wait with her at your place. It's better for her to be home."

"No, I think Laura has someone over."

"Oh, well, if she's home, can't I just leave Maude with her?"

"Mom, please, can you just do what I ask?"

"Okay, okay. You're welcome, by the way."

"Thanks." Vivs hangs up.

I'm about to mentally gripe that this happens more than it should, and Raj doesn't seem to be pulling his weight. But then I think of how wonderful he has been these past few weeks. He has such a quiet strength and is able to keep Vivs from popping off most of the time. I think being in business together has really helped their relationship. She doesn't snap at him nearly as much as she used to.

The thought of an afternoon with Maude puts me in a much better humor. I call the dentist, then I get back to the laundry with gusto until it's time to pick Maude up.

✦ ✦ ✦

The kids in Miss Dawson's class file out, each holding a pink frosted cake pop and giggling. Maude runs out with a big grin that fades when she sees me.

"Where's Mommy? I have this for her." She holds up the cake pop.

"Oh sweetie, you can give it to her at home. She and your dad had to work." We start walking out of the school. I can tell Maude is thinking about something.

"Gee Gee, you can have it if you want."

"Oh, that's okay. I know you made it for your mom." I'm not going to lie; it looks really tempting. "Why don't you eat it?"

This makes Maude burst into giggles as she gets into her car seat.

"What's so funny?" I ask and look a little more closely at the cake pop. She just shakes her head.

"We're going to Gee Gee's house, okay?" I tell her as I start the car.

"Can we get Lamby first? I forgot her today and I miss her."

Maude's security blanket is a small pink lamb's head with a little blankie attached. She never goes anywhere without it. We had to have it FedExed back from India when she left it there at Christmas. Vivs and Raj are still recovering from the ten-hour plane ride home without Maude's emotional support toy

"Oh, sweetie, I don't know." I'm worried about crashing in on whatever Laura is doing.

"PLEASE, GEE GEE!" Maude goes from zero to hysterical in five seconds. "I haven't seen her ALL DAY!" She is crying real tears, and I don't have the energy to deny her.

"Okay, sweetie. Of course, we can. Let's go right now."

I call Laura on the way to their apartment to give her a heads-up that I will be stopping by.

"I'm not home, Mom. I'm at work."

"That's weird. Vivs thinks you're having a meeting or something."

"I don't know why she thinks that. I told her ten minutes ago where I was."

I'm confused about why Vivs would tell me that. Unless she's working at home and doesn't want to be bothered. But that doesn't make sense either.

When we get to their building, I tell Maude to bring the cake pop and we will leave it in the fridge for her mom.

"Gee Gee, can I tell you something?"

"Sure."

"It's April Fool's Day."

"I know. Did you play any tricks on anyone?"

"Uh-huh." She nods and laughs. "On Mommy."

"Really? That's funny." I'm only half listening because I'm having trouble with the lock, and I can hear the TV blaring inside the apartment. When the lock finally clicks, I open the door and am treated to the sight of Vivs and Raj, half-dressed, making out in the kitchen. They don't hear me because the television is so loud. But they do hear their daughter screech their names in delight.

"Mommy! Daddy!"

They break apart and Vivs yells, "Mom! What the hell?"

I don't even know how to respond to that. For Vivs to be on the attack in this scenario is pretty rich. Raj zips up his pants and scoots to pick up Maude.

"Hi, Moo Moo, how was school?"

"Good. Look what I have for Mommy!" She shows him the cake pop.

I'm still processing the implications of what I've just walked in on. First, are Vivs and Raj back together? And if they are, why are they keeping it a secret? Second, clearly no work is being done here. Did they actually make me cancel my dentist appointment so they could have a little afternoon delight? And third, do they always do it in the kitchen?

"Mommy, here." Maude hands Vivs the cake pop.

"Thank you, baby." Vivs takes it and kisses Maude's head. Thankfully, she has put her shirt on. Her face is unreadable.

There is a palpable tension in the room that Maude is clearly oblivious to when she yells "Eat it!" to her mother.

"Okay, okay!" Vivs playfully pops the whole cake pop into her mouth and chews. About three seconds later, she violently spits it out on the floor in front of her.

"Gagh! What the . . . ?" I can tell Vivs is censoring herself. We all look down at the floor and see chunks of green mixed in with the pink frosting.

"April fools!" Maude yells and claps with delight. "Mama, it was a brussels sprout!"

"I can see that, Maudey!" Vivs doesn't look pleased as she wipes her mouth.

"I bet you thought you were getting cake!" She laughs again. Raj starts laughing too, and soon we all are.

"I did. That was so gross! Was it Gee Gee's idea?" Vivs asks with a glance my way.

"No. Miss Dawson helped us make them! Gee Gee wouldn't do that."

"Ya, I'm more of a Saran wrap on the toilet seat kind of girl," I offer up. "Maude, go get Lamby so we can go to my place."

"Actually Jen, it's okay. We've got her," Raj says with a confirming glance at Vivs. Who *are* these two?

"Uh, okay. Well, I'll be off. Vivs, can you help me with something in the car?"

"Real subtle, Mom," she gripes, but she follows me out.

I wait 'til we get in the elevator to say anything.

"Spill it."

"Spill what?" she grumbles.

"Don't even start, Vivs."

She sighs out of what I'm hoping is defeat.

"We've been thinking about getting back together," she says plainly.

"How long have you been thinking about it?"

"Since Thanksgiving."

"That long?" The elevator door opens to let us out, but I just stand there.

"Mom, come on." Vivs pulls my arm.

When we get outside, I barely notice the warm spring sun on my face. I'm too busy trying to put this new information together.

"What about Coach D and that woman Raj was seeing? You were with them after Thanksgiving."

She sighs. "I know. When Raj saw me with Dana at Thanksgiving, he got jealous. And I wasn't thrilled when he was taking Maude to whatshername's house for family time."

"So?"

"So we started talking and hooking up."

"While still dating other people," I clarify.

"Yes, Mom. Yes, we were dating other people. We don't feel good about that."

"And what about Maude?"

"Maude's the reason we're keeping it a secret. We don't want her to get her hopes up if it isn't going to work out."

"Well? How's it working out? I mean, you looked pretty 'together'"—I use hand quotes—"when we walked in just now."

Vivs smiles for the first time. "I don't know if it's just because we're sneaking around, but it's been really great."

"What's changed? I mean you've dumped this guy more times than I can count."

She shrugs. "We're older, and we have Maude. There are just more reasons to be together than apart, I guess."

"You'd better not be guessing," I warn her.

"No shit, Mom, thanks for stating the obvious."

As I'm getting in the car, something occurs to me.

"So every time you told me you were working and couldn't pick up Maude, you were having a booty call?"

Vivs groans. "God, I hate when you try to sound hip."

21

To: CLOP
From: Jen Dixon
Re: Apologies
Date: April 11

Dear CLOPpers:

Let me start by apologizing for the incident at the match on Saturday against Atchison. My emotions are obviously running high these days, but that isn't an excuse for what happened. Contrary to what some will lead you to believe, I really would love to participate in the fundraiser this year, but I just can't. To paraphrase Coach D, my head would not be in the game. But I promise I will be there to cheer on whoever is wrestling!

We have a bye this weekend, but next weekend is our overnight road trip to Dodge City. I'll send out a separate email detailing travel, chaperones, and roommates next week, once I think of a good joke about Dodge City that doesn't involve "Let's get the hell out of Dodge!"

Thanks!

Jen

I hope that smooths things over. I still cringe when I think of my little meltdown in front of everyone at the match on Saturday.

The evening started off well. The boys were winning their matches, and besides a decidedly awkward few minutes when Max grabbed a full boob while wrestling a girl named Jasmine, it was all good. Sadly, he lost the match, but on the bright side, he can now brag that he has made it to first base. That's got to be worth something in seventh grade.

It turned into a god-awful mess when I crossed paths with Mimi on the way to the bathroom, and she asked me if I had been training for our match. I told her I hadn't, but it didn't matter because I wasn't going to participate.

"What?" She seemed more annoyed than surprised. "Why not?"

"Because my father just died," I said plainly.

"I really think your father would have wanted you to do it," she said as if she knew him.

"You didn't know my father." My voice was made louder by the echo in the hallway outside the gym. "You have no idea what he would want!"

"Look," Mimi said in what I think was a conciliatory voice. "This is a big fundraiser for the league, and in case you haven't noticed, you and I are the main event."

"I, I . . . I don't give a shit!" I sputtered out.

No surprise that by this time we had attracted a crowd.

"I knew you were full of it."

"Why? Because I don't want to wrestle a month after my dad died?" I was yelling at this point. "I can't believe I'm even having this conversation." I glanced around. "I guarantee you *no one* expects me to even be there let alone participate."

"It'll be *two* months by then," Mimi corrected me. We glared at each other, and she looked away first. It was a small victory, but I took it.

"There's something really wrong with you," I told her. Then I turned and sprinted through the league members who were watching us before they could see me burst into tears.

Franny called me later that day to make sure I was okay. My note to the league was her idea. It really hadn't occurred to me that anyone would still expect me to wrestle, but I got the sense from Franny that they would all be disappointed if I didn't. But she was a lot nicer about it than Mimi was.

I run upstairs and don the mom uniform, brush my hair and my teeth, and grab my purse. My mother still isn't talking to me, so today is the day I take matters into my own hands.

✦ ✦ ✦

I haven't been to Riverview Assisted Living in a long time—not really since my parents stayed there two years ago after the carbon monoxide scare in their house. When I walk in the main entrance that opens to a great room with a piano, I'm half hoping to have Shirley greet me with her usual "Hello, are you here to see me?" but Laura told me she died last year. Sadly, that happens a lot around here. I read a study that said the average assisted living resident stays for just over a year before they die. I find that a brutal statistic. If it's true, it means the person I am here to see is living on borrowed time.

"Can I help you?" the young woman behind the desk asks with a cheery smile.

"Uh, yes. I'm here to see Sammy Leighton."

"Is he expecting you?"

"Actually, it's kind of a surprise," I tell her. Sammy has no idea I'm coming, and I wasn't sure he would want to see me, so I didn't give him a heads-up.

"Oh, that's so nice!" the girl whose name tag says Hadley tells me. "I'll call his room. What is your name?"

I think about lying but decide to go with the truth. If he doesn't want to see me, I'll know immediately.

"Jen Dixon," I tell her, and she makes the call.

"He'll be right out. He just got back from his bath."

Ugh. TMI. I make my way to a chair in the great room and sit down to wait for him. No one is playing the piano today, but the memory of Isabel, the woman who knew only one song, makes me smile. I start humming "Pennies from Heaven" as I sit and wait for Sammy. I haven't really decided what I'm going to say to him, but I do know I'll never be able to make it right with my mother if I don't have him on my side.

He shuffles out ten minutes later looking much older than I remember. He has on a burnt-orange cardigan, a white button-down shirt, and a pair of khakis on his slight frame.

"Mr. Leighton." I stand and offer my hand.

"Jen." He nods and takes it. "This is quite a surprise."

"Thanks for seeing me," I mumble. We sit down in side-by-side armchairs covered in a gold chenille. The next closest person is three chairs away, and he's sleeping.

"So what can I do for you?" Sammy asks without a smile.

I take a breath and decide to wing it . . . I mean, speak from my heart.

"I owe you an apology for the way I behaved at my father's funeral. I'm sorry I made such a scene."

He nods. "It isn't often I get accused of murder."

I smile. "Hardly ever, huh?"

He smiles back. "It's been years."

He waits for me to continue.

"I really don't have an excuse except I was grieving and not quite in my right mind."

"I can understand that, but those feelings didn't come out of nowhere."

Smart man.

"No, you're right. I had been feeling for months that my mother was spending more time with you than was necessary and neglecting my dad—just fobbing him off on the rest of us."

He nods. "And with everything you know about your mother, does that sound at all right?"

"No," I admit contritely. "But she was here all the time. And you two would go out for lunch while one of us was home taking care of Ray."

"In fairness, that happened only a handful of times before she started bringing him with her."

"I think that might have been worse for him. She had him out all day long, and it exhausted him. It was like she didn't care if he was uncomfortable." I can feel my cheeks getting hot, and I remind myself I came here to mend fences, not break them.

Sammy sits thoughtfully for a few moments, then leans his forearms on his knees. "Jen, Kay came here because she was lonely. She needed someone to talk to. Can you imagine suddenly not being able to talk to your husband, your life partner? And not just conversation, but input into daily decisions and even bigger life decisions. She had no one to talk to. I can't tell you how many times she just sat in my room with me and talked about their finances, and insurance and real estate. That or she just cried. My God, she loved your father so much. It was breaking her in half to see him slip away."

"Why didn't she come to me?" His words are making my heart ache.

"It's a funny thing." Sam looks off into the distance. "We as parents never want to burden our children. Part of it is we never want you to see us as losing the ability to take care of ourselves. Plus, she told me how busy you are with the girls and Max and Maude. She didn't want to put any more on your shoulders."

I'm trying to reconcile what he is saying with the demands my mother did put on me. She asked me to stay with my father at least once a week whether it was convenient for me or not. As if reading my mind, Sammy continues.

"I do know she wanted you to have as much time with Ray as you could, and that's probably why she left him with you when she did."

I think back on the times I spent with my father in the car, or walking, or hanging out with him in my kitchen. I'm not sure when I started crying, but tears are now streaming down my face. I look at Sammy.

"Thank you for telling me this." I wipe my eyes and let out a chuckle that ends with a sob. "You know I really thought you guys were having a fling."

Sammy gives a genuine guffaw. "Oh God, your mother would never see me in that way. She thinks of me as the skinny nerd who had a crush on her in high school. She only ever had eyes for Ray. But I am happy to call her my friend, and I hope you won't object if we continue to see each other."

Man, when I get it wrong, I get it epically wrong. This man is a saint. A kind, sweet, gentle saint sent to help my mother through the worst time in her life. And I'm the idiot who only saw something bad.

"Now I really owe you an apology. I had no idea about any of this."

"Your mom didn't want you to. She's very proud of you, you know."

"Really?" I sniff.

"Of course. You remind her of Ray."

Well, that pretty much flattens me. I start to cry all over again at the thought that my mother sees even a bit of my father in me. It couldn't have touched me more if he had told me I look like Cindy Crawford from the nineties.

We sit in silence for a while, and I'm startled by the announcement over the PA that lunch is being served. I take it as my cue to get going.

"Thank you so much for this. I feel like I've been reborn," I tell him.

We stand and he tentatively hugs me. "I'm very glad you came, Jen. Can I tell Kay I've had a visit with you?"

"Sure." I smile and blow my nose. "Have a good lunch! I wonder what Laura has made for you today."

Sammy looks confused. "Laura? Your daughter? She stopped working here about two weeks ago."

✦ ✦ ✦

"When the *hell* did I officially become the last to know everything?" I mutter as I dial Laura hands-free from the car. When she answers I bark out, "Where are you?"

"At work. What's wrong? Do you need something?"

"I need my daughters to stop lying to me!" I yell.

There is a moment of silence, then Laura says, "Did I not tell you I left Riverview?"

"No. You did not tell me you left Riverview."

"Oh. Sorry. It's been so crazy the past few weeks, and with you and Nana fighting, I didn't want to bother you," she says matter-of-factly.

"Good God! Someone please *bother* me. I feel like I don't know what the hell is happening in my own family. Where are you working?"

"At the new space. I've been cleaning the kitchen for like a week."

"What new space?"

"Oh, I thought you knew. Doug Willy found us the perfect space right near Hawthorne Plaza."

"You are kidding me! Why didn't you ask me to come and help you?"

"I didn't think you were up for much of anything, Mom. You've been kind of absent."

Ouch. There's no way she's turning this one on me.

"Did it ever occur to you guys that I might be hurting and in need of a little support?"

There is silence as she considers my question.

"No," she says without a hint of sarcasm. I'm speechless.

"You know, we should all have dinner," Laura suggests. "Then everyone can give you an update." She sounds like she's placating a child, but I ignore it because as ideas go, it isn't a bad one.

"Okay," I say, a bit defeated. "Sunday? It would be nice to start the weekly dinners again." We had stopped when Ray died, and because of the riff with my mother, we hadn't started them again.

"I'll call everyone," Laura promises. "But I doubt Nana will come."

I hang up, pull out of the parking lot at Riverview, and turn up the radio. SiriusXM's 80s on 8 is playing *American Top 40—* the Casey Kasem version. It reminds me of my childhood. I used

to listen every weekend, and I just loved the long-distance dedi-
cations. Today Casey is reading a letter from a boy named Trevor
from Toledo who met a girl named Wendy when his family was on
summer vacation in the Catskills. Trevor wants Wendy to know that
he will never forget the kiss they shared by the bonfire, and he wants
Casey to play "Don't You (Forget About Me)" by Simple Minds for
the girl he calls his first love.

As the song plays, I start to cry all over again. I miss my father,
but at this moment I miss my mother much more. And while it bugs
me that my daughters didn't think I needed help or support, I
wonder if my mother feels I've made the same assumption about
her. How could I ever have doubted her love for and loyalty to my
father? I'll be fifty-six in a week and I'm still clueless.

On impulse, I say "Call Mom" to my onboard computer, but it
goes straight to voicemail. For the first time, I don't blame her.

22

To: City League, Overland Park
From: Jen Dixon
Re: Thanks
Date: April 22

Hey CLOPpers!

Thank you so much for all the birthday wishes and the cupcake at practice the other day. Kudos to Franny for knowing that asking me to do her a favor by picking up the singlets would get me to show up! I really didn't feel much like celebrating, but it cheered me up to see everyone. So cheered in fact that I have decided to do Just for the Smell of It after all. So, Mimi, I hope you're ready to rumble.

Speaking of seeing everyone, are we all ready to bring the pain to the Dodge City Dragons this weekend? The carpool caravan leaves from the rec center Friday at 10 a.m. With a half hour stop for lunch, we hope to be there by dinner time, get the kids a good night's sleep at the Comfort Inn, and be ready to compete Saturday morning at 9. Carpool assignments are attached, and I don't care if you think I'm a bad driver, Georgina. You're stuck with me.

Have a lovely day.

Jen

I send the email and brace myself for the replies of delight and questions about why I changed my mind and decided to fight. I credit it to the day I turned fifty-six, which started off about as welcome as a hemorrhoid flare-up.

I was really hoping everyone would just forget, but no such luck. Ron started it off with breakfast in bed (well, a protein shake in bed), then my spin class surprised me by singing "Happy Birthday" to me, and Jodi, the manager of Fusion, slipped me a fifty-dollar gift card to the juice bar at, you guessed it, Fusion Fitness.

"You spend enough money there," she said by way of explanation.

Not lately, I thought to myself. I haven't done an after-class meet and greet in months, and I have no idea when I'm going to feel like starting again.

So, when Franny called me later that day and asked if I could pick up the Comanche's laundry for her, I was happy to do something mundane. But when I got to the rec center, about ten of the mat moms had shown up to sing "Happy Birthday" and give me a cupcake. It was so sweet of them, and I have to say, it sort of made my day. That is, until a few asked me if I had changed my mind about participating in Just for the Smell of It, and I had to let them down, yet again.

I spent a good part of the day licking my wounds because my mother hadn't upheld her tradition of calling me on my birthday morning to tell me how she remembers every minute of the day I was born, and proceeding to tell me the story again for the fifty-sixth time. I never thought I'd miss it, but I did.

Kay's ability to hold a grudge should be in the Guinness World Records. It had been over a week since I had gone to see Sammy Leighton, and still, she hadn't called. I know he put in a good word for me, but I guess it wasn't enough.

The icing on the cake of my day came when I was leaving the rec center and Ron called to say he'd gotten pulled over for speeding coming back from the studio in Lee's Summit and needed me to go to the Overland Park studio and get his driver's license and drive to where he was pulled over.

"You don't have your license?" I asked, frustrated.

"I took it out this morning and forgot to put it back in my wallet. I'm sorry, sweetie."

"Well, happy birthday to me," I said as I turned the Palisade around and headed to Om Sweet Om. Rush-hour traffic was a bitch, naturally, and it took me a good forty-five minutes to get to Ron. When I found him, he was alone.

"Where's the police?" I asked without even trying to hide my annoyance.

"He didn't want to wait." Ron shrugged. "He told me if I bring it in to any station tomorrow, they'll drop the driving without a license charge."

"Well, why didn't you just do that to begin with?"

"I didn't know that was an option."

I rolled my eyes and got back in the car. "See you at home."

Ron waved and jumped into Bruce Willis (the nickname he has for his BMW), revving the engine once he started it. To piss me off even further, he peeled out and sped by me.

"I hope you get another ticket," I yelled to no one.

When I pulled into the driveway some forty minutes later, Bruce Willis was already covered up for the night. I wondered if Ron had thought to order something for dinner. I knew he wouldn't expect me to cook on my birthday.

I trudged in the back door and was hit with the intoxicating smell of roasted chicken. The girls were in the kitchen along with Raj, Maude, and even Max, home from practice early. They all screamed "happy birthday!" and ran to hug me. My eyes filled with tears because I really didn't deserve this. I said as much to them, and they laughed. Then a voice pierced through the noise.

"Of course, you do, Jennifer! Really, who doesn't deserve a party after the year we've all had?"

And there in the flesh was my mother, looking pale and petite but nicely put together in a green cardigan sweater and jeans. I felt like I hadn't seen her in a decade.

"Mom!" I sobbed and ran to her. She opened her arms and

hugged me like she used to when I was a little girl—stroking my head and whispering "shhh" in my ear. Then she held me out at arm's length, looked me in the eyes, and said, "Enough now. Dad would have hated this."

For some reason that made me giggle and sob at the same time, and I hugged my mother again. The place deep down where I had been hurting was finally soothed, and I took what I think was my first full breath in weeks.

"Well thank God that's over." Vivs's voice broke the silence, and we all started to laugh. Laura had made an incredible dinner of my favorite roast chicken with lemon and thyme gravy, roasted potatoes, baby carrots, and, for dessert, homemade chocolate cake. We sat around the table and had a really good catch-up—talking about Good Clean Grub, Om Sweet Om, my mother's recent trip to Riverview to help them start planting a garden that will be named after Ray, and finally my daylong birthday palooza.

When dinner was finished, the girls insisted Kay and I go into the living room, and they would clean up.

"I'm so happy to see you," I told her when we were alone. "How are you feeling? You're looking thin."

"It's that grief weight coming off," she acknowledged. "But I'm feeling okay."

"I'm so sorry . . ." I began.

"Listen, Jennifer. Let's just call it a day on all that, okay? We were both hurting. I'm not going to lie, I don't think I've ever been madder at anyone in my whole life. But I was very touched that you went to see Sammy."

"He's pretty great," I conceded.

She nodded. "He's a good man. Not up to your father's level, mind you, but a good man nonetheless. He's a good listener."

"I could tell. I really misjudged . . ."

The ringing of my cell phone interrupted me. I looked and it was Georgina from wrestling.

"Hang on, Mom, I think this is about the wrestling trip to Dodge."

I answered, "Hey Georgie, what's up?"

"I don't think you're a bad driver!" is the first thing out of her mouth.

I laughed. "I know that! It was a joke!"

"Oh, okay. I just know how sensitive you are these days, and I wouldn't want you to think I said anything about you."

"I didn't," I promised her.

"While I have you," Georgie said, "can I just make one more push for you to do Just for the Smell of It?"

I stole a glance at my mother, and she was smiling at me. I held up a finger to say one minute.

"You can, but there isn't much to say."

"I know. But I promised Franny I would."

"Well, my answer is the same. It's too soon after my dad."

"I get it. Sorry I had to ask."

"Don't worry about it. I'm going to let you go because I have my mother here . . ."

"Really—she's talking to you? I'm so glad!"

"Yes, me too." I laughed. "I'll see you Friday."

"You got it."

When I hung up my mother raised her eyebrows.

"What is too soon after your father?"

"Oh, it's this fundraiser the mat moms do for the City League." I shrugged.

"A fundraiser? Since when do I have a daughter who doesn't donate her time to a fundraiser?"

"I'm going to go and support the team, but they raise money by wrestling each other—the moms, that is—and I really don't think it would be appropriate for me to take part."

Kay stared at me as though she was trying to solve a puzzle.

"Because of Dad," she confirmed.

"Yes."

"And what do you think your father would have to say about this?"

"I don't know, but I don't think he'd blame me for not wanting to wrestle."

"Are you scared?"

"Scared to wrestle?" I thought about that for a minute. A vision of Mimi crashing me to the ground and pinning me made me shudder. "Maybe I am."

"What scares you? That you'll lose?"

I laughed. "Oh, I'm definitely going to lose. That doesn't bother me."

"Are you scared you'll get hurt?" Kay pushed.

"I mean, I'd rather not get injured. I wouldn't be able to teach." I paused. "Do you think I should do it?"

"I think you should do what you want." She kissed my cheek, stood up, and headed toward the kitchen. "Just don't use Dad as an excuse. He wouldn't tolerate that."

I knew she was right, so it was there and then I decided I would fight in honor of my father instead of *not* fight in his honor.

✦ ✦ ✦

So the first task this morning is to find a wrestling coach. I'm filling in for one of the instructors this morning so maybe I'll ask Jodi if anyone at the gym wrestles.

Jeremiah's class is used to high-energy EDM so I put together a compromise playlist of songs from the top ten on Spotify. When I walk in I'm happy to see two familiar faces: one is a guy who started taking my class in the new year and the other is Lynnie.

"Do you always take Jeremiah's class?" I ask her as I'm putting my shoes on.

"Hell no, I hate EDM. I heard you were teaching."

"How did you hear?" I ask, wondering if we are back in stalker territory.

"I came in yesterday to drop off a bunch of towels I've been taking home by accident, and I heard Jodi talking about it."

That actually sounds legit, so I climb on the instructor bike, put my microphone on, and say, "Good morning Jeremiah's ten o'clock!" In my cheeriest voice. I hear Lynnie give a small *woo hoo* but the rest of the half-full class just stare at their handle bars. Clearly I have my work cut out for me.

✦ ✦ ✦

After a fair to middling class, I take my sweaty self to the front desk to talk to Jodi.

"Subbing is a bitch," I tell her.

She laughs. "You should see the poor souls who have to sub for you. You have some very vocal riders. Especially this one." She gestures toward Lynnie.

"I have no doubt." I laugh. "Hey Jo, does anyone at this gym teach wrestling or know anything about wrestling?"

Jodi pauses before she says, "I don't think so but I can—"

"I do," Lynnie interrupts.

"You do?" Jodi and I say together. I'll admit I'm a little skeptical. "Who?"

Lynnie shrugs. "My brother."

I stare at her. "Your brother is a wrestler?"

She nods. "I told you."

This is one of the downsides of Lynnie talking as much as she does. Sometimes I zone out.

"When you say he wrestles, do you mean on a team?" I'm hoping Lynnie doesn't consider rolling around in the rec room "wrestling."

"Ya. His high school team went to the state championships this year but they lost, so maybe you don't want him."

"No, I do. Does he ever come to the city?" I ask her.

"No, thank God. He'd drive me crazy. He's only seventeen and he thinks he knows *everything,* and he never stops talking. It's so annoying."

I can only imagine. I tell her I'd love to have him give me some wrestling tips.

"When do you want him?" she asks.

A month ago, I think to myself. I'd love to start this weekend, but I have that Dodge City tournament, so I suggest next week.

"I'll call him and let you know. His name is Lyle bt-dubs."

Lynnie and Lyle. A lot of alliteration.

"Great, thanks." Then something occurs to me.

"Aren't you going to ask me why I want to learn to wrestle?" I ask her.

She gives me a guilty look. "I sort of already know."

"How?" I say much too loudly.

"I overheard your mom friends talking about it when they came to spin. I tried to tell you I could help you, but it wasn't about the class, so you didn't want to talk about it, remember?"

Lynnie has to be the most skilled eavesdropper in the greater KC area. But for once, I'm not annoyed.

"Lynnie, you're the best!"

I give her a hug and tell her to have a nice weekend to which she replies, "Dude, I'll see you tomorrow!"

And so she will. I'm teaching my regular class before I join the caravan to Dodge. That means I will literally have an hour to shower and get from Fusion to the rec center—no time to go home so I will have to have my luggage and Max's gear ready to go tonight.

On my way to the grocery store I stop by the space that will be Good Clean Grub once they finish fixing it up. As with everything, the work turned out to be a bit more complicated than simply cleaning the kitchen, but thankfully Raj is an architect, so he drew up an easy renovation and has been doing the work himself in his spare time.

He is on his own at the shop when I arrive, and I think it's because the girls are out selling their food.

"Actually, they are training two new people," Raj tells me excitedly. "We have officially hired a staff, such as it is." He laughs.

The place is looking great to my untrained eye. Fresh paint, clean windows, and a spit-shined counter make me think they could open tomorrow. The back kitchen is a whole other story. It's like an

Amazon truck backed up and dumped its entire load of boxes onto the no longer clean floor.

"Ay ay ay" is all that comes out of my mouth.

Raj laughs. "I know. It looked great a couple of days ago, and then we got this huge shipment of supplies."

"Need help unpacking?" I ask with very little enthusiasm.

"No, that's okay. Vivs says she has a whole system worked out in her head. I wouldn't dare start without her."

"You're wise beyond your years, Raj," I joke.

I wonder if Vivs knows how lucky she is. She has kicked this guy to the curb so many times, and he has always come back. I really want to ask him why, but I don't know how to phrase it. I mean, Vivs is my daughter and she's a smart, beautiful, ambitious young woman. But she's also occasionally a raving bitch who can make you want to tear your own hair out with frustration.

As if reading my thoughts, he says, "She's mellowed out, Jen."

"Really? I haven't noticed that." I laugh.

"Trust me. I wouldn't be here if things hadn't changed."

"Well, I admire you for being able to see the good."

"What can I say?" He shrugs. "I love her."

I shake my head. "I hope she knows how lucky she is."

"I tend to remind her every now and then." He smiles.

I hope he does.

"Hey, how's our little Maude doing?"

He beams as usual. "Great! She loves school, but I guess the teacher had to talk to her about being a bit of a tattletale."

"Oh no! Who was she telling on?"

Raj rolls his eyes. "Everyone. She was a regular visitor to the teacher's desk to air her complaints about the other kids."

I laugh. "You know Vivs used to do the same thing."

"That doesn't surprise me at all." Raj shakes his head. "Anyway, Miss Dawson suggested she try thinking of nice things to say about her classmates instead. We'll see how that works out."

I can just imagine Maude determined to make that pivot but having a bit of a struggle. She is nothing if not Vivs's daughter.

Daughter number two comes waltzing in about five minutes later with someone I'm guessing is her trainee—a tall athletic-looking girl with dirty blond hair pulled back from her face with a headband.

"Mom! Hi. I was just going to call you." She gives me a hug and nods to Raj.

"About what?" I ask her with a glance at the tall girl.

"Oh, sorry. This is Naomi. She's going to be working with us."

"Hi, nice to meet you," I say to the girl. She smiles and shakes my hand.

"I've heard a lot about you, Mrs. Dixon," she says with a giggle.

"Uh-oh, that can't be good." I'm laughing but also a bit worried. God knows what my daughters say about me behind my back.

"Mom, you're going to Dodge tomorrow, right?"

"Yup. We're going to have a ball." I pause for a laugh that never comes. "Get it? Dodge ball."

Laura looks horrified and says simply, "Why?"

"I've been trying to think of a good Dodge City joke." I shrug.

"Well, I can promise you that isn't it."

"Thank you, Laura. I so need comedy advice from you."

"Mrs. Dixon?" Naomi interrupts. "I just googled jokes about Dodge City and there aren't any."

Raj and Laura burst out laughing. I have to wonder if she's joking because if she is, she's brilliant.

I stare at her trying to figure it out. I conclude she's dead serious.

"Thank you for checking," I say sincerely.

"So do you have room for me in the car?" Laura asks.

"Right now?"

"No, going to Dodge City."

"Oh! You want to come?"

"Ya, I want to see Max wrestle."

My brow furrows as if on autopilot.

"Really? That's . . . random. I do have room if you don't mind sitting in the back with two tween boys."

"Great!"

Something about this isn't ringing quite true. Laura loves her brother, but it's more of an across the bridge to Kansas City, Missouri, kind of love, not a seven-hour road trip love.

"Does this have something to do with Dana?" I query.

Laura avoids eye contact and doesn't say anything, so I press on.

"Did he reach out to you?"

"No . . . I mean, not yet."

"Sweetie, it's been three months since Vivs broke up with him."

"I know. I think if I bump into him by accident it will remind him I'm around."

"So your plan is to follow him to Dodge?"

"I just think if he *sees* me, he'll remember that it was me he meant to call in the first place."

I see this particular delusion hasn't gone away. I can't believe my daughter has turned into the crazy girl who keeps making excuses about why a guy hasn't called.

"Laurs, I don't think ambushing him while he's working is the best way to get his attention. Why don't you set up a meeting with him to talk about snacks?"

"I wanted to, but he isn't involved with City League snacks. The parents take care of it."

I actually do know that since I made the sign-up sheet,

I weigh the pros and cons of Laura's plan in my head.

"Well, we're staying overnight, you know. Do you want me to book you a hotel room?"

"Umm . . . I'm not sure."

I glance at Naomi, who seems to be practicing TikTok dance moves while she stands there.

"I'm booking you one," I say definitively. "And if you want a ride, meet me at Fusion at nine forty-five. We're leaving from the rec center at ten."

"Can't you pick me up?" She has a trace of a whine in her voice.

"No, I'm teaching. Either meet me at Fusion or at the rec center, but don't be late."

23

To: CLOPpers
From: Jen Dixon
Re: Victory!
Date: April 26

Hello CLOPpers!

Have you sobered up from all the celebrating yet? I don't know about you, but root beer goes right to my head.

Congrats to our Comanches for their sweeping victory in Dodge City. I don't think I've ever seen our kids fight so hard or smell so terrible afterward.

A quick note about switching cars for the ride back. It isn't really a good idea as evidenced by Charmaine and Teddy having to scramble to find a ride when someone took their seats in the car they had come in. A good rule of thumb is you dance with the guy who brought you, okay?

This weekend Wichita comes to us, so there will be full practices on Tuesday and Thursday.

Over and out!

Jen

Dodge was our last road trip of the season, and thank God for that. Driving fourteen hours in two days isn't on anyone's bucket list.

The line in the email about switching cars was for an audience of one—Mimi had decided she didn't want to drive back with the group she had come with and just invited herself into Maize Cornfield's (yup, that's her real name) car. So, when Charmaine and Teddy showed up, there wasn't any room for them. Thank goodness not everyone had left, and Maria had room in her minivan.

While the team's decisive win was a highlight, the lowlight for me was watching Laura resign herself to the knowledge that Coach D seems to have a new girlfriend.

After six solid hours of sleep on lumpy beds at the hotel, Georgina, Laura, and I piled into the Palisade with our boys and went to the gym where the boys would be wrestling. I really didn't have a lot of confidence that they would do well because they all looked exhausted from yesterday's travels. Laura was the only one with a spring in her step, but that was quickly tempered when we walked into the gym and couldn't help but notice Coach D having an engaging conversation with what I can only describe as the female equivalent of him—tall, dark skinned, and gorgeous.

"Is that one of the parents?" Laura asked me immediately.

"Not from our side," I assured her.

As we watched the two hug and the woman take a seat on the coaches' bench, Laura started hyperventilating and turned back toward the gym door.

"Oh my God, I'm so stupid. I'm so stupid! What was I thinking?"

I grabbed her arm and turned her around. "Look at me. Look at me!! You're not stupid. You didn't know. For all we know Coach D is a big player with a girl in every port."

"Mom, please let go of me. I have to get out of here before he sees me."

"Where are you going to go?"

"I don't know, but just let go. I'll wait in the car."

Before I could argue, she wrenched her arm out of my grip and walked away.

I watched Coach D take a seat next to the beautiful woman and put his head near hers to continue their conversation. But I couldn't worry about that because Max was digging through his bag and calling my name loudly, wanting to know where his jock itch cream was.

The tournament was great, but the ride home was brutal. I don't think Laura said five words.

My doorbell rings and I look at the clock. I love punctual people. I open the door to Lynnie and her brother, Lyle, who is here to start my wrestling training. I was surprised he was available on a Tuesday, but Lynnie assured me that it's the second semester of his senior year so he basically never goes to school.

Lyle is a handsome young devil with dark curly hair and a stocky frame that screams "*I wrestle.*" His arms don't seem to rest easily by his sides because they are so bulked out, but his hand is soft when he shakes mine and he says he's glad to meet me.

"Lynnie talks about you *a lot*." He grins and shows me the gap between his two front teeth.

"I do not." Lynnie punches him.

We all head up to Max's room, which is set up with a mat and, of course, Dwayne. I'm glad to see he opened the window before he left for school, so the stench is more at skunk level than the usual raw sewage and wet dog level.

"Okay Lyle, I'm in your hands," I tell him.

"Ya, dumbass, show her what you know," Lynnie ribs her brother.

Oh God, this is going to be torture.

✦ ✦ ✦

We work out for a good ninety minutes. After the first thirty minutes, I send Lynnie down to the living room to watch TV because she won't stop talking.

After we go through a few holds, I ask Lyle to show me some tricks that Mimi won't see coming.

"There are no tricks, Mrs. Dixon. And there are no shortcuts," he says solemnly. "Your best bet is to stick with the basics. A good single leg takedown or cradle is what wins matches. Or in your case helps you put up a bit of a fight."

Lyle makes me practice those two moves over and over again and then shows me how to use Dwayne when I'm alone.

When we join Lynnie, she's sulking in front of the TV.

"Do you guys want some lunch?" I ask them.

"No thanks. I'm meeting my mom," Lyle says.

"I'd stay but I have to drive this loser to meet her." She rolls her eyes at me.

"Lyle, thank you so much for this." I give him a hug.

"No problem. I can come back before your match if you want." He shrugs. "I think you should learn some defensive moves, too."

"That would be great! I'll call you."

"You can just call me," Lynnie inserts as they head out the door. Lyle flashes me a peace sign as he gets into the car.

24

After lunch I pick up my mother and we head to Good Clean Grub to help in any way we can. They are planning to open their doors in a week while still providing salads and snacks for the Om studios, so they need all hands on deck.

"Sweetheart, you don't think they'll ask me to cook, do you?" my mother wonders.

"I'm pretty sure you'll be on packaging duty, Mom. Or cleanup."

She nods her acceptance that this will be okay.

Kay's grieving period is over. At least I think it is. She is one of the most practical people I know and sitting around being sad is just not in her DNA. Without Ray to worry about she is filling her time with lots of volunteer work.

"It's never hard to find someone to help," she has told me for years. "You just have to know where to look."

The girls have been going full tilt boogey since they got their kitchen license. It was expedited thanks to the persistence of Raj and Mary Willy's husband, Doug. With the help of their new employees, they think they'll be ready for opening day. As we pull up, a man in a white hat is painting something on the window under the Good Clean Grub logo. It says, *Fresh Food Made Daily*. My heart has a little burst of pride. My daughters did this. They made this happen for themselves. And they didn't kill each other in the process. What more could a mother want?

"Right. Put me to work," Kay commands after the greetings are done.

"Nana, come in the back with me," Laura says. "We'll put you on sticker duty."

"That sounds just about my speed." My mother laughs and follows her granddaughter through the swinging doors.

I'm alone with Vivs at the front of the store, having been given the task of cleaning the windows. I take the opportunity to ask her how it's going.

"Fine. Good, actually. I really think we're going to be ready."

"Where are your employees?" I ask, because I can never remember their names.

"Naomi and Holt are out there"—she nods toward the buildings that share the parking lot—"handing out flyers for the grand opening."

"I can't believe this is really happening."

"Gee, thanks, Mom." Vivs is her usual curmudgeonly self.

"Oh, you know what I mean. I'm really proud of you girls."

"Truthfully, bringing Raj in was the best decision we made, or well, I made. His business savvy has helped us level up big-time."

"And how's the romance going?"

Vivs pauses her task of writing the menu on a chalkboard and glares at me.

"Oh stop with the looks, you big bully."

"We're good," she says evenly. I feel like she wants to say more, but the moment passes.

"What about Laura? How's she doing after Dodge City?"

Vivs shakes her head. "I can't believe you actually drove her there. I could have told you it was a bad idea if anyone had thought to ask me."

"She was following her heart," I answer defensively.

"You know she still believes that insane scenario she concocted about Dana mixing up our names."

"I know. Let's hope she never shares that with him."

"I told her if he liked her, he would have called after I broke up with him."

"I hope you were nicer than that."

Vivs shrugs. "Mom, what she needs is tough love. You can't let her live in a fantasy world."

I decide to change the subject. "I had my first wrestling lesson," I tell her.

"With that weird girl's brother?"

"Yes. And she's not weird, she's just . . ." I can't seem to find the word, so Vivs helps me out.

"I'm sticking with 'weird.'"

"Okay, she's a bit weird, but her heart is in the right place. And her brother really helped me."

"When is this thing again? Nana says we all have to go."

"It's the Thursday before Memorial Day weekend."

"Huh. That's pretty soon."

"Don't remind me."

"Hi Gee Gee!" Maude comes running in the front door dressed in a blue jumpsuit that reminds me of the old gas station attendant outfits. Raj is three paces behind her.

"Hello, you!" I say and immediately think of my dad because that is how he always greeted me. The now familiar hollow ache in my heart presents itself yet again. It's always there, just in varying degrees, and I expect it always will be.

"I did this today." Maude shoves a large piece of paper in front of me with what looks like a sunny day at the beach drawn with Cray-Pas. Out of the corner of my eye I see Vivs flinch.

"This is beautiful! Is it for me?"

"No. It's for Mommy."

Vivs smiles at her daughter.

"Does this look like the place, Mommy?"

"What place?" I ask.

"The place where Mommy and Daddy are going to get married," Maude tells me.

I look from Vivs to Raj with my mouth open.

"Maude! That was supposed to be a secret, remember?" Vivs tells her.

"It's just Gee Gee." Maude shrugs.

I find my voice and turn to Vivs. "Really? This is happening?"

She nods and rolls her eyes at Raj. "I told you she couldn't keep a secret." He seems amused.

I get up from my knees, throw my Windex to the side, and give them all a big hug.

"When?" I ask, already picking out the flower arrangements in my head.

"Memorial Day weekend," Raj tells me.

"That's so soon! You haven't given yourselves much time to plan."

"We're keeping it really small, Mom. Just the three of us, on a beach in Florida."

I hear her words, but they don't register immediately.

"We need to find a venue . . ."

I barely notice Raj take Maude into the back of the shop.

"Mom." Vivs touches my arm to get my attention. "It's just going to be me, Maude, and Raj."

"But . . . why? We all want to see you get married."

"I'm sure you do, but hear me out." Vivs leads me to a chair behind the counter. "First, we don't want to spend a lot of money."

"But we can . . ."

"And don't say you can help. We don't want anyone spending money on it. We're taking a quick weekend to go someplace warm and exchange some vows. Second, we'd have to invite either everyone or no one. We can't afford to fly Varsha here, and this way we can assure her that she didn't miss some big party. And third, this is what we want. Period. Full stop."

I'm doing a terrible job of hiding my dismay. After a brief, soaring high, I'm now completely deflated.

"Mom." She softens her tone. "You must have known I'd never want to play the blushing bride at a big wedding."

It's taking all my will to manage my disappointment.

"I guess there's always Laura."

"Exactly. She'll want the biggest, fanciest wedding you guys can throw her."

I take a deep breath and nod. "Okay. I get it. But you have to let me watch you tell Nana. She's going to have a fit."

Vivs cracks up. "I'll tell her now if you like. It can be the highlight of your day."

And indeed, it was.

25

To: City League, Overland Park

From: Jen Dixon

Re: Tonight's the Night!

Date: May 25

Helloooo CLOPpers!!

I have it on very good authority that this has been the best season City League has seen in ten years, and I'm happy to take full credit. It must have been my snappy emails that made the difference this year. It couldn't have been the die-hard dedication of our kids, the guidance of the wonderful coaches, or the supersized support of the CLOPpers. No, it was me, and that's what I'm choosing to believe, until someone tells me otherwise.

Please turn in all gear that does not belong to you by tomorrow. We want to get it all catalogued and put away for next year. Also check out the lost-and-found table at the fundraiser tonight. Someone has yet to claim the mouthguard we found a month ago, among other things.

I'm looking forward to seeing you all tonight for my public humiliation. I hope you guys aren't expecting a good fight. At best you'll be able to admire my new teal singlet and matching headgear before I'm carried off in a stretcher. Kidding of course! My singlet is black.

Don't forget to bring the heat tonight!

Jen "Cage Match" Dixon

"Well, I'm as ready as I'm ever going to be," I tell Ron as I send out my CLOP email.

"You were looking pretty strong with Lyle yesterday," he agrees as he sits down at the kitchen table with a protein bar. "What a nice kid."

"I thought so too until he told me I have heavy hips."

Ron laughs. "It was a compliment. Max wishes someone would say that to him."

Lyle ended up coming a total of three times to coach me. He made me stick with the two moves he had originally taught me, plus two evasive moves to avoid getting pinned, and I'm pretty good at them, thanks to my "heavy hips." Don't ask me to do anything else, though. That's all I've got in my arsenal besides Bengay and Advil.

Lynnie was with him, of course, but thankfully she limited her heckling to saying a few times, "You're an asshole."

"What's your day looking like?" Ron asks. It's a Thursday morning, but for some reason he hasn't gone into the studio yet.

"I have to do a little grocery shopping for the long weekend if you want to come along."

"I was thinking we'd do a little reading this morning." He puts his hands on my shoulders and starts rubbing them.

A few months ago, this offer would have been most unwelcome, but thanks to Mary Willy and of course Greta, I spring to my feet, grab his hand, and pull him up the back stairs.

✦ ✦ ✦

After grocery shopping, I stop by Fusion to grab a green juice and double-check that Jodi has found someone to fill in for me tomorrow. I'm not sure what is going to go down tonight, but I've been thinking I'd better take tomorrow morning off. I'm surprised to see Carmen at the front desk when I walk in.

"Hey! What are you doing here?" I give her a hug.

"Taking a class. Are you teaching?" I think she sounds hopeful, which I take as a compliment.

"Nope. Today I'm just here for the juice. How's everything at Om?"

"It's really great." She lowers her voice. "That husband of yours is like the best boss I've ever had."

"Aww. That's sweet." I glance toward Jodi's office and am glad to see the door is closed.

"So, I keep meaning to ask you, how did it go getting to know all your riders?"

I remember that she hadn't seemed that enthused when I told her I was doing this.

"It was interesting." I think of all the riders who have helped me this year—Dr. Superbitch, Mary and Doug Willy, even Lynnie, in the long run. "You know, I'm glad I did it."

I laugh at the look on her face. "Why do you look so surprised?"

"Well, you probably don't remember this, but I got close to a bunch of my riders a few years ago. It was fun for a while, but then things got weird. If I went out with one, another would call and ask why she wasn't invited, and then they started fighting over front-row bikes. It all got pretty crazy. You can ask Jodi about it. She had to sit down with a bunch of them for a *Leave Carmen Out of It* intervention."

"Yikes. That sounds terrible. Was I taking your class back then?"

"I honestly don't remember. But I swore I would never blur the lines between teacher and friend ever again."

"So that's why you wished me luck with it."

She laughs. "Ya. I didn't want to scare you, but I knew you might have some issues."

"Well, nothing like *that*," I assure her.

"I'm glad you had a good experience." She smiles.

"Maybe you should try again," I suggest, to which she barks out a laugh and gives a hearty "no thank you!"

Once she heads toward the spin room, I feel saddened by her absence. Carmen is one of those people who can make a room better just by being in it. When she's with you, her aura casts a spell of happiness that lingers for only a very short time after she's gone.

It's like you get a little bit high just being in her orbit. No wonder people fought over her attention.

Jodi is on the phone when I poke my head into her office, but she gives me the thumbs-up that I'm all good for tomorrow, so I take my juice and jump in the Palisade.

✦ ✦ ✦

Good Clean Grub isn't exactly on my way home, but I make a detour to stop by. The opening a few weeks ago was a bit underwhelming. The girls didn't have a lot of resources for a big ad blitz, so the only people who showed up were friends and family. I think they were hoping for a slam dunk home run (pardon the mixed metaphors), but it looks like they'll need to be patient.

I pull up to the shop, planning on lending some moral support to whatever situation I run into, and I am confused when I see a sign on the door that says, *We Are Closed*. I look at the dashboard and see that it's two o'clock. I try the door, but it's locked. Shit, has it been that bad?

I don't see Vivs's car in the lot, but she could be parked in the back. I bang on the door loudly.

Raj pokes his head out from the back kitchen and waves, then comes to let me in.

"Hi. Sorry the door was locked. We didn't know you were coming."

I follow him to the back and see Vivs sitting on the counter and Laura standing by one of the fridges.

"Why are you guys closed?" I demand without even greeting them. "Did something happen?"

"Uh, you could say that," Laura says, and Vivs laughs.

"What? What happened."

"We ran out of food." Laura giggles then fist-bumps her sister and Raj.

"What? How? Didn't you order enough?"

"Obviously not." Vivs chortles.

"Why are you guys so giddy?" I ask them, and they all crack up.

What the hell am I missing? Out loud I say, "Have you been drinking?"

This sends them into another peel of laughter.

"Alright, that's enough. Someone tell me what's so damn funny?" I'm really annoyed.

"Mom, chill!" Laura breaks from the hyenas. "We thought we might sell a lot today because we papered the neighborhood with two-for-one flyers, but we ended up selling three times more than we expected!"

"We got slammed," Vivs adds.

"We had to close at one-thirty because we had no more food!" Raj boasts. "Can you believe it?"

I can't, and I tell them as much.

"Did you lose money with the special offer?"

"Nope. The specials today were all salad based, so we came out ahead."

I'm not going to pretend I understand that logic, but they obviously had a successful day, so I decide to join in the revelry.

"We should do something to celebrate," I suggest.

"Oh, we are. We're going out to see our awesome mom get the crap kicked out of her at a wrestling fundraiser." Laura puts her arm around me.

"Well that just sounds like so much fun!" I snark. "Maybe when I'm recovered from whatever the hell is going to happen to me, we can hit J. Gilbert's for dinner."

I get a round of approval for that suggestion.

I look at my phone. "Yikes, I've got to get going."

"Are you ready for tonight?" Vivs asks.

I sigh. "I'm ready for it to be over, that's for sure."

26

I arrive at the rec center with Ron and Max in tow. The whole ride over was a big pep talk, with Max reminding me what not to do and Ron telling me how hot I look in my black singlet. Neither was helpful.

We enter the gym under a larger banner that reads, *Just for the Smell of It Fundraiser*. Even though I took over the reins at CLOP this year, Franny wisely stayed in charge of this particular soiree, and I'm grateful. There's no way I could have done anything other than show up for this.

The place is already half-full with parents and kids, everyone with signs for their favorite mom. There's pop music blasting on the PA system, the aroma of hot dogs and popcorn provide a mask for the usual stench of the gym, and there is a general buzz of enjoyment . . . except from me. I feel like I'm walking around in someone else's body. Such a fun night can't really end in me wrestling someone, can it?

I see Dana and two other coaches who agreed to be referees huddling in a corner. I hope to God Laura doesn't decide to share her theory with him tonight. I have enough to worry about.

I'm nervous. There's no two ways about it. I'm reminded of

how I felt the first time I ever had sex. I really didn't know what I was doing; I just knew it was going to hurt.

More people are streaming in, and before long the gym is full. I see my mother, my daughters, and my granddaughter sitting in the stands, all holding signs for me. Maude's is my favorite because she made it herself and it just says *GO GEE GEE* in bold lime-green letters. I give them all a wave, then make my way over to the rest of the twenty or so CLOP moms who are also sacrificing their dignity in the name of making money to keep this league alive for our kids.

As I understand it, matches are chosen by pulling names out of a jar. This is for the first round anyway. After that, people can challenge each other. Lucky me, I've already been challenged! I told them I wanted only one match, so I get to play spectator for the first hour.

I see Mimi stride in with purpose, her four redheaded sons trailing behind her along with her husband. She is wearing a tie-dyed singlet, and I have to say it looks really good, especially compared to my plain black one.

"You're a rock star for being here," Maria says to me. "How are you feeling?"

"Uh, pretty good. I've been practicing, so I shouldn't do too badly."

"You're going to be surprised how much you picked up just from watching the kids all year." Yes, that would be a nice surprise.

Franny gets on the microphone and welcomes everyone to the fourth annual Just for the Smell of It Fundraiser. She gives a grocery list of thank-yous in her typical low-key style, and, as always, she gets huge rounds of applause from her wrestling community. Then she starts pulling names out of the jar by twos and reads them out loud. She reads her own name first, and then that of her opponent, who is Kyle's mom, Irene. Kyle of course is the other kid who got drunk on white wine at our Halloween party. Those two are followed by Maria and Maize Cornfield, Georgina and Charmaine, and so on until all the names have been pulled. Mimi is doing a warm-up match against a mom I don't know very well, and it makes me wonder if I should have done the same.

Franny and Irene take the center ring as Franny's husband, Trent, announces the fight. They are both dressed in joggers and T-shirts and look pretty evenly matched, body-wise, but once the match begins, Franny takes Irene down almost immediately. She lays her body across Irene's shoulders, and before you can say, "Get off your back," Coach D has called Franny the winner by pin. She holds her hand out to Irene and they hug and laugh.

"Wow!" I exclaim, clapping loudly along with everyone else. "Go Franny."

"Franny is the best wrestler of all the moms," Maria tells me.

"Even Mimi?" I ask.

She laughs. "Now that's the match everyone wants to see, but Franny refuses to fight Mimi."

Before I can ask why, Maria's name is announced, and she runs to the mat for her match against Maize.

She takes her place on the center mat facing Maize, who has a good twenty pounds on her. Both their sons are ringside ready to coach their moms if they need it. This match lasts much longer, mostly because Maize keeps pushing Maria out of bounds, and neither of them can stop laughing, despite Maize's son yelling at her to take it seriously. It's hilarious to watch, and the crowd loves it. After five minutes they are both exhausted, and the match is called a draw. They hug and run off the mat to huge applause. I'm so glad to see it's all in good fun and no one is taking it seriously.

I have some time before the challenge matches, so I join my family in the bleachers.

"Gee Gee, I want to see you wrestle!" Maude hugs me as I sit down.

"This doesn't look too bad, Mom," Vivs notes. "You won't get hurt if you just take a dive in the first ten seconds."

"Don't you have a wedding to go to?" I give her a jab.

"Leaving tomorrow," she whispers because she doesn't want to rile my mother up again.

Kay's reaction to their planned elopement was everything I could have hoped for. Among her *many* choice words were two Kay classics.

"Well, Vivs, I expect this type of behavior from your mother, but not from you." And, "If you get married in secret like this, people are going to assume the worst."

But it seems all is forgiven as Kay sits beside Raj and shares her popcorn with him.

"I'm proud of you, Jennifer. Now who is your opponent?" she asks me.

I point out Mimi as she takes to the mat.

"Oh, look at that hair!" is my mother's only comment as Mimi ties her orange mane into a bun. She and the poor wretch she's fighting get into ready position and start to go at it after the whistle is blown. I can see why a match between Franny and Mimi would be good, because Mimi too has made mincemeat out of her opponent in seconds flat.

"Wow. She's good." Kay states the obvious.

I didn't get much of a sense of Mimi's fighting technique in those brief seconds, but I did note that she used a double leg takedown, and thanks to Lyle I know exactly how to deal with that.

Once the first set of matches are done, the music starts up again so the refs can take a much-needed break. My gang all head to the bathrooms, then hang out by the hot dog stand.

I see Laura eyeing Coach D, but she doesn't approach him, thank goodness. Instead, she asks Max if his girlfriend is here tonight.

"Does he have a girlfriend?" Max asks.

"You know, the girl who was with him in Dodge?" Laura prompts.

"What girl?" Max is confused.

"She sat beside him on the coaches' bench." I decide to be helpful.

"You mean Michelle?" Max scrunches his face. "That's Coach D's sister."

"His sister?" Laura and I say together.

"Ya. She's really cool."

Laura turns and makes a beeline to where Dana is sipping a soda and talking to some of the dads.

"Don't!" I yell to her, but all I get is the back of her head. I think about running after her to try to spare her the inevitable embarrassment, but I can't because my name is being called to come to the mat. I guess Mimi and I are first up in the challenge round.

My mouth is dry, and the adrenaline is pumping so strongly that I can hear white noise in my ears. As I get to the center of the mat, I see Coach D coming toward the mat but also backing away from Laura as she talks at him. Crap.

Mimi is the last to join us on the mat in all her tie-dyed glory. I really do look like the villain with my black singlet and T-shirt. I mean, I wore it because I thought all black would be slimming, but maybe I *am* the villain? It wouldn't be the first time I wasn't aware I was in the wrong.

But as I look into my opponent's eyes, I see just how much she wants to win this. I realize I'm probably the first wrestling newbie who hasn't bought into her alpha mat mom BS, and she needs to win this to keep her fiefdom intact.

"Come on, Mom!" I hear Max's voice from the side. I turn to give him a wave and see Lyle is standing beside him. I get a little choked up that he has come all the way from Wamego to see me fight. I notice Lynnie for the first time standing off to the side and holding a sign that says, *Jen Dixon Eats Melon for Breakfast*. I salute her then and turn back to Mimi and Coach D. There are no smiles between us, so Coach D reminds us we're here to have fun.

"Alright, moms, let's keep it friendly. The kids are watching." Mimi and I crouch into starting position, and even though I know people around us must be yelling, the only sound I hear is my own breathing and the coach's whistle as it blows.

27

To: CLOP

From: Jen Dixon

Re: It Isn't a Party 'til Something Breaks!

Date: May 26

Happy Weekend CLOPpers!

I just wanted to send a note to thank you for an amazing night. All in we raised $2,712 for the league, ensuring we will be well funded for next season. Franny, you are a superstar.

And for those who asked, Mimi and I are fine. We all know nose and mouth bleeds look much worse than they are. And after only a few hours at the emergency room, Mimi's shoulder is back in its socket where it belongs. We both thank you for all the calls of concern.

Happy Memorial Day!

Jen

I hit send and hope I sound more cheerful than I feel. I return the ice pack to my nose and mouth and take a sip of coffee from the straw I'm using.

My phone rings and its Vivs.

"Boy, you'll do anything to keep me from getting married without you," is her greeting.

"Didn't you go?" I'm genuinely surprised. She and Raj and Maude were supposed to be on a plane to Tampa this morning.

"Not yet. Maude is refusing to go anywhere until she sees you. Can I bring her over?"

"I don't know if that's wise. I look like hell. Maybe I can just talk to her on the phone."

"Maude!" Vivs's yell rattles my eardrum. "Want to talk to Gee Gee?"

I have to wait only a moment to hear her footsteps running and then her little voice saying, "Gee Gee, are you okay?"

"Of course I am," I say with a little too much jolliness.

"Can I come and see you?"

"Oh, Maudey, not today. I'm going to be cleaning all the toilets." I choose this chore because I know it's her least favorite when she's "helping" me.

"Pew," she says, giggling.

"Besides, you need to go on a plane today with Mommy and Daddy and watch them get married."

"But who's going to take care of you?"

"I can take care of myself! And I need you to watch the wedding so you can tell me all about it." I hope I'm convincing her. I feel like my relationship with Vivs depends on it.

"I have a pretty dress for it," Maude says.

"I know you do. So go and have fun, and I'll see you in three days when you get back, okay?"

"Okay. But Gee Gee, I don't want you to wrestle anymore."

"I promise I won't. Bye, baby."

"Bye," she says, and I can hear her yelling to Vivs that she's ready to go before she hangs up the phone.

I still wish I could be there, but as it turns out, I wouldn't be able to travel today anyway. My nasal passages couldn't take the cabin pressure.

"There's my Million Dollar Baby!" Ron says as he walks in the back door after taking Max to school. We let him sleep in this morning because of all the drama last night. "How are you feeling?"

"Better," I tell him. "I look worse than I feel."

And that's no lie because I look like a bruised raccoon. It turns out, I put up quite a fight in my one and only match last night. Once the whistle blew, Mimi and I both immediately crouched and started circling each other, and before I knew it, she had her arms wrapped around my upper legs.

"Legs back!" I heard Lyle yell, and I immediately shot my legs out behind me, so Mimi only had a hold of my hips, and my torso was above her. Lyle and I must have practiced this move at least fifty times, but no one was more surprised than I was that it actually worked.

"Whizzer! Whizzer!" Lyle yelled, and I immediately took my right arm and put it over Mimi's armpit, which effectively stopped her from raising her arm. I knew I was supposed to get my legs to the side now, but Mimi picked me up by my torso and pushed me away. The whole thing took about six seconds, but I felt like I should be declared the winner just because I was still standing. Next time Mimi came for me she grabbed my shoulders and put her head against mine. Her breath smelled like garlic and tuna fish, and not in a nice way. I couldn't help but wonder if this was part of a strategy she uses to unsettle her opponents. I can tell you it made me want to get as far away from her as possible. While trying not to dry heave, I used the strength in my "heavy hips" to push her out of bounds. It took me a good thirty seconds because she also has "heavy hips," but I finally did it.

I noticed that Mimi was breathing heavily, as if she'd just sprinted around the gym. I, on the other hand, was barely winded, and I was thrilled to see that my cardio stamina just might be my saving grace in this match.

The next time we reset, Coach D insisted we start on the ground with me on my hands and knees and Mimi above and behind me. I glanced over at Lyle and Max and they both looked crestfallen. I figured this was going to be it for me, and frankly I was relieved. This was way more wrestling than I had ever expected to do.

I didn't fully understand what happened next until Georgie sent me the footage she had shot.

I got down on my hands and knees as I've seen the boys do, then Mimi got behind me with her boobs pressed against my back and her arms around my chest. Her tuna-garlic breath made the closeness all the more uncomfortable, and I started to panic. When Coach blew the whistle, I flailed and writhed and did anything I could to get Mimi off my back, to no avail. I heard Lyle yell something about putting my hip down, but Mimi rolled right on top of me and threw her body across my shoulders. At this point I probably should have just given up and let her pin me, but I was frantic for her to be off me, so I couldn't let myself relax. I was wiggling and undulating like a wild animal caught in a trap, and there was no way for Mimi to keep me down.

I somehow grabbed her left arm with my hands and pulled as hard as I could. I heard a pop and a gasp and then felt the back of Mimi's fist hit my face. We both stopped fighting immediately—like two unhanded puppets—Mimi screaming that her arm hurt, and me trying to stop the blood gushing from my nose and mouth.

People were beside me, pulling my hands away from my face, and I heard someone yell, "Call nine-one-one." I could hear Mimi screaming, and I wondered what the hell I had done to her and if I could go to jail for it. *I wouldn't do well in jail*, I thought to myself. A lot of people take an instant dislike to me.

Then Ron was beside me, lifting me to a sitting position and shoving a T-shirt in my face to catch the blood. I screamed as he applied pressure, so he stopped. Time didn't seem to be moving as I sat on the mat. I saw the concerned faces of my family among the people surrounding Mimi and me. I tried to tell them I was fine, but the words came out as a gurgle.

I looked up to see paramedics dealing with Mimi. She wasn't bleeding, but she hadn't stopped screaming, "My arm, my arm," and I thought I heard someone say, "We heard it pop out." They finally got her on a stretcher, and that was the last I saw of her.

As my adrenaline slowed, the pain got much worse. Ron lifted me to my feet and walked me toward a young EMT—a girl who introduced herself as Dutch. She took the T-shirt away from my face and felt around my nose and mouth area, which made me cry out in pain, so I punched her in the arm.

"I don't think it's broken," she said, ignoring the hit I had landed on her. "But if you want to be sure, you can go to the emergency room."

"I want to go home," I told Ron. I was very near tears and felt like I might throw up.

I didn't find out until this morning that Raj had taken Maude home as soon as the blood started gushing, and she was borderline hysterical until she went to sleep, poor baby. The rest of the family followed us home and kept vigil until I was asleep, which, thanks to the pain meds I was given, was only about twenty minutes.

"Do you think I'm in trouble?" I ask Ron as he chugs a large glass of water.

"With who?"

"Uh, the law."

He laughs. "I know Mimi's litigious, but I don't think she can sue you for dislocating her shoulder during a charity wrestling match."

My phone rings.

"Hello?"

"Jen, it's Franny. I just got your email. How are you feeling?"

"Um, I'm a bit better. The drugs are helping."

"I'm really sorry this happened to you . . ."

"Franny, I'm the one who's sorry. Ron told me the night was pretty much over once the paramedics showed up."

"Oh please. It's actually making us rethink the whole moms-wrestling-moms thing."

"Really?"

"Honest to God, I don't know how it took four years for some-one to get hurt. What were we thinking?"

"Have you talked to Mimi?" I ask her.

"Yes, I just got off the phone with her."

"How is she feeling?"

"She's a little sore, but, you know, she's Mimi. Talking about suing everyone for everything."

"Oh no!"

"I wouldn't worry. She's generally all hat and no horse, if you know what I mean."

I really hope she's right. Personally, I just want to forget the whole thing. But I know I won't be able to until I see Mimi face-to-face.

But not today. Today I'm planning to lie in bed and watch as much guilty pleasure TV as I want.

✦ ✦ ✦

"Are you up for a visitor?" Ron pokes his head into the bedroom and interrupts my *Gilmore Girls* marathon.

"Who is it?"

"It's me." Laura bumps past Ron and flops on the bed beside me.

Ron looks annoyed, but I let him know it's okay.

"How are you feeling, Mommy? You look terrible."

"Well, aren't you sweet," I tell her.

She laughs. "I'm sorry. It's just, wow. I've never seen you like this."

"It looks bad, but I'll be fine. I'm just a bit tired from the pain pills."

"Can I stay and watch TV with you?" she asks.

"Of course."

Laura snuggles down next to me like she used to when she was little, and we watch the episode where something crazy happens in Rory's love life.

At one point Laura's phone rings. She looks at the display and bolts upright, jostling me as she does.

"Holy shit."

"What?"

She waves me off and takes her phone into the hallway and closes my door. I pause the show and end up dozing off waiting for her to come back.

I wake up as she sits back down beside me.

"Who was that? Is everything okay?"

Laura grabs a pillow and screams into it.

"That was Dana!" she exclaims.

I remember seeing Laura talking to him last night.

"Oh really?" I smile.

"He wanted to see how you're feeling."

"Uh-huh."

"And he wanted to continue our conversation from last night." She's grinning like an idiot.

"Tell me," I encourage her.

"Well, last night when I found out he didn't have a girlfriend, I just said to myself, screw it. I just wanted to say my peace, you know? So I walked over and just straight up said, 'Did you mean to call me instead of Vivs?'"

"Way to rip the Band-Aid off." I nod. "What was his reaction?"

"He was like when? So I was like when you asked her out. And he was like no."

"Ouch."

"Ya. That's what I thought. But he had to go referee your wrestling match, and then all hell broke loose so we never got a chance to finish."

"But at least you got your answer. He had always meant to call Vivs."

"That's what I thought. But he just told me he did like me at first, but he didn't think I liked him, and Vivs basically threw herself at him . . ."

"He said that?"

"No, I said that, but he didn't disagree. So we just talked for like an hour, and now we're going out tomorrow night." Laura ends with another big scream into the pillow.

"Oh, sweetie, that's so great."

"He wasn't sure how you guys would all feel, but then I told him Vivs is getting married tomorrow so he shouldn't feel weird at all."

I'm guessing the first few family gatherings might be a bit awkward, but if there is a generation that is able to just get over it, its theirs.

28

Text from Lynnie:

> Hi, just checking in again. Hope you're
> feeling better. Send me a picture of your
> nose! When will you be back to class?
> Jodi's been filling in and she sucks.

Say what you want about Lynnie, she's devoted. She isn't the only rider who has texted me, but she *is* the only rider to text me five times in one day!

I text her that I will be back in class tomorrow, which is Friday. It's been a week since the "Rumble at the Rec Center," and I think I've taken enough *me* time to last for quite a while. My bruises are now a light yellow, the swelling in my nose has gone down, and my teeth don't feel like they've been pushed to the back of my mouth anymore.

Mimi and I had a face-to-face at my insistence. I met her at the Donut Hole yesterday and I think the look of me took her by surprise. She may have had her arm in a sling, but I looked like hell and got stares of either horror or pity from everyone.

I sat down, and she asked me how I was feeling, which I thought was very generous. I asked the same of her, and I feel like we were both satisfied by the degree of each other's misery.

"You were pretty good," she said to me out of the blue.

"Pretty good as what? A punching bag?"

She smirked. "No, you held your own. I should have been able to drop you in the first ten seconds, but you had some moves."

"I had exactly three moves, and I had used them all," I assured her. "That's why I started flailing like a mad woman. I swear I didn't mean to pull your arm so hard."

"Well, believe it or not, I didn't plan to punch you in the face. It was an impulse reaction."

"I get it." I nodded. "Can we just put this behind us? I mean, we have a good five years of wrestling ahead of us."

"I'm up for that." Mimi sighed and suddenly let out a laugh. "Oh, and by the way, I only hung out with Cindy Dixon like, twice."

I shrugged. "No judgment."

"Is she really your husband's ex?"

"Yup."

"Wow."

"Why? What did she do?" I asked her.

"Well, for one thing, she never stopped talking about *you*."

"Really? That's so flattering."

Mimi laughed. "Ya, I don't think it was meant to be."

I laughed along with her. Maybe someday we can go out and swap stories over a glass of wine.

Everyone is coming for dinner tonight to celebrate Vivs and Raj and watch the wedding videos they took. It's potluck, thank goodness, so all I have to do is set the table and make a corn salad.

Laura and Coach Dana are the last to arrive, and he seems genuinely happy to be back in our home. He and Vivs greet each other warmly with a long hug, and then he and Raj hug and swap some overly aggressive back slaps. There doesn't seem to be any awkward-ness surrounding who has slept with who (except internally by me) so that's good.

Dana regales us at dinner with horror stories about the wrestling world and has us all wincing, especially when he tells of a terrible herpes outbreak on his high school team. But when he claims that it spread like wildflowers, I laugh much louder than I should have. I glance at Vivs and her look says, *I told you so.* I want to tell her that I don't care. Laura has finally found a nice guy and if saying the wrong phrase every now and then is the worst thing about him, I'm okay with that.

After dinner my mother and I take a seat on the back patio to enjoy the warm June evening. She tells me she thinks she'd like to move out of her condo.

"Are you lonely, Mom?" I ask her.

"My heavens, Jennifer, I wish I were lonely. Ever since your father died, I'm like catnip to every widower in the building."

"You're kidding." I laugh. "What do they do?"

"They're always coming to my door asking if I need anything fixed. Then if I let them in, they expect a meal! I fell for that a couple of times before I just stopped answering the bell."

"So where do you want to live? Riverview?"

She scrunches her face. "I thought about it, but I really don't think I need that much care."

I'm inclined to agree. Kay's a tour de force these days. A place like that would only slow her down.

"So where?" I ask.

"Well, how would you feel if I moved in with you?"

It takes me a second to comprehend what she's saying.

"Here? With me and Ron?"

"And Max," she adds and pats my knee. "Just think about it." She stands up and takes her cup of tea inside.

While I'm absorbing the bomb she just dropped on me, Kay pokes her head back out the door and says, "Kidding! You're not the only one with a sense of humor, Jennifer."

She heads back into the house chuckling at her cleverness.

I'm glad she's kidding but it makes me wonder if I could live with Kay. Given her age and circumstances, it's not out of the question at some point. Nina and Garth are facing it right now.

I mean, I did live with her for a lot of my life, but that was in *her* house, under *her* rules. In my house, under my rules, it would be very different. Or would it?

I'm going to have to consult Yvette's guides about this one.

Acknowledgments

Thanks to everyone at Henry Holt for encouraging me to write another chapter in the Class Mom series even though most reviewers seemed to think *Yoga Pant Nation* was the end of the road for Jen and the gang. Surprise! It will never be over. Mwa ha!

Thanks to poor Serena Jones, my editor, social conscience, and personal cheerleader. You are a wonderful guiding force.

Maggie Carr, you were a rockstar copyediting this book and pointing out things like Kay and Ray had a carbon monoxide leak, not asbestos poisoning. The devil is in the details and you had them all.

Pilar Queen and UTA, I'm so happy just to be in your orbit. Let's keep this gravy train going!

Paige Baldwin, thanks for your invaluable input every time I write a book. I encourage you to write your own so I can return the favor. I know you can do it!

Thanks to all the mat moms who gave me an inside look at the wonderful world of junior high wrestling, and most especially Kelly Ripa, who knows how to put a funny spin on even the most disgusting details.

To all the authors I have met in the trenches, I admire you all so much for your commitment to the written word and the generosity of spirit with which you treat each other. I'm so proud to be a part of this community.

And, as always, I save the best for last. Michael, Jamie, Misha, and our new addition to the family, Billie the wonder dog . . . I couldn't imagine doing any of this without you!

About the Author

Laurie Gelman spent twenty-five years as a broadcaster in both Canada and the United States before trying her hand at writing novels. The author of *Class Mom*, *You've Been Volunteered*, and *Yoga Pant Nation*, Laurie has appeared on *Live with Kelly and Ryan*, *Watch What Happens Live*, and *The Talk*, among others. She lives in New York City with her husband, Michael Gelman, and their two daughters.